GUARDED BY THE WARRIOR

A Conquered Bride Novel

ELIZA KNIGHT

KNIGHT
MEDIA

ABOUT THE BOOK

A lady in need of protection...

Suffering through a short marriage to an enemy of Scotland, Lady Emilia MacCulloch manages to escape just before her husband dies. But the Ross Clan will stop at nothing to get her back, for she plays a big part in their plans to thwart Robert the Bruce. She fears not only for her life, but for her family who will be labeled traitors. Placed by her king as a governess in the household of a devastatingly handsome warrior, Emilia finds herself drawn to the man when she had previously sworn off love altogether. His passion, charisma, loyalty, and strength shake the very foundation she's built around her heart.

A warrior in need of saving...

Ian Matheson has spent his entire life trying to prove himself. To belong. When his father passes away and his mother takes her vows at a nearby abbey, he is suddenly left in a position he was wholly unprepared for. And then his father's dozen illegitimate children arrive on his doorstep in need of a father figure of their own. They are adorable and reckless, and he's certain they'll drive him mad. Just when he thinks he might actually need to find a wife to help him, Lady Emilia is presented to him by the king. She needs his protection and he needs her help with the bairns. Ian is tempted by her angelic face, her fiery tongue, and the secrets that surround her. He must resist the growing desire that's laying claim within him. He must prove to his clan that he is a worthy leader. But maybe, just maybe, he can have the respect of his people and Emilia, too.

FIRST EDITION

November 2016

Edited by: Scott Moreland & Jennifer Jakes

Cover Design: Kimberly Killion @ The Killion Group, Inc.

For Katie, always my sister, always my friend.

PROLOGUE

Ross Castle
Scottish Highlands
February, 1303

Ina Ross, laird of her clan by default—due to the untimely murder of her father—seethed with fury. To be sure, she was an angry woman by nature and she had been since the day she came screaming into the world. She knew this. Her father had known it, and now, even her miserable husband was hyper-aware of her changing moods.

Sitting opposite her was her simpering, English fool of a spouse, Marmaduke Stewart. Why she'd ever agreed to marry him was lost to her these days. Once, there had been a great fondness she'd felt for him. However, when she looked back upon it now, she realized it was no great affection but, instead, a mutual need for vengeance. It just so happened the people they respectively wanted to punish were married to each other, which made the planning all the more sweet.

But that sweetness had long since turned into a bitter, harsh tonic that ate away at Ina's stomach day in and day out.

The more children Magnus Sutherland produced with that calculating witch, the deeper Ina's knife wounds to her pride cut. Och, but Arbella would pay, if it was the last thing Ina ever did.

"Will ye stop sipping like that?" Ina's voice was sharp, which caused Marmaduke to suck harder on the ale in the pewter mug.

When she made a move to swipe it from his hand, he set the cup down and did his best to divert her attention.

"What will we do now?" The imbecile sat forward in his chair, laying his impotent arms on the table. His body was frail since his fall from a horse the previous month.

"*We?*" Saints, but even she hated the shrill tone of her own voice.

He had done nothing to help her capture Arbella. A simple siege at the castle had been a complete waste of time, not to mention 'twas an embarrassment to her. The blasted maggot couldn't even keep his seat on his horse, falling off and having to be rescued by their men—half of whom perished. Now she had to deal with dozens of widows holding their hands out for a crust of bread to feed their whining children.

Marmaduke flopped back in his chair, his eyes glazing over—as they normally did most days. "Aye. *We.*" His voice was tired.

What did he have to be so tired about? She was about to ask him just that when he interrupted her thoughts.

"I am your husband, whether or not you let me into your bedchamber."

Ina held back the bile that threatened the back of her throat. "What has that to do with anything?"

"Only a reminder that, perhaps, your plots for revenge should center more around filling our nursery with heirs.

People will come to you, be loyal to you, if they see you are doing your duty."

"My duty." Her tone was strangled and it was hard for her to keep a hold on her temper. She wanted to let it fly like a bird of prey and scratch his eyes out.

On their wedding night, she'd stomached his intrusion into her body, his flopping around. When it was over, she'd sworn to him that he would only be allowed entry into her person one time a year—on the eve of their wedding anniversary and that he'd best make the most of it. Perhaps it was that night that she realized what a mistake it was to be joined with him. It'd been four years since they were wed and, lucky for her, the previous anniversaries had always seen her indisposed with her women's courses. Thus, he'd been shunned from her chamber.

Despite their lack of nuptial congress, Ina had managed to birth a bairn just nine months after they were wed. When she'd found out she was with child, she'd loudly boasted of her English husband's powerful seed, but only because her clansmen wanted to kill the idiot. Otherwise, she wouldn't have gone to such lengths to make him feel good about himself. The English were full of themselves enough as it was. And her husband's wounded pride at having been snubbed by Arbella, his intended bride—and Magnus, who'd stolen her away—well, it was a wound that festered and needed the kind of constant stroking Ina had no patience for.

When her child was born, a son, he luckily took after his Scottish roots, which made it easier for Ina to pretend the bairn was from the man she truly wanted—Magnus.

They'd been betrothed, set to marry, before that saucy harlot, Arbella, crossed the border and stole him away.

Ina fisted her hands, her fingernails biting into her palms. *Arbella*... Why hadn't Ina killed her when she had the chance the previous month? There had been more than enough time, more than enough occasions to see it done. But after successfully abducting her, Ina wanted to torment her, tease her. And then the bitch had gone and escaped. Run right away back into the arms of Ina's man.

Magnus, Magnus, Magnus...

The one and only true Highlander.

"Aye, your duty. You need to see it done. *I* need to see it done."

Ina felt a small thrill in her belly. One she would equate with desire if she were to feel such things. But she wasn't. So she quickly shoved it aside.

"Ye'll be getting there soon enough," she growled.

His eyes sparked determination. "I'm counting down the days. You'll not be escaping this time." There was a sinister glint in his tone, as though he could possibly be serious.

Where was this coming from? She'd not seen him so blisteringly angry since before they'd wed.

Ina narrowed her eyes on him. She prepared to tell him just what she thought of his idiotic notions, but a stirring from the courtyard caught her attention. "Someone is here," she said.

Marmaduke shoved away from his chair and walked toward the arrow slit window to look down into the courtyard. He motioned for the guards to stand ready at the heavy oak door that led down a wide spiral stair and to the main doors of the tower.

"'Tis your cousin," he mused. "Padrig."

"Why the hell would he be *here?*" she asked sharply under her breath. Ina shoved her husband out of the way to see a large warrior carrying her cousin's limp and bloody body through the bailey. "Ye didna say he was wounded!"

She didn't recognize the man who carried her cousin, nor

the colors he wore. And why, oh why, were they here? That was a more pressing question on her mind than what had happened to her wayward relation. Padrig had escaped the priory where he'd been sent to languish at for a minimum of five years, a prison sentence so to speak. Magnus Sutherland was behind his temporary confinement, but Ina had no doubt that it was Arbella's idea. When he'd escaped, Padrig had come to Ross Castle first and Ina had given him a task. One that even Marmaduke was unaware of. Showing up now, broken of body, sent a torrent of anger rushing through her. Padrig had failed.

Marmaduke snickered and shrugged. "What difference does it make? He escaped the priory, and the Sutherlands want him dead. With him here, he'll only be a burden on us."

"Nay, that is not true." She stared hard at her husband, hoping he would see that she thought *him* more of burden than her own cousin. "He is my blood and the second heir to the Ross Clan."

Marmaduke looked at her pointedly. "Away from the priory where you wanted him kept. Now he'll be causing trouble all over again."

Ina huffed a breath. Marmaduke had no idea what an asset Padrig could have been if only he'd been able to infiltrate the Bruce's camp and see to the task she'd set for him.

Saints on a spitfire! This put a considerable wrench in her plans. If Padrig was no good to her in a priory, he was even less so bleeding in her bailey. Perhaps, her husband was right and Padrig was a burden. Mayhap she should see him tossed in an oubliette.

Ina regarded Marmaduke with conflicting feelings of disdain and interest. He went against most things she believed in, but worst of all, he hated Magnus Sutherland. Though Ina wanted Magnus' wife dead, she wanted *him* very much alive. Could she forgive Marmaduke for hating the man she loved? Probably not. But, she could respect Marmaduke's concern for her and her clan and the trouble her cousin was causing them. Her husband was right about that. Whoever had harmed Padrig could have gotten information out of him, portions of Ina's plans.

A moment later, Padrig was carried, unconscious, into the great hall by a great, hulking warrior. The stranger was plainly dirty with ratty clothes and boots with a large hole in the toe. His scraggly beard and knotted hair spoke of a hard life. Ina wrinkled her nose at the scent that was brought in with him.

"Lay him on the trestle table," Marmaduke ordered.

Padrig's large, limp body was placed on the table. His face was pale and blood spread all around his middle. He made not a sound. If not for someone whispering they could still feel a weak pulse, Ina would have thought him dead.

Ina addressed the oafish man without looking at him. "What happened?"

"Took an ax to the back," the warrior said. "If he lives, he'll likely not be walking again."

An ax to the back. He'd been fighting. A battle. Probably at Robert the Bruce's stronghold. Ina shivered.

"Who are ye?" Ina asked, not bothering to hide her disdain. "Why did ye not leave him to die?"

The dirty warrior bowed. "I am Ahlrid, my lady. Padrig bade me bring him here, his last wish, he said."

"Who are ye to my cousin?"

"I am no one. I found him on the road, barely breathing, and he told me what happened."

Ina didn't believe him. For some reason, Ahlrid did not want her to know he'd been fighting the Bruce. Well, Ina didn't have the time or the inclination to find out exactly what his reasoning was. And she, quite frankly, didn't care.

She waved to Old Man Angus. "Give this man a warm meal and a few coins for his trouble, then see him on his way."

"My lady," Ahlrid said, fear flashing in his gaze. "If I might beg a night afore your fire? There's a storm brewing."

Ina pinched the bridge of her nose, squeezing her eyes shut and forcing herself not to order him to the dungeon. He had brought her cousin home, so at least she knew Padrig's mission had failed. That deserved something.

"Nay. Nay. Nay," Ina muttered. "Now, go with Angus, else I change my mind about feeding ye at all." She pointed toward the kitchens where Old Man Angus had waddled off to.

"If he lives and he canna walk," Marmaduke mused, walking toward the table, "then he will be within our power. If he lives and 'twas because we saved him, then he will be within our power."

Ina perked up at hearing this. She drew closer to her cousin's body. Annoyance melting away. "And we can use him to our own advantage."

Marmaduke met her gaze, a cruel smile on his lips. "Aye. He will be at our mercy."

That strange feeling of desire rolled in her belly again. What was that? And why the hell was she feeling it whilst staring at her husband? Was it the cruel glint in his eye? The sardonic curl to his lip? The very idea that he wanted to use her cousin to their advantage? Whatever it was, she was suddenly hot. Before she could pull the words back, she found herself saying, "Come to my bedchamber. I have need of your... assistance."

CHAPTER 1

Scottish Highlands
Terrel Tower,
August, 1308 (five and a half years later)

"Da, I dinna want to marry." Lady Emilia faced off with her father, Laird MacCulloch, with a glower she hoped mimicked her mother's expression when she was ready to toss the laird in a fire.

"Ye've no choice. We've made a good match for ye. Padrig of Clan Ross is heir to the Ross Clan now that the wee bairn succumbed to fever. One day, ye'll be the mistress of the castle. Is that not what ye want?"

What she wanted? Nay. Not entirely. Aye, what a dream it would be if she could be mistress of her own castle. Every little lass growing up dreamed of such things. But at what cost? Certainly not the loss of her freedom, her sanity. Nay, married to Padrig Ross was not what she wanted in the least —and lady of the castle, it would never happen.

Beyond that, the Ross Clan was aligned with England.

Traitors to the Scots. How in good conscience could she willingly wed traitors?

Wrinkling her nose, Emilia gave her father a look she hoped conveyed all the doubt she felt. "The man is not much younger than his cousin. Ina Ross and Marmaduke Stewart will continue to rule that clan—even from the grave. Beyond that, the English will expect an alliance from ye. The Bruce will name ye a traitor to all Scots!"

The laird clucked his tongue, his mood obviously souring tremendously. He did not like when she talked back to him, but what good daughter would allow her father to believe something that was false? And how could she ever face her reflection in the looking glass if she simply allowed herself to be given over without even trying to dissuade her father?

"Ye know 'tis true," she grumbled, crossing her arms over her chest.

To this, her father growled. "Nay, ye're wrong, lass, and ye shouldna stick your pert little nose where it doesna belong."

Oh, saints, Emilia should keep her lips firmly closed, but she could not. "How is me being forced to marry into that clan none of my business? How can I turn a blind eye to my family's peril? I should say it is exactly where my nose belongs." She was quick to stand, fearing her father may just come after her, tossing her over his shoulder, and throwing her in her chamber until the papers were signed and the priest waiting only for her consent—which she would never give.

Having lived a much-sheltered life, Emilia had not many chances for romance, but she'd tried her best to flirt with some of the younger warriors, to tease the stable hands, and even found herself kissing a merchant's son who was just passing through. She'd not yet fallen in love and, though she didn't expect to be in love with the man she was to wed, she at least had hopes of respect. Wasn't respecting one's spouse essential?

Gooseflesh tingled over her arms, and she resisted the urge to rub them. She also resisted the urge to tug at her eyebrow, which she often did when distressed, a sure sign to her father that she was extremely bothered. Neutral was what she needed to remain. Completely neutral. Especially with the way her father's face had gone from an angry red to a purplish rage.

Mayhap she shouldn't have goaded him so. And, perhaps, she should not have made him out to be an ill provider and protector of the clan. But... wasn't that the line he was crossing?

Laird MacCulloch sucked his breath in on his teeth, hands fisted at his sides. He stood so rigid that Emilia feared he might just fall over. "'Tis best ye take yourself off to your room, for I've an itch to take a lash to your behind!"

"I'm a grown woman!" Hands fisted at her sides, it was a practice in willpower not to stomp her foot. She cursed herself for not doing exactly as he said, but she was stubborn to a fault and when battle lines were drawn, she couldn't help but leap over them.

Her father's chest swelled, his harsh eyes slashed with anger. "Then act as such and accept your duties with the pride a lady should."

Emilia gritted her teeth. Her father was right that she was not behaving as she ought to have been. She was more than aware of it. Her compulsions had gotten her into trouble plenty of times. But he was also wrong in this, she was certain. How could she get through to him?

MacCulloch lands bordered Ross lands. How many men of her clan had been lost to a skirmish with the devils? How many of their cattle, sheep, and other livestock had been stolen? How many crops burned? How many of their people harmed, killed? Crofts burned? Fences chopped? The list was endless.

Why was her father insisting she marry the enemy? Laird MacCulloch was a good man. He loved her, she knew that. She was the eldest of his daughters . Her younger sister, Ayne, was already at Nèamh Abbey. Her eldest brother had been killed during a battle. Her youngest sibling, Dirk, took up his grooming to be laird and was betrothed to the Sutherland's eldest daughter, Belle. They'd not be wedded for at least another decade or so.

And this left all the marrying for alliances up to Emilia. "Why a Ross, Da? Why not any other clan?" Softly, she added, "They are our enemies."

Her father's face fell, mouth going slack with regret. With his gaze toward the thin window, he took several steps toward her. "My darling daughter, in this world we have alliances and we have enemies. The only way to bring our enemies close to our breast is to offer them something in return."

Her heart clenched. "I am an offering?"

MacCulloch cleared his throat. "Of a sort."

"What are ye not telling me?" Emilia locked eyes on him, upset when he blinked away. "Da, please, why am I to be the sheep?"

Her da grabbed on to her hands, squeezing them tight, all the anger gone from him. "Please believe me when I say I've no choice."

"How can I when ye willna tell me anything but words steeped in mystery?" Anger burbled up the back of her throat. If she wasn't careful, she'd be screaming and stomping her foot in minutes. "Does mama know about this?"

Emilia glanced around her father's study, half-expecting to see her mother hiding in a corner, unable to face her. Lady

MacCulloch was no simpering female, but she was honest to a fault. The lack of her presence was telling.

"I will only tell ye that our clan is in trouble, that Ina Ross approached me about forming an alliance. Rather, than having me pay the dowry, she was willing to double it in return."

That was unheard of. And even more terrifying... Ina Ross thought of Emilia as some kind of commodity. "I am to be sold."

"Nay, 'tis not the way of it." Though he denied it, the truth was evident in his tone.

Emilia ground her teeth, stubbornly yanking her hands from his grasp. "Aye, Da, no matter how ye've convinced yourself otherwise, it is the way of it. Ye sold me to the Ross witch."

"Nay, ye're to marry her cousin."

Emilia shook her head, incredulous. She let out a bitter laugh. "Is there a difference? No one, not even her husband, has the willpower to deny her. All of Scotland knows this." She let out a deep, disappointed sigh. "I love ye, Da, I do, but ye've broken my heart this day."

Laird MacCulloch's features hardened, his mouth forming a thin, hard line. "Best not bring matters of the heart into it, lass, for there is no place in marriage for it. When ye get to the altar and ye repeat your vows before God and all, remember this: ye saved your clan from utter ruin. Your sacrifice did that."

Utter ruin. How? Wasn't her father hurtling them all onto the wrong side of this great war for independence?

She opened her mouth to ask him to explain but he held up his hand. "Dinna speak another word of it, for I'll not listen. I've made up my mind. Your mama has already begun packing for ye."

Emilia's heart lurched into her throat, and she swayed on her feet. "Packing? Da! When do I leave?"

"Ye'll be married by proxy in the morn. Marmaduke Stewart will act as stand-in. Then ye'll leave with him to greet your husband at Ross Castle."

The walls around her shifted, breaking from their mortared places and closing in on her. The light from the candles grew long, then short, then long again, and the floor beneath her feet buckled in waves. With a shuddering breath, she closed her eyes to compose herself. To force her mind to put everything back in its place. "How long have ye known?"

At this, her father had the decency to look embarrassed. "Long enough to have the paperwork drawn up and signed."

Emilia's heart set into brittle stone. Before she could stop herself, she rushed headlong into a passionate speech. "I will remind myself daily that I've done this to save my clan and that I was sold to the highest bidder in order to save MacCullochs from whatever mystery that plagued them. But I will also tell myself that my father betrayed me."

With that, she whirled around and hurled herself from the room, rushing up the stairs fast enough that she tripped and banged her shins painfully on the edge of the stone steps. Tears tracking her face, she burst into her chamber to find her mother, who looked up sharply, guiltily, from the trunk she was stuffing full of garments.

"My darling," her mother whispered, tears gathering in her eyes. Her hands moved to her mouth as though she wished to hide every word that would rush from her lips.

"Dinna speak to me," Emilia hissed. "Dinna call me your darling. Ye could have warned me. Could have prepared me. But ye are no better than he is. Ye have both betrayed me."

Mama looked helpless, her shoulders sagging. "Daughters

must marry who their fathers choose. Alliances must be made."

Emilia marched to the trunk and pulled out a wad of fabrics, tossing them to the floor. "I dinna argue the merits of my duty to ye, to Da, to MacCulloch. I curse that he sold me to our enemies." She tossed her boots near the hearth and reached in to tug out all the lovely silken scarves. "I curse that he willna tell me why. I curse that the both of ye hid the truth from me. Now that my heart is breaking, I've not the chance to let it sink in. Instead, I am to be shipped off at first light—with our enemy." Her fingers touched on a brooch with the MacCulloch crest and she flung it toward the window, hitting the arch and watching it clang against the stone before falling to the floor. "Who is to say they willna slit my throat once I've crossed onto their lands? Who is to say they willna sell me to someone else to recoup their loss?"

Lady MacCulloch shook her head, having the nerve to look as though she pitied Emilia her anger. She walked around the room gathering the items Emilia had tossed. "Knowing anything wouldna have changed the course of things. A daughter must marry." She dumped them back in the chest.

"Why, Mama? At least tell me that much." Emilia stared at the mess she'd made, her energy waning.

Lady MacCulloch fretted her hands on the items in the chest, refolding them neatly. "We are in trouble, my dear. We've no coin. Our men are depleted, our walls crumbling, our people starving."

"Because of the Ross Clan! And ye would give me over!"

"They have filled our coffers, restored our flocks, and filled our granary. Ye have saved us." She gently closed the trunk.

No matter how many times they said it, Emilia still didn't

want to accept that as the answer. And yet, as both of her parents said, she had no choice.

A subtle knock sounded at the door and Laird MacCulloch pushed through without waiting to be let in. "I've posted guards outside your door, lass. In case ye have any ideas of escape."

Emilia perked up, brushing aside any hurt at her father's distrust, for he'd given her a thought. Escape? That was not something she'd even considered. What a grand idea. Where could she go? To the Sutherlands? They were enemies of the Ross Clan; they were allies to her own. They may take her in, but they would likely not risk the alliance with her parents. All the same, she could try. She could warn them about her parent's alliance and what it meant in regards to the English and the Scots. The Sutherlands could talk sense into her parents; bring them back to the Scots' cause. Mayhap even give them a loan so they could pay back Ross. She had to do something, or else all of them would be doomed.

Dirk was too young to be brought in to the center of this war. Her sister needn't worry about anything other than her prayers. Obviously, her parents had lost their sense and it was up to Emilia to gain it back for them.

Turning her back on her parents, she walked to the thin window that overlooked the back gardens of the castle. In the morning, when the time came, she would be meek. She would be agreeable. She would be pathetic.

Marmaduke Stewart would let his guard down, thinking her such a weakling, so biddable. And then when he least expected it, she would run. And if no opportunity presented itself upon the road, she would run after she was at Ross Castle.

"I am verra tired," she said. "I would like Cook to bring my dinner to my chamber. My last request."

"Nay, Daughter, there is no need for ye to eat alone," her mother hurried. "We would eat with ye."

"I am verra tired and not feeling at all myself. I need to be alone. To think." To plan. To slip a dagger into that chest and another under her dress. To properly prepare herself for what was to come.

What she wanted to do was curl up in a ball on her bed and cry. To rage at the world for the injustice of how she felt. She desired to take her dagger and cut the ever living hell out of something.

But that would only draw the attention of everyone in the castle. While she had a wicked temper that sometimes got the better of her, she didn't often like to make a spectacle of herself.

Her parents quietly left the room, no utterances of apology—not that she could have truly expected they would. Still, that didn't make it hurt any less.

Emilia traced her fingers over the stones surrounding her chamber window. Would she ever see this view again? Would she ever touch these stones once more? Would she pick the apples from the trees in the garden beyond or was traipsing through the orchard not something she'd likely experience in future?

When her throat swelled and her breath caught, she turned away from the window and went about the task of finding the few daggers she'd hidden about her chamber. One could never be too careful when enemies lurked about. Besides, blades were a passion of hers.

She'd once seen a woman, Aliah de Mowbray, who was now married off to one of the Sutherlands. That woman was wicked with a blade. They'd had a knife throwing contest at a tournament. The way the lady had whipped her blades through the air, silky locks coming loose of her braid, determination set in her brow, a satisfied smile when she met her mark, had caused Emilia's own obsession. Her oak wardrobe sported many cuts on the inside back panel from where she'd open the doors, emptied the contents, and practiced throwing. An attempt at hiding her hobby from her mother and father. As of yet, they'd not noticed or, at least, they'd never said anything. Her maid had always kept her secret.

Well, soon, Ina, Marmaduke, and Padrig Ross—if they didn't allow her to escape—would feel the brunt of her blade. After all, her father might have sold her to the enemy, but never would she dare give away her soul.

CHAPTER 2

Balmacara Castle
Inverness-shire, Highlands, Scotland
September, 1307 (one month later)

How many months had passed since he'd been with a woman? Two? Three? And why now had he decided to develop a conscience?

Laird Ian Matheson followed the line of female servants going about their duties with his eyes, watching the swish of their hips in rough woolen skirts. Some tall, some short. Some thick, some thin. Some curvy, some narrow. He wasn't picky. Didn't matter the size; all women were beautiful to him. And as long as they were warm, willing, and able, he was happy to bring them to bed for sport. Well, he used to be happy. Now everything had changed.

One particular lass kept boldly looking over her shoulder as if she knew his exact line of thoughts and was happy to oblige.

Ian gulped his ale, meeting her gaze for one longing moment before pulling away. If his father hadn't borne a slew of bastards, he might have invited all the women to bed right then and there. But as the newly appointed laird of his clan, he didn't want to overstep the boundaries between leader and subject, a line his father had never recognized. There was also the fact that his new role was tenuous at best. He needed to prove himself to his people, to the elders, else he be forced to step aside.

Ian stood from his chair and turned his back on the servants, walking toward the hearth. As much as he wouldn't mind a little afternoon dalliance, today was not the day for it, nor did he see any in the near future. There had once been a time he'd eagerly leap at the opportunity to take one of them upstairs. Those days were long gone.

'Twas unreal, being named laird. His entire life he'd never thought it would happen. Though his father had trained him to be so, had often boasted loudly of it, feelings of inadequacy made Ian doubt it. He scrubbed a hand over his face. To be sure, he was well trained for the position. At twenty and nine years of age, he'd seen plenty of battles, had the scars to prove it, defended the castle, attended negotiations between clans, saved his mother, and saved his father. Ten times over he'd proven his worth. But there was still that one thing, that one little piece of the puzzle he was missing. And it was an heir of his own.

"What shall we do with them?" Alistair, his second-in-command, asked with a noticeable hitch of nerves in his tone.

The them that Alistair referred to was about a dozen lads and lasses who'd been brought to the castle that morning by a harried elderly woman and her husband. The lot of them scampered around the bailey laughing, screaming, and causing all sorts of general ruckus that, foretold at some point, disaster was certain to happen.

Alistair looked unnerved. He'd been Ian's best mate for as

long as he could remember. As a young lad, Alistair had washed up on the shore of Loch Alsh. No one knew who he was and no one ever came to claim in. But Ian did. Alistair and he had been inseparable ever since.

"Tell me again what they said?" Ian was still having a hard time figuring out just what the hell was going on.

"They are your bastard brothers and sisters. Your father left them all in the care of the generous couple, but now they are too old to take care of them."

Ian nodded, though he agreed to nothing.

His father had passed away a few months before. The laird had been just past sixty years, hale and hearty. His death was unexpected by everyone, especially by Ian. 'Twas at that time the female servants, one and all, began offering him the special services that they used to provide to his father. That was also precisely the time Ian had become celibate.

"We must find out who their mothers are." Ian ran a tired hand over his chin. "They shall be returned to their mothers. I will pay a generous allowance to each of them per annum. 'Tis no apology, but hopefully it lessens the pain of my father having taken advantage."

Alistair nodded. "In the meantime?" He shifted. "The wee ones are running through the barn, disturbing the horses."

Ian frowned. He turned back toward the female servants in the great hall, noticing how very few males there were. He'd remedy that tomorrow. "Attention!" he called.

They all stopped what they were doing to face him.

How to ask? Ian decided for bluntness. This business needed to be taken care of straight away. "How many of ye birthed bairns by my father?"

The lassies all turned to look at one another with wide eyes, as though they'd never expected to be asked such, nor admit the truth if they had. He wasn't surprised. Such wasn't discussed.

Tentatively three of them raised their hands.

"Go, then, and get your bairns."

They shook their heads, worrying their lower lips, and wringing their hands around mops and rags.

"Why not?" he demanded, his frown deepening. This was the respect he needed, expected as laird if, that was, he deserved to be laird.

Two firmly clamped their lips shut and the third stood with her mouth agape and no words coming out.

Saints preserve him. Ian blew out an exasperated sigh. "Ye have permission to speak. I am not a monster, nor a hypocrite. I'll not punish ye for telling the truth."

One of them finally quit her silence. "We wouldna know which was ours, Laird."

"What?" Exasperation slapped him on the back with a mighty whoosh. Unfortunately, his outburst had them all clamping up again. "Again, I swear it, ye'll not be punished. I pray ye'll tell me what in blazes is going on afore the lot of them destroys the bailey completely."

Another stepped forward, her gaze toward the ground. "They were taken from us when they were wee bairns. We'd have a hard time recognizing them, given we haven't seen them in so long."

The situation couldn't get any worse, could it? First, his father seemed to have bedded every woman in the castle. Now he'd taken their bairns away so they couldn't recognize them. Lord, help him. Ian had always taken it for granted that a mother would recognize her child should she see it finally. Had hoped that such was true. For orphans everywhere.

Beside him, Alistair was all too quiet. This news was a blow to him, for he'd often confided that he hoped to one day be reunited with his family, a sentiment Ian couldn't agree with more.

But right now, there was no time for sad thoughts or the like. Ian didn't have time for this. There was a wall to fortify, a roof to fix, horses to work, men to train, letters to be written, ledgers to be checked, crofters to be found, autumn crops to be harvested, and food stores to be prepped for winter. The list went on and on. And at the very top of it, was getting twelve little imps behind secured doors before they made his list of things to repair even longer.

Ian glanced at Alistair who slowly backed away, shaking his head. Damn. The man had figured him out. Tasking his second with this madness was out of the question.

"All right then, the three of ye will go and gather the bairns and take them up to the nursery. Clean them up and feed them. No longer are ye to clean the castle, ye'll be nursemaids now. 'Haps in time ye'll come to know who is yours."

One of them fainted straight away. One dropped to her knees, her hands in supplication mouthing *thank ye, thank ye, thank ye*, and the other simply stared at him with ice in her eyes.

"Ye want us for breeders?" she asked, shocking him.

"What? Nay. That is an insult to my character." His anger was obvious in his words and she immediately paled. "But I understand why ye said it. I am... different." He hadn't the heart to put his father down. The man had done well in raising him, even if he saw fit to impregnate only God knew how many women. "He was a great laird but he had great faults. I willna repeat them. Now go, afore they destroy my castle."

Rousing the woman who'd fainted, the three women rushed from the great hall, but that didn't give Ian any sense of relief. What was he to do with twelve children? He couldn't turn them away. They were his father's blood and they were children. Cruelty wasn't in his nature. Besides, he felt extreme guilt for their circumstances, though they were not of his doing.

A moment later, one of the maids returned carrying an infant in one arm and holding the hand of a toddler with the other. The look of love in her eyes was enough to move even Ian, who was often hardened to such shows of affection. The infant could have been this woman's. He'd returned her child to her. That would mean something to his people, wouldn't it?

Next came two lads, aged five perhaps, who were laughing and chasing each other. An older boy of about ten years followed slowly, looking quite annoyed to be there. The second maid entered with two girls around the same age as the boy, looking rather fearful.

The third maid returned, bairns of perhaps one year on each hip. "Ye said there were twelve?"

"Aye."

"We only found nine."

"Bloody hell," Ian grumbled. Again, he looked to Alistair, who avoided eye contact altogether. "Come on, help me round up the last three, it canna be hard as all that."

His second grumbled something under his breath and then brightly said, "Aye, my laird."

Ian laughed. "Only ye could show me such blatant disrespect and get away with it." And that was the truth, for he was working damn hard to gain the full respect of everyone else in this castle.

Alistair clapped him on the back. "And only ye could take in twelve bastards. Any other laird would have turned them out."

Ian shook his head. "My mother wanted many children, I know she did. And perhaps by keeping the bairns hidden, it was my father's way of sparing her feelings. Now that they are both gone from here..."

"Your mother will catch wind of it."

Ian sucked on his teeth. "Likely."

Lady Matheson had sequestered herself at Nèamh Abbey in Skye, where a cousin of hers was abbess, after his father's death. Though she'd taken her vows and devoted the rest of her life to God, she continued to send Ian a letter once a month like clockwork. She'd mothered him well and he loved her deeply. He wanted to make her proud.

However, Ian prayed that her work with the church would keep her well away from Balmacara Castle. But he feared that if she caught wind of the dozen children now inhabiting the walls she'd come calling—and not in a good way.

Ian twisted his neck from side to side, cracking the tension out. Blowing through the large oak door of the castle, he found himself in the midst of chaos, indeed. What did the maid mean when she said she couldn't find the three others?

For there they were, tiny heathens, destroying everything in their path. Two lads and a lass, perhaps aged seven or so, were running circles around the stone well as they chased a goat, which in turn was running amok, knocking down crofters with push carts of vegetables and hay. The goat bleated piercingly as its horns got caught on the fabric of a washerwoman's skirt, tearing it as it dragged her to the ground. Not to mention that each of the little urchins was so brown in the face, they might have bathed in a tub of mud. Chasing the children were two stable hands. Rushing from inside the stable, at that moment, was a furious Master of the Horses, who was white-knuckling a whip in each hand.

"Halt!" Ian shouted, but the chaos was so immense that no one seemed to hear him. "Enough!" This time, when he bellowed, even the ravens on the rooftop flew away.

Everyone in the courtyard stopped mid-stride, save for the goat that escaped around the side of the castle with an apple speared on each horn.

"What in the bloody hell is going on here?" Ian marched toward the three menaces, who had the foresight to look down at their folded hands. "What possessed ye to tear my castle apart?" He stood, hands on his hips, looking down at the three bowed heads.

"Be—begging your pardon, Laird," the lass said, "but we wasn't tearing apart the castle, just the bailey."

If he'd not been so furious, he might have roared with laughter. His lip twitched, but he ground his teeth to keep himself from letting it loose. Och, but he'd been quite a menace himself at that age. He and Alistair had gotten their hides tanned more times than he could count, but it never stopped them from causing more mischief. The fun of it had outweighed any consequences. Still, his clan was looking at him to punish these children for their disruption and he needed them to know he'd make a good leader. But the whip? Nay, he'd not do it.

"Unacceptable," he said, his tone harsh, though he spoke quietly. From the sides of his eyes, he watched people gathering round. "The three of ye will clean up this mess at once, no supper."

Three tiny heads popped up to look at him in horror. He didn't blame them; the job would be no easy task even for a grown man. And they looked as though they'd missed supper for the past fortnight already.

"Go on now, ye can start by picking up the vegetables ye knocked out of the cart. How are we supposed to feed ye tomorrow if ye treat the food we grow like rubbish?"

"Feed us?" The lass once more acted as their spokeswoman. Each of their eyes widened at the prospect. "Tomorrow? Ye promise?"

Ian narrowed his eyes. "Aye." He looked closer at each one of them, their tiny bodies floating in their ragged and dirty clothes. Perhaps 'twas more than a few meals they'd missed. Whole days and weeks even.

They looked at each other, then ran to help right the cart and fill it back up with everything they'd spilled. Even for their young age, they worked rather well, surprising Ian.

The older couple that had brought the children eased slowly toward the exit, their faces filled with guilt. Perhaps the whip should find its mate on their backs.

"Halt!" Ian roared. And when they ran, he yelled, "Close the gates. Dinna let them pass." The guards immediately stepped in the path of the older couple.

Ian marched with purpose in their direction. When he reached them, he put his hands on his hips, glaring down at their obstinate, lined faces. "I dinna know the arrangement ye had with my father, but I doubt it included starving the wee things. How much was he paying ye?"

Their chins thrust up, but they didn't answer.

"How much?" Ian growled.

The man grumbled something inaudible.

Ian stepped closer, invading their space, intimidating them with his sheer size. "Speak clearly."

The man cleared his throat. "There was no exchange of coin."

"What then?"

He looked to his wife who subtly nodded.

"We've not had to pay tax nor rent on our land."

"Ye've been living for free then?" Every crofter owed a yearly coin tax, in addition to rent, typically in the form of a portion of their crops, livestock or other goods. Despite what a boon that was, Ian couldn't imagine that his father would only give them a free living. "What else?"

"A few gifts with each child."

"What kind of gifts?"

"Jewels, plate, furs, the like."

Ian tried to hide his exasperation. In some cases, those items may be worth more than a bag of coin. None of the ledgers bespoke of these missing items from his household and he'd never taken an interest in his mother's jewels. In fact, when she left, he'd assumed she'd taken them with her. Now it was obvious, her personal collection may have dwindled much over the years. He'd have to write her to ask and pray she'd tell him, and not question why he was inquiring.

"What have ye done with it all?" Ian asked.

"Raising twelve hellions is no easy task," the woman said bitterly. "We've nearly starved for it."

Ian frowned all the more. "Clearly ye both havena." They were plump, healthy of color, and their clothes well cared for. "Though the children have."

"We did the best we could."

"I highly doubt it. I'll need ye to make a list of the gifts and who ye sold them to."

"I dinna—"

"Ye will do it, else I'll throw ye in the dungeon. Ye have robbed my kin. From this day forward, ye'll pay your share like everyone else. I'll expect the first payment in a fortnight, along with the list." He wanted to punish them further, but they had kept twelve children alive and fairly well, if not a bit hungry. Then a thought occurred to him. Could there have been more? Ian cleared his throat. "Are these all the children?"

To this, the woman lowered her head and shook it. "There

were seven other bairns. Three... didna make it past the first year. Four have gone elsewhere."

A pang made his chest swell at the loss of three. But he swore he'd find the other four. "Where?"

"Moved away." The woman shrugged. "They didna tell us."

He gritted his teeth at her indifference. Did they mean so little? "Find out where."

Seeing he was serious, she nodded emphatically. "I will try."

"And who was their nursemaid?" Because clearly, this elderly woman wasn't nursing all the bairns.

"Our daughter."

"Send her to me with the tax and list."

"Aye, my laird. We truly did the best we could. We are old. We simply canna do it any longer."

Ian grunted. "I am glad that ye have brought them to me." That was all he could say. He turned away from them to help his three wayward wards clean up the mess they'd made.

To his surprise, many of the clan joined in helping, a few even with appraising looks. Was it possible they liked how he'd handled the situation?

Mayhap.

The wee bairns worked hard, smiles lighting up their faces, melting his heart with every passing moment. Saints, but he couldn't deny them supper, even if he had to sneak it up to the nursery himself.

Twelve bairns.

Ballocks... He'd been a bachelor of the highest order not three months past. Now he was a laird and had twelve bloody bairns to raise.

Heaven help him, but a thought crossed his mind, one which he'd been pushing off since he reached his majority: He was in need of a wife.

CHAPTER 3

Emilia glowered at the man lying before her, withered from what he'd professed had been a form women loved. He wasn't that much older than she was, but miserable years confined to a bed had aged him, and not in a good way.

Today marked the third month she'd been wed to him, and her thirtieth thwarted escape. It would seem that no matter how meek and simple she appeared, Ina Ross knew better. That woman was always one step ahead of her.

"I am dying," Padrig said, his voice gravelly with sickness. "Soon I should think."

Emilia folded her hands before her to stop from wringing them. She rarely visited this room. The few times she had, had been very unpleasant. Clearing her throat, she said, "I am sorry for that."

He snickered. "I know ye're not."

"Nay," she shook her head. "I can say with all honesty, I *am* sorry for ye, Padrig. No matter our personal circumstances."

His yellowed eyes met hers, hardening with an anger she

was certain simmered hot as the blue of flame in his heart. "I dinna want your pity."

"Ye have it all the same." She stood a little taller. This might have been the most words they'd ever exchanged.

Padrig coughed; hard, wracking coughs that shook his entire body. When he was done, his hand was covered in blood. "Ye're a tiresome fool."

Emilia soaked a linen square in the water basin and handed it to him. "And ye're a pathetic fool. We're both fools, it would seem. At least we have something in common."

A laugh escaped him that sounded like coarse stones scratching against one another. "I'm lucky to have lived long enough to have had several wives, though I'm sorry to say none of them were ever mine, in truth."

Emilia smoothed her skirts, unable to look him in the eye. He'd had more than one wife? She was not the only one? What had happened to the others? The night they'd been wed had mostly been a blur to her. She'd drunk many cups of wine when physical escape proved impossible. At least her mind could be elsewhere. Unfortunately, she still remembered vividly her wedding night. Ina and Marmaduke gathered round the bed as she sat there in her thin chemise, shivering, and drunk.

They'd shouted at her to lift the sheet. Beneath it, a servant had already undressed Padrig. His legs had shriveled from years of disuse and though he'd been washed, she could still smell the stink of sickness. *Touch him*, Ina had instructed. *There, on his pizzle.* Emilia had tried, doing as they instructed despite her own discomfort, until Padrig had thrown her from the bed, and Ina Ross had declared her a failure.

Emilia squeezed the memories from her mind. They were horrid, awful, embarrassing.

She'd barely been able to look at Padrig since, though

there had been four more times that Ina had forced them to bed without results. Padrig had not even tried to kiss her.

"I need ye to do something for me," he was saying now.

Emilia shook herself back to the present. "Why should I do anything for ye?"

"Ye shouldna if ye dinna wish, but 'tis for ye as well."

"For me?" That got her attention. In the three months since she'd been there, no one had ever tried to do anything for her benefit.

"Ye need to escape. Ye need to run. To Robert the Bruce."

"Robert the Bruce? But he is Ina's enemy. And," she said bitterly, "do ye not recall the dozens of times I've tried already?"

Padrig smiled bitterly. "I admit I wished ye'd been able to. Out of them all, ye've been my favorite."

She ignored what he implied, not wanting to think about the others. This horrible castle, or its inhabitants. "Why do ye want me to escape?"

"Because I never will. Because I've been a pawn my entire life. Because ye will carry out my revenge."

"Revenge? For what?"

Padrig met her gaze, his eyes filled with fury, regret. "I was a pawn, just like ye, lass. I was to marry a beautiful woman. But then my cousin decided I was best used as collateral, to rot away in purgatory, to pay for her sins."

"Ye mean the priory?" What she wouldn't give to be locked away in one right now.

"Aye. A veritable hell for a man like me. I've said my prayers, made my confessions, but I'm a man of the world. A warrior. A lover of women. An imbiber of heavy drink. And I had to give those things away. When I snuck them, I was punished severely. But it was worth it. If only to give my cousin the fear that I might be sent to her enemies and the hope that I just might make it."

"But now ye would have *me* go to your enemies?"

Padrig shook his head. "Ye're already in the house of my enemies. I would have ye go to the Bruce and I want ye to give him something."

"What?" Was he saying what she thought he was saying? The Bruce wasn't his enemy?

"The key to the castle."

"The key?"

"Aye." He motioned her forward with the crook of his finger and, without thinking, Emilia walked forward. "Here, in my sleeve." He withdrew a roll of parchment. "That is a map of every tunnel and hidden entrance to the castle."

Was this some sort of trick? Emilia turned to look behind her, expecting to see a guard there, or Ina, someone waiting to shackle her in a dark dungeon while they sought an annulment to this farce of a marriage—or worse, they would tell everyone she'd simply disappeared. But there was no one there.

"Lass." Padrig's voice was serious.

She turned back toward him, taking in his grave expression. If this was a test, he was doing a very good job at playing his part. "Ye want me to give it to the Bruce?" she whispered.

"Come now, I may call ye a fool, but I know ye're bright." He shifted in the bed, wincing, as he tried to sit up more. "I've lain here for more than five years, suffering at *her* hands. One bride after another, I made excuses. This one was ugly, this one smelled bad, that one had rotted teeth. I've had more annulments than a good man should. But between Ina's attempts, I gave her hope that I could still...be with a woman. I snuck gifts to the maids to brag loudly of their carnal nights with me, none of which were true, hoping one day, the perfect bride would come along for me."

Emilia swallowed. "And that is me?"

"Aye. I've told Ina I felt...that ye were the one to heal me. I did that to keep ye safe, because I had hope on that verra first night when I looked into your defiant eyes. Ye were still strong."

"I dinna understand."

"Lass, ye're good, where the rest of my wives were broken. And those who live in this household are devils." He pressed the parchment into her hand. "Ye're the one to see to this task. Ye must leave tonight. Before I die. For when I do, they will have no use of ye as a widow and they've paid a pretty penny for ye as a bride."

Emilia nodded, though she didn't understand. "What... will they do with me?"

Padrig's face darkened. "Ina is barren. She has birthed only one child and he fell ill soon after. They will breed ye, lass, one way or another. They need an heir. If not by me, then by Marmaduke. They canna risk their clan's legacy falling into someone else's hands."

Emilia shuddered. But she knew he spoke the truth. Marmaduke had been making subtle hints to just that lately. Ina had been eyeing her as though she were a prized mare. While she'd not comprehended their plans before, she did fully now.

"I will go," she murmured.

"Good girl." He patted her hand. "The guards change at sundown. Listen carefully, because ye've not much time until then. If ye get it wrong, I fear ye'll be lost to their machinations as I have been."

Emilia nodded, her stomach twisted up into knots. "I am listening."

Padrig gave her detailed instructions on how to get to one of the secret tunnels. There would be a man waiting for her at the end, Ahlrid. He'd been going to the tunnels every night for a fortnight to make certain no one else was using them. Padrig and Ahlrid had once made the escape plans for himself; though it was obvious he'd never be able to use them now. "Ahlrid will take ye to the Bruce. Stay with him. He will protect ye. But I warn ye, the man is not to be trifled with."

"Who is he?"

"He was my personal guard for many years."

Emilia was dizzy with fear, with anticipation. She wanted to leave. To be free, and this seemed the perfect opportunity. "Thank ye, Padrig. I will never be able to repay ye."

"Och, lass, but ye will, when this map gets into the hands of Robert the Bruce."

Emilia tucked the parchment in her own sleeve. "Godspeed, Padrig. I will pray for ye."

Padrig smirked. "It'll do me no good. Now go, afore they come searching for ye. I've paid the guards outside the door to look the other way."

Emilia rushed from her husband's sick room, through the door that linked their chambers. She didn't bother to pack anything, possessions would only hold her back, but she did need her knives. She'd given them a home these past few months. One beneath her mattress, one hidden in a nook by the slim window, and the other strapped to the outside of her thigh never left her, though she'd had to be careful to keep it hidden.

Armed, she carefully opened the door to the corridor. The two guards posted, true to Padrig's word, did not look at her at all. Each seemed to concentrate quite hard on the wall opposite them. They would be punished for her escape and she hoped they'd been paid well for it, for every other guard she'd thwarted had disappeared.

She whispered a prayer for them but could think on their sacrifice no more.

Emilia scooted down the opposite direction, keeping her back to the wall, hands sliding along the stone. She wished she could sink into it. Become invisible.

The castle sounds remained the same with servants bustling about below. Warriors outside. Merchants. Nothing amiss. Still, every little noise, normal as it was, made her leap out of her skin.

She made her way, largely unnoticed, down to the bottom of the back stair. But rather than sneak out the door as she'd done during several previous escape attempts, she continued on to the bowels of the castle and into the cellar where the wine, ale, and whisky were kept.

The room was dank, smelling of wetness and must. A single torch was lit, illuminating the cramped space. She hurried to the far back, finding the wooden shelf with the nick on the top corner that Padrig had told her about. She couldn't shove it aside with casks, jars, and barrels holding it in place. Her heart thumped loud enough she feared she'd not hear if anyone approached. She was running out of time!

In order to move it out of the way, to get to the hidden door behind, she'd have to empty the shelves.

Emilia worked as fast as she could with slickened hands, afraid, more than once, that she'd drop a jar on the floor and the entire castle would come running at the clatter. She'd be strung up, whipped, but kept whole enough on her lower extremities that Marmaduke could mount her. Breed her.

Fear gave her strength and a speed she didn't normally have. Soon, she was pushing the shelves out of the way and counting eight stones from the bottom of the cellar floor up, until she found the hidden latch that clicked the door open.

Foul, musty, old air whooshed out from behind the closed door. Air that had not been stirred in who knew how long. She gasped, closing her eyes at the dust. 'Twas dark beyond. Childish fears of spiders, rats, and ghosts leapt to the forefront of her mind.

Childish? Perhaps. But real? Very.

She grabbed the lone torch on the wall and rushed into the tunnel, tugging the door as closed behind her as she could. Whoever found where she'd gone would see the shelves emptied and follow. Down the dusty stairs she hurried, not daring to look back, and fearing every second that Ross guards were chasing after her.

Down and down she ran. Then up a slim circular stair, her gown catching on God knew what a thousand times until she finally reached the top, and apparently the end—a wall loomed tall and devastating.

"Nay!" she shouted in frustration, pounding her fist against it.

Had she gone the wrong way? Had she taken a turn she shouldn't have? Was this all a farce for Padrig's amusement? Was this a game they were playing, laughing so hard tears came to their eyes?

Emilia punched at the wall again, only to hear a scraping on the other side. A breath later, the wall slid away and a man, larger than a mountain and fiercer than any of her nightmares, stood before her.

"Took ye long enough," he grumbled.

"Ahl—Ahlrid?" Emilia chewed her cheek praying it was the man Padrig told her meet. If not, she might as well offer up her prayers to heaven for a quick death.

"Aye. We've no time for introductions. No time for fancy

37

travel." He opened a wineskin and dumped some of the contents onto her torch, extinguishing the light.

Was light a fancy thing?

No matter. She breathed a sigh of relief that it was Ahlrid and, so far, Padrig had been true to his word.

Ahlrid continued, "And certainly no time for any feminine whining. We will travel fast and hard. Else we're both dead and, trust me, while I might have given my life for Padrig, I'll not be giving it for ye."

Emilia opened her mouth to respond but found she had nothing to say, so she simply nodded.

Ahlrid turned his back on her and rushed through the darkened woods.

She chased after him, getting whacked in the face more than once with a wayward branch. Freedom was worth the sting. And try as she might to avoid them, it was a lost cause as she needed to hold up her skirts, else trip over them. Perhaps women's clothes were also too fancy for an escape.

Clouds covered the moon, and she found she was literally running blind. Ahlrid was nearly silent ahead of her, while she crashed through the forest like a wild boar.

At last, she managed to catch up with Ahlrid without having fallen and with only a few cuts on her face.

"Get on." He nodded toward the large warhorse beside him.

"I—" She cut herself off. She didn't know how to mount a horse without help. There had always been stairs or a stable hand to help. But she couldn't ask for help, he'd think she was whining.

After watching her struggle for several moments, Ahlrid blew out a disgusted breath, urged his horse forward, gripped her around the waist and tossed her on the mount's back.

"Can ye ride? Or is mounting not your only weakness?" His voice was filled with disdain, but she didn't care.

"I can."

"Then ye'd best keep up. I'll not hesitate to leave ye behind." Ahlrid took off at a rapid pace.

Emilia adjusted her seat, took the reins, and begged the horse to keep pace and follow Ahlrid—thank the saints it did.

CHAPTER 4

Alistair cleared his throat. "Bad news, Laird."

Ian looked up from the mountains of paperwork on his desk. His eyes burned from lack of sleep, and his head ached as though a dozen tiny pairs of feet had leapt upon it. Perhaps they had.

"I tell ye, man, I canna hear another bit of bad news. Take ye to the devil."

Alistair chuckled. "'Tis a pretty bit of bad news."

"I dinna care if 'tis pretty with eight breasts and a rear even a saint would mount, I banish ye from my study." He pointed toward the exit for good measure.

Alistair only roared with laughter. "Shall I tell ye again what they're calling ye in the Highlands, Laird?"

Ian scowled. "Nay."

But that didn't stop his second from speaking. "Papa Matheson."

"I see ye canna follow a direct order." Ian tossed down his quill, prepared for an onslaught of insults.

Alistair straightened, his laughter gone though it still danced in his eyes. "There's a saucy bit here to see ye."

Ian crossed his arms over his chest and shook his head. There'd been a number of them every single day. "Give her a bag of coin and tell her we're not breeders."

Alistair poured Ian a dram of whisky and set it on the desk in front of him. "I dinna think that will work this time."

"Pray tell me ye dinna speak of my mother?" Oh, saints, if it was his mother... He downed the whisky, hoping it would take some of the pain away from his head.

Alistair slapped his knee. "I say, Ian, ye're in a right ornery mood! And your jests, why they have never been better."

Ian narrowed his eyes. "Have I ever told ye how much I want to stab your eyes out when ye poke fun at me?"

"Aye." Alistair grinned widely and nodded. "Now, about the minx in the great hall. Her companion is, by far, more intriguing."

"Oh, for the love of God." Ian pushed away from his desk and stood. Shoving past his second-in-command, he stormed down one flight of stairs, ignoring the calls from Alistair who followed. He burst into the great hall, exclaiming with great vehemence, "We're not breeding anyone!" But his bellow fell from his lips too quickly and, at once, he was contrite. He paled, placed his hand over his heart and bowed. *Bloody hell...* "Majesty, please accept my most sincere apology. I was led to believe ye were someone else."

"Breeding? Pray, do tell," Robert the Bruce said with amusement.

Alistair stepped into the great hall beside Ian with a weary nod and a worried brow. Och, but Ian was going to beat him into a pulp later. He couldn't truly say it was a stunt the man played, but he'd blame him for letting Ian embarrass himself this way all the same.

Ian cleared his throat. "'Tis nothing, my lord. I do apologize. A simple misunderstanding."

"Someone looking to breed?" The Bruce seemed genuinely interested.

Ian stifled a groan. Och, but he wanted to die. To simply turn around and run. Nay, better yet, to grab his friend by the hair, drag him outside and force him into hand-to-hand combat. The air vibrated behind him. He could practically *feel* Alistair laughing.

"Indeed, my lord."

"Horses? Dogs?"

Ballocks! "As a matter of fact, it seems my father was... Never mind. Pray dinna ask me to explain." He changed the subject before the king could question him further. "To what do we owe the pleasure of your company, my lord?"

Robert the Bruce wagged his finger at Ian. "I will get the answer from ye soon enough, Matheson, but ye're right, for now we must get to business." His king stepped aside, revealing the minx Alistair must have been referring to.

Only, she did not look like a minx. Her hair was the color of spun gold, shining with luster against a gown of deep green. Across her middle she wore a sash of royal plaid. Her skin was creamy white and a rush of pink color filled her high cheekbones. Until that moment, her eyes were downcast, a froth of thick lashes against those cheeks, but then she raised her gaze to meet his and Ian wondered if he'd ever seen anyone more beautiful.

Her eyes were a deep amber color, wide, innocent at first, but he realized that innocence was only a facade. This woman was intelligent, observant. At once, he saw the obstinate side of her as she pursed her rose-red lips at him and raised a questioning, if not sardonic, brow.

"This is my...cousin," the Bruce said, capturing the lass' hand and ushering her forward to be presented. "I hear ye've recently come into being a ward of sorts."

Ian gritted his teeth. If the Bruce said Papa Matheson, Ian would literally take himself outside for a beating. "Indeed."

"I but thought that Lady Emilia here would be a good fit."

This was a joke. He was the laughingstock of the entire country. How would he ever gain the respect he needed? "Forgive me, my king, but I canna take in any more wards. We've a dozen already."

Robert the Bruce chuckled. "Nonsense, Matheson. Lady Emilia is not to be your ward, but your governess. She's not a nursemaid, mind ye. She's well-educated and will help school the children. Keep them in line."

"Huh." Ian grunted. Perhaps he wouldn't need to get a wife after all if he had a governess. Why had he not thought of that before? This would solve two problems at once. The offer was a good one and he wanted to leap on it, but he also had reservations. The Bruce did not simply do favors for his lesser lords. He expected things in return. Ian's father, though loyal, had not involved himself much in the affairs of the country. Was this what the Bruce would require? Many years before, Ian had joined the Bruce on campaign and he'd received much honor for doing so. Perhaps, he'd be able to gain the esteem from his people if they were to see him as a warrior, as he truly was. "I do appreciate the offer of your cousin and her services but I must ask, what do ye need from me in return?"

"Ye're a shrewd man, Matheson." The Bruce nodded his appreciation. "I like that."

"I only want to be certain ye get what ye wish, in return for doing me such a great service."

"'Tis ye who will be doing me a service, Matheson. More than ye know. I wish for Lady Emilia to be safe."

Ian narrowed his eyes. How was she *not* safe? "She will be, ye have my word. And I will pay her for her services, of course, as well."

"Good. That is all." The Bruce made no moves to explain further.

All? Truly? Ian didn't believe him, though he should. Trust was important among sovereigns and their loyalists, but Ian knew better. The king would not have come all this way and chosen him, just to simply employ his cousin. There was something more to it. What had happened that forced the lady into needing protection? Hiding, really.

"I see ye doubt me," Robert said, nodding. "And I understand why. We've not seen each other in several years, but I havena forgotten what ye did for me. For my wife. My cousin is in need of protection. Of placement. I trust that ye'll see it done without question."

In other words, do it and shut up about it. No questions asked. Well, he might not ask his sovereign, but he'd find out one way or another.

Ian placed his hand over his heart again. "Without a doubt, my lord. I am your loyal subject and at your disposal however ye may need me."

"Excellent! Then 'tis settled."

Ian did not feel that it was *settled* in the least. The lass was glaring daggers at him. She was distractingly beautiful, magnetic. If she kept it up, he might just give her permission to throw real daggers at him.

"Alistair, will ye see to the king's refreshment?"

With his second seeing to the king, Ian approached the lass and gave her a slight bow. "My lady, welcome to Balmacara Castle. I am pleased to have ye, as I know the children will be."

She pursed her lips some more, eyeing him up and down. He felt a shiver pass over him with every inch she regarded. When was the last time a woman made him feel that way? He couldn't recall. The answer might seriously be, never.

"'Tis good of ye to accept me into your home, Laird Matheson."

Oh, heaven help him. Her voice was throaty and seductive. A bedchamber sound that belonged to a woman borne of pleasure and, yet, she was as prim and proper as she pleased.

"Shall I escort ye to the nursery to meet the children?" *Please.* He needed the diversion. Potent desire was making his thought process hazy.

The lass winced. "I..."

"Go on, lass," Robert the Bruce urged from the trestle table where he sat with Alistair, drinking ale and eating cold chicken.

Ian offered her his arm, keeping his gaze toward the doors. "They will be glad to meet ye."

"Will they?"

"Aye. Right now, they've three nursemaids. Their mothers, truly."

"Mothers?" Lady Emilia slipped her slim fingers around his arm, settling her palm properly on his forearm.

Saints, but maybe he shouldn't have offered his arm. "'Tis a long story and I'm certain to tell it to ye one day. Needless to say, the little imps are a blessing to the castle."

"'Tis good to hear ye say such about your children." Her voice was tight and she walked stiffly beside him.

"My children?" Ian chuckled. "Nay, lass, they are not mine."

That seemed to shock her, for she was silent for many moments. "Ye would take in so many that were not your own?"

Ian cleared his throat, a hard edge to his tone. "I may be a warrior, but I am also a charitable man. They were my father's bastards. I couldna let them starve."

The lass stiffened all the more beside him. "I do apologize if I've offended ye, Laird Matheson, that was not my intent. I am simply... stunned."

As was he. Mayhap it was best for him to change the subject. A task he was becoming increasingly good at. "Have ye worked as a governess before?"

"Nay." She spoke so quickly that he was a little taken aback.

"Then why is our king so certain ye will be good at it? I must warn ye, they are adorable, but diabolical, too."

Lady Emilia let out a soft laugh that stroked along his ribs. "I was once that verra way."

"Perhaps ye still are," Ian found himself teasing, falling into an easy pattern of flirtation. Too easy. He pulled back. "Forgive me. I've not had sleep for the past fortnight."

"Why ever not?" she asked, scooting around his flirtation.

Above them, the sounds of singing, laughing, and screaming could be heard amid stomps and what sounded like the roof itself caving in. "Is it not evident, yet?"

Lady Emilia paled. "Is that the...wee ones?"

"Aye, my lady, or we've been invaded by a lot of other worldly creatures. If ye last a month, I will put in a good word for ye with the church, nominating ye for sainthood." He chuckled.

"Oh..." Her voice trailed off as another thud overhead caused plaster to rain down from the ceiling.

There was a true look of fear on her face. Just when she jerked away from him, perhaps to run, Ian placed his hand over hers.

"I am grateful that ye've come, lass. I was at my wit's end, thinking it was going to be them or me. I've never... had children."

"Are ye not married?"

A line of white dust covered her forehead. Without thinking, he swiped it away with the pads of his fingers.

"Nay. Never. Though I might have been, until... verra recently."

She nodded. "Marriage doesna suit me." Bitterness laced her words, igniting his curiosity. Was marriage the reason she was hiding in his castle?

He held his tongue, else she ask him why he wasn't married yet. His father had never broached the subject with him before. And now, the few letters he'd sent out had been returned exponentially faster than he would have anticipated. No one wanted to marry him. No father would *allow* his daughter to marry him.

Alistair brushed it off that 'twas because of the wards and because of his father's behavior, but Ian new better. They didn't want to marry *him*. For reasons he well understood.

"Perhaps not me, either. I thank ye, my lady, for saving me." Och, but she had no idea the humiliation she was sparing him. No more letters. No more pointless asking when he'd only be denied.

"I think it is the other way around," she pointed out, though her wary glance toward the ceiling gave away that she also agreed with him.

"Shall I introduce ye to the heathens?" he teased.

Amber eyes flashed on him. For the moment, her pursed lips turned to a delicate, closed-mouth smile. "I see no other better time."

"After a flagon of whisky may be better," Ian jested.

The true smile she gifted him made his chest constrict. Saints, but if he'd thought her beautiful before, she was positively glorious now. Two rows of beautiful, white teeth, one top tooth coming slightly over the front of its neighbor to ruin perfection and make her all the more real.

"If I were to imbibe in a flagon," she said, "I fear I'd sleep until they reached their majority."

Ian laughed and chucked her on the chin. "Ye're going to get along here just fine, my lady."

Lady Emilia blushed and ducked her gaze. "I am eager to start anew."

"As am I." Whatever she was running from had her on edge and his curiosity was thoroughly piqued.

He'd have to ask the Bruce about it, again, hoping he wasn't given the runaround once more. 'Twould be easier to protect her if he knew just what she was escaping.

Before he could think on it more, a door banged open and footsteps skittered over the steps above, followed by the shout of one of the nursemaids for the escapees to return.

"I see ye'll be getting a taste firsthand of the little imps," Ian said, bracing himself for impact.

Emilia laughed softly. "I am in luck then."

They waited patiently where they were until the young lass, whom Ian had the pleasure of facing off with in the bailey the very first day, appeared before them.

"Zounds, but ye had to be here." She pouted something fierce, coming to a halt and crossing her arms over her chest.

"Alice, I'd like to introduce ye to your new governess, Lady Emilia."

"Governess?" Alice asked, scrunching up her nose. Her ginger curls were washed and pulled back into a plait, her face was scrubbed and her clothes clean. A far cry different than her situation a fortnight ago.

"The proper response is: A pleasure to meet ye, my lady," Lady Emilia said. "And a little curtsy wouldna hurt, either."

Ian winged a brow, waiting for Alice to explode into a litany of excuses as to why she should not obey.

Well, she shocked him speechless with what she did, instead.

Damned if wee Alice didn't bob a rough curtsy and say, "A pleasure to meet ye, my lady."

"And ye as well, my dear. Would ye kindly show me to the nursery so I might meet the other children?" Lady Emilia slipped her hand off his arm and offered it to Alice, who took it and led her up the stairs.

Ian watched them go, not only speechless, but apparently unable to move as well.

CHAPTER 5

Thank goodness she'd been able to remove her hand from the devastatingly handsome laird, for she was certain, at any moment, to begin trembling. Then he would know just how nervous she really was.

Emilia allowed Alice to lead her up the stairs, theoretically allowing the child to present her into her new life. Realistically, she allowed the girl to tug her along when she truly wished to run for the hills.

So much had happened in the past two weeks that she could barely comprehend it. That this would be her new situation for the time being was, in and of itself, nearly incomprehensible. For a lass who'd spent her entire life in one castle, she was now finding herself under the fourth roof.

To top it off, she was supposed to play a governess? Emilia knew nothing of mothering children. Not rearing them. Not guiding them. Nothing.

She, herself, had a hard time following the studies put to her by her various governesses and tutors. Things of a studious nature never seemed to capture her attention, whereas adventure and pretending to be the lovely Aliah de Mowbray, often did.

But the Bruce had insisted. Ina and Marmaduke were hunting for her. She belonged to them, or so they perceived it to be that way. They'd stop at nothing to see their investment fully returned to them.

And she knew why. Padrig had made that fact perfectly clear. The thought of being so ill-used turned her stomach.

Thank God for Ahlrid, Padrig, and the Bruce.

Poor Padrig had, indeed, died that day he'd sent her away. News had traveled fast. As soon as he'd heard, Ahlrid had faded into the mist and she'd not seen him since. The Bruce had taken her in quickly, thanking her for Padrig's missive— the key to the castle. Almost at once, he'd told everyone she was his cousin, not once mentioning her ties to Padrig, Ina, or Marmaduke. Not even her bloodline. Never once was Clan MacCulloch mentioned, nor summoned for her protection. She'd asked after them, but the Bruce had, instead, worn a brooding look that brooked no argument.

That hadn't stopped her from telling him more than a dozen times that her parents weren't traitors. She explained that they were simply beaten down to the bottom of the barrel, and they longed to climb out.

He asked if she blamed them for her situation, and she said not at the heart of it. She knew it was the Ross Clan that was at fault. But that was not the complete truth. Aye, they'd been raided, depleted, and left with not much more than nothing, but still... she thought her father could have done better by her.

The king had been so grateful she'd escaped Ross Castle with the key for him that, just that morning, he'd agreed to pardon her family should they ever go against him. Though he also warned that if they went against him, he would be forced to retaliate, but he would only do so after offering them the chance to change their minds.

Emilia had to accept that it was the only option open for them. They may have been backed into a corner by the Ross Clan, but misfortune, misguidance, and whatever other nonsense could have been at the heart of their problems, but they were, all in all, good people.

"Ye're verra pretty," Alice said quietly beside her, stopping just a few steps shy of the landing. "Like an angel."

Emilia squeezed the little girl's hand with reassurance. "Why thank ye. I assure ye, I'm no angel, love, simply a governess."

Alice nodded very seriously for a girl her age. "I confess, I'm glad ye're not."

"Why is that?"

"I thought ye were coming for us."

Emilia cocked her head to the side in question. "Coming for ye?"

"Like the other angels did, when the bairns passed on."

Emilia's heart skipped a beat and she bit her lip, unsure what exactly Alice meant. "I have come only to teach ye how to be a proper lady."

"And the boys?"

"To teach them to be gentlemen, until they are ready for their training to be warriors."

Alice tugged at her braided hair. "Do ye think they will be warriors?"

Emilia daintily shrugged her shoulders, realizing, perhaps, she should not have mentioned it. Mayhap they wouldn't be. She didn't know the plans the laird had for the children and she did not expect to be here when the time came. "I suspect some of them will be."

"And the others? What will they do?"

Emilia looked behind her. Where was Laird Matheson? Why wasn't he up here helping her? "I suppose some may decide they wish to join the church."

Thankfully, Alice nodded as this seemed to make sense to her. "I had two older brothers. One went to the church and one went to work as an apprentice."

"Impressive. Ye should be proud of them."

"I am. But I miss them so. Do ye have any brothers?"

Emilia swallowed. She itched to run. "I have one brother alive and the other passed on. I also have a sister."

"I have many sisters. Some passed on, some married off, and the rest are in the nursery right now."

At last, an opportunity to leave off from such personal topics. "I should like to meet them."

Alice smiled. "Ye have a good smile." She touched Emilia's face.

Hearing their voices, one of the nursemaids rushed to the door, but stopped short. "Oh," her hand came to her chest. "My lady, I'm so sorry."

"There is no need for apology."

"Alice," the nurse clucked her tongue. "Ye're bothering the lady. Quit touching her and come up here to wash up."

Emilia offered a tight smile. "She's no bother. I'm Lady Emilia, the new governess."

The nursemaid pulled up straight to her full height then, giving Emilia a once over that left her feeling slightly lacking. "Governess?" she asked, a twinge of disdain in her tone.

"Aye."

"His lairdship didna say anything about a governess." She folded her arms over her chest and blew a stray hair out of her face.

"'Twas a rather sudden arrangement," Emilia tried to explain. But when the nursemaid was joined by two more and they each exchanged a worried glance and a few whispered words, Emilia was pretty certain she knew exactly why.

Just what, exactly, was the laird's reputation?

He'd come storming into the great hall, lamenting he wasn't a breeder of women and even just now had denied these children were his. But certainly, they were of an age they could be... He had no wife and didn't seem inclined to get one. She knew now from experience how much an heir meant. Just what was Laird Matheson willing to do to see his legacy passed on?

"I'd like to meet the children. Observe them a little, so I know just what they need from me."

"Ye've not the look of a mother," the tallest of the nurse-maids said.

"I'm not. And I'm not here to replace any of ye, simply to add to the children's education. Wherever it may be lacking."

One of the nursemaids laughed and they all seemed to warm once they realized she wouldn't be taking away anything from them. "Love, they'll need ye for everything. These bairns havena learned a thing in their life other than survival."

The thought, brushed off as normal, tore at Emilia's heart. She swallowed back her pity for the young ones. "Survival. Ah, but then they are well trained for most things, for the desire to remain alive, to move forward, is that not most of the battle?"

The women wrinkled their brows and stared at her as though she'd spoken in a language not yet discovered.

"No matter," Emilia said, waving away this and any other conversations. "I shall come in now." She pushed past the women, who'd seemed rather more interested in keeping her out.

The nursery was clean of dust, the bedclothes pressed,

but that was the only clean thing about it. Children's toys, clothes, food, and drink littered the floor. Several bairns sucked their fists inside cradles, while a few little ones toddled around the room knocking over whatever they could and running away from a maid who attempted to stop them. Some who were older jumped from bed to bed, shouting, and ignoring the maids who clapped their hands and called for order. The very oldest three, a boy and two girls, sat at a table playing what looked like a game of bones, their expressions dutifully bored, and, she took note, linen stuffed in their ears to ward off the noise.

It was utter mayhem. The noise alone gave her an instant headache.

Emilia cleared her throat, but that did no good. She stuck two fingers in her mouth and gave off a shrill whistle that had them all stopping in their tracks. They stared at her in horror, the youngest of them started to cry, but was quickly soothed by one of the maids.

"This is Lady Emilia," Alice said. "The proper way is to curtsy and say, pleased to meet ye."

One by one, those who could walk approached. Those who could, curtsied or bowed and mumbled the words Alice had imparted on them, even the eldest of them.

Emilia inclined her head. "I am so glad to meet all of ye," she said. "I'm to be your new governess."

Oh, saints, but if her father could see her now, he would fall to the ground laughing. She'd been the most stubborn, the most obstinate child. He'd often said if she ever had children they would return to her the heartache she'd given him, by tenfold.

Considering she was still a virgin, perhaps in his visions, he'd only seen this part, missing the fact that she wouldn't actually be the mother to them.

The laird then came into the nursery, commanding the attention of the children and women by his sheer presence alone—including Emilia.

He took her breath away and her heart seemed to beat a faster pace.

Emilia had not missed his wicked good looks. Laird Matheson had striking blue eyes. As deep as the sky on a summer afternoon. His hair was ginger-gold and hung in rugged waves down to his chin. A day or two's worth of stubble graced his chiseled-from-stone chin and cheeks. A wide, slashing mouth with near perfect teeth, smiled at the children.

The laird was tall, broad. Judging from the way his shirt-sleeves clung to the bulges in his arms, he was quite impressively muscular. She followed the swath of his plaid from shoulder to waist, the line of his hips and thighs, to defined calves covered halfway by woolen hose and leather boots. Aye, indeed, he cut a striking figure. Just looking at him gave her belly an odd flipping sensation. Saints, but she'd never felt this way about a man, simply from staring at him. How could he have that effect on her?

The children gathered round and he tugged from his leather sporran at his waist, treat after treat. Every one of them clutched it to their chest like a treasure before running away to eat it without interruption.

He might swear they were not his and that they stole his sleep away, but he couldn't hide that he cared for them.

"How do they fare today?" he asked the nursemaids, who tittered behind batting lashes and simpering compliments.

The way he grinned, he was used to it, took pleasure in it. This made Emilia roll her eyes. From one fool to another. The laird may be a god in boots, but he was just as vain as they could come, she was certain.

When he was done preening, he glanced up long enough

to catch Emilia's eye, and then he winked at her. The gesture was accompanied by a slow, lazy grin. That was a knowing, conspiratorial wink. She gasped. What on earth did he mean by it? She'd not conspired with him. Not about anything, she was certain.

Emilia straightened her shoulders and lifted her chin, not smiling back. She didn't want to encourage whatever that was.

"The children have already done verra well with their first lesson," she said. "Introductions."

"Marvelous. I'm not surprised. They have Matheson blood in their veins. Mathesons are strong and smart."

Was he hoping she'd agree? Expecting her to give him a compliment? For he was simply being a braggart now.

Emilia pursed her lips, a gesture she'd noticed herself doing much more lately than usual. She forced herself to stop, realizing the same pursing of lips was what one did when they were going to get a kiss—and as braggart as this laird was, she wouldn't be surprised if he mistook her pursing lips for something more. She was most certainly *not* looking to get a kiss. In fact, kissing was the very last thing she ought to be thinking about. Except...her gaze was suddenly drawn to Laird Matheson's mouth.

When his grin widened further, she forced her gaze away, back toward the children. Her heart was suddenly pumping wildly and she noted that she'd been holding her breath. She could swear she heard the man chuckle softly.

"Shall I take ye back down to your cousin?" Laird Matheson asked.

Her cousin.

Before the week prior, Emilia had never seen Robert the Bruce, let alone called him cousin. Padrig could not have known her desire to meet the man and attempt to atone for her family. What had he put in his letter? The Bruce never showed her and she'd never unrolled the parchment. At best, she guessed he must have asked the Bruce to see her well protected from his family.

"My lady?"

Emilia realized she'd been staring at space above his head without answering.

"I think I should like to stay here." She regarded all the tiny faces peering intently at her. So much heartache they must have been through recently. She didn't know their story other than the rumors that had been boasted upon the road. But she knew what it was like to be forced into a new situation, out of everything you'd ever known.

"Are ye certain?"

Nay she wasn't. She had no idea what to expect from a dozen children and three irritated nursemaids, but it was better than what waited her in the great hall—Matheson and his charm. "Aye."

Laird Matheson nodded. "I will have the staff bring in your luggage and set up your chamber, which will be just a floor below the nursery."

Emilia nodded. "I am grateful." What would they say about how little luggage she had? There was just one small satchel, filled with a few borrowed items from the Bruce's wife. A kindness, she would add to the long list of kindnesses she owed. She'd never be able to repay them for finding her a safe haven.

And she did feel safe here. Though, she knew she'd not be able to sleep at night. Not with the images of Ina and Marmaduke running through her mind.

"Will ye join us for supper in the great hall this evening?" Laird Matheson asked.

"Do ye normally take your supper in the great hall with those in your service?"

He shook his head. "'Tis a special occasion with the king here."

A special occasion. Saints, but the man had no idea...

The Bruce had his men camped outside the walls. From here, they would travel to Ross Castle and attempt to infiltrate it. And then she'd have nothing to fear anymore. Her enemies vanquished.

She was about to deny him, but then he said, "I insist," leaving her no other choice.

She inclined her head and then regarded the children, all staring wide-eyed and full of concentration. "Do the children ever eat with ye?"

"Nay, lass."

"Then that is something we will work toward, but perhaps not tonight."

"Ye're a brave woman." He lifted her hand to his mouth, brushing his lips lightly over the top of her knuckles before letting her go.

'Twas brief. Too brief. Yet, that told her it was actually long enough.

And judging from the glares centered on her by the three nursemaids, the gesture and its significance had not been lost on them.

"Ye'd best be returning to the king," she urged.

Distance would be her savior, for she couldn't fall for this man. Not when one marriage had already been her undoing.

CHAPTER 6

I an made a good show of pretending everything was as it should be. As though he had the king in his home all the time and that the beautiful woman upstairs in the nursery didn't have him questioning his own desires.

He sipped from his mug of ale as he spoke about politics and glories of battles past with the Bruce, Alistair, and with several of the Bruce's top generals who happened to travel with him—one of whom was the infamous Magnus Sutherland. The man commanded all of the Sutherland lands north of here and had been an asset to the Bruce for nearly a decade. Not to mention, the man's brother, Ronan, who was also present, was married to the Bruce's half-sister.

Ian was in the presence of the elite and he felt like a fraud. If the news of him taking in his father's bastards had traveled so fast, wouldn't news of his own past have also gotten to them? And yet, no one mentioned a thing. They treated him as though he were one of them.

'Twas these moments that were the hardest. These moments in which he found himself doubting. Growing up, Ian had earned his place. As an adolescent, he earned his spurs. And when he was a man, running headlong into battle, he earned his place at the forefront of the line. With women, he charmed himself into their beds—again, earning it. He was not a fool, he knew all of this. Ian had earned himself a place within the clan, but was he worthy of being their leader? Aye, his father had thought so, but nearly everyone agreed the man's personal judgment had not been the best.

So while on the outside Ian laughed, shared, and clapped the men on their backs, on the inside, he was twisted up in knots. For bloody hell's sake, if he didn't get a hold of his whirling mind soon, he might step down before anyone had a chance of challenging him.

Speaking of challenges... Where was the lass?

What was he going to do with a lass?

What was she going to do with the twelve children upstairs?

Better yet, would either of them survive this?

He downed another large gulp of ale and signaled to a waiting servant to refill his cup.

"I thank ye for your hospitality," the Bruce was saying. "The men are always glad to have a good meal and plenty of ale afore the night of a battle."

"Battle?" Ian shifted his attention back to the conversation.

"Aye. We're on our way to Ross Castle at daybreak."

Laird Sutherland was nodding, anticipation sparking in his eyes. "Finally."

"I had heard they caused a good bit of trouble some years back," Ian started. "What have they done now?"

The Bruce grunted. "We've word they are gathering allies and forces, reinforcements for the English who will invade come spring."

"We're planning to take them out afore they get a chance," Ronan offered.

"Can I offer my men? Myself?" Ian asked.

The Bruce nodded. "If ye can spare a score of archers, we're in need. But I need ye to remain here, Matheson. Keep an eye on my cousin. Protect your borders."

"I will have my men ready in the morning," Ian said. "And I will keep my borders safe and your cousin, I swear it. The Matheson Clan is true and loyal to ye, my king. No amount of English coin, bribery, or beatings could change us."

The Bruce clapped him on the back. "Ye're a good man. I knew that already, which is why I came to ye."

"I wish ye luck on the morrow."

"Luck? We'll need the Lord on our side, for we're dealing with the devil," the Bruce muttered as he sipped his ale. "Evil things going on in that castle."

The men all agreed, privy to something Ian wasn't. "More evil than plotting against your own country?" he asked.

"Ye jested of not needing any breeders," the Bruce said, bumping his shoulder against Ian's. "'Tis not a jest there."

Ian frowned. "What do ye mean?"

"Ina Ross is barren. They lost the only bairn they ever created. She, and that bastard Sassenach she's married to, have tried to breed her invalid cousin to nigh on ten lassies. None of it worked."

Ian's stomach soured. "That's heinous." He could only imagine the suffering of those women. To be forced into such... He shook his head. At least the women his father had relations with seemed to have enjoyed themselves.

"Indeed." The Bruce's scowl deepened, and he seemed on the verge of saying more, but then a hush fell over the great hall.

Ian followed the line of everyone's regard to the door.

Holy Virgin draped in satin...

Lady Emilia.

The sight of her knocked the wind from his lungs. 'Haps it was best to ask the Bruce to take her back with him. Find someone else to protect her. For if she stayed, he may be the one needing protection from his own desires.

She was a vision, wearing the same green gown as before, but it had been recently brushed free of debris from their ride and the creases pressed free. Her golden locks had been arranged in artful curls around her face. Her hands were demurely folded before her.

She kept her gaze downcast as though she were shy.

It was a practice in restraint not to rush forward and take her hand. Not to bow before her and offer up his most charming flirtations.

"Cousin," the Bruce belted. "Come, have a cup of wine."

The lass, shy as she pretended, floated toward them with grace and ease, looking at them through her thick lashes. She accepted a cup of wine from Magnus and took a dainty sip. Her gaze flicked over Ian with what he hoped was more interest than she showed the rest. Nay, nay. Interest was not what he needed from her—even if it was what he wanted.

She took another, lengthier, sip of wine. Her sigh of relief and pleasure did not go unnoticed by Ian. She was just as filled with tension as he. If they'd been in private and he not forcing himself into celibacy, he might have placed his hands on her shoulders to rub the tension away.

Alas, that was not the case. So he, too, took a long sip of his ale.

"Ye look well rested," the king observed.

"I am, thank ye, my lord." She nodded to Ian. "The children were so verra kind to keep quiet for an hour or so and allow me a short nap."

"I confess I am quite surprised. Ye must be an enchantress, for I've not yet experienced the same."

Lady Emilia laughed softly. "Ye might try a bit of bribery next time. No sweets unless they quiet down. They seemed verra taken with your treats."

Ian grinned. "And how did ye bribe them?"

A teasing glint came into her eye, and she rested the rim of her cup on her lip, staring at him a moment before taking a sip. "Oh, well, I might have used your name with that."

"Tell me how ye used me."

The rest of their group watched, equally interested. From what he'd heard, Magnus and Ronan had a slew of children at home. Perhaps they hoped to learn something.

"I told them that I'd heard ye say ye'd not be giving them any more treats, but that if they were mighty quiet for one hour, I would convince ye otherwise."

Ian's mouth fell open. "Ye have ill-used me and made me a villain!"

"And I the hero." She laughed, a tinkling sound that made his insides clench with need.

"Clever."

Magnus frowned hard. "I do believe my wife, Arbella, is already using that trick."

"Arbella?" Emilia's face blanched white, and she took a step back.

"Are ye all right?" Ian asked, touching her elbow.

"I am fine." She shook her head, looking into her cup. "It would seem I drank my wine a bit too fast on an empty stomach."

"Come, I will sit ye at the table." He led her to the high table that ran horizontal to the trestle tables where the men would sit.

He pulled out her chair and tucked her into the table after

she sat, catching the scent of rose water as he did. He breathed in deep and then took a wide step back. How was he to sit beside her for the duration of this meal if she smelled so good?

Ian nodded to a servant and called for supper to be served. A grand feast it would be. Most often, the main meal was at noon and a small repast was served in the evening. But Ian had wanted to show his king hospitality, to make an impression on the man he'd pledged his loyalty to.

At the high table, the king flanked Ian on his right and Lady Emilia on his left. The Sutherland brothers took the two outside seats near the king, and then two long lines of trestle tables filled the great hall with warriors from both his own army and the highest ranking men from the Bruce's. Though they couldn't fit everyone, Ian had ordered ale and warm bread to be sent out to the men in the fields. They'd been allowed to hunt that day and the scent of roasting meat filled the land for miles.

The great hall was soon filled with the sounds of men rejoicing, supping, and sending up cheers and prayers for the coming battle.

While Ian was interested in more of what the king had to say in regards to the state of their country, he was also concerned with the lass at his side. He'd done a fair amount of ignoring her, but he couldn't help but take note of how uneasy she was. Lord, but he knew that feeling.

"How did ye fare in the nursery, prior to telling the children I disliked them?"

Emilia let out a small laugh and glanced up at him. "I didna tell them ye disliked them. Only that it was time they started to earn their treats."

"I shall have to have Cook bake them a massive cake on the morrow to make up for it."

"Ye will do no such thing," she teased back. "Else they are spoiled rotten."

Ian chuckled. "'Tis no less than they deserve for the harsh life they've led up until now."

"Will ye share with me what happened to them?"

"Aye. But first, tell me, how did they treat ye? I'm curious because they seem to run circles around the nursemaids, poor lassies. I've heard them whisper they were better off cleaning the chambers."

"I survived. I think they may have taught me that lesson."

"A lesson in survival?"

"Aye." Her voice grew quiet, dark, and she turned away from him to stare at her plate. She picked at her bread and tore off a tiny piece, popping it into her mouth. "One would think survival was an instinct and, to a degree, I suppose it is. But first, ye have to want it."

"They would be good teachers in that, then."

"They are lucky to have ye."

Ian chuckled. "I keep hoping the feeling will be mutual," he teased. "So tell me, what is on the agenda for tomorrow?"

"If I wake," she teased, "I plan to start them on their letters in the morning, followed by a few games that will teach them to trust one another, and me. In the afternoon, we will work on arithmetic and then we shall go over verses. I hope ye dinna mind, but I've invited the chaplain to join us. While they break their fast and during the noon meal, we will be working on etiquette."

"Ye have a verra rigorous schedule planned."

Emilia reached for her cup and swirled the contents before taking a tiny sip. "I do. I will be pleased to call it a success if we get through a third of it."

"And the children's mothers? Are they treating ye well?"

She stabbed at a piece of venison. "As well as I would

expect them to treat a stranger. They feel I've come to replace them, though I've assured them I havena."

The women of the clan were often the hardest to break through in terms of allowing someone new into their fold. How many years had Ian been a part of the clan? Still, they had a hard time accepting him. "I will speak to them about it."

"Nay, please dinna." She pleaded at him with her eyes and massacred her bread into at least thirty tiny pieces. "They simply need to get used to me. That is all. I am new. Soon we shall all get along just fine. Though I daresay me being asked to join ye at supper in the great hall may press a kink into whatever progress I've made."

"And why is that? Ye're a lady and the king's cousin. Ye might be offering your services to my kin and me, but that doesna diminish your station. There are many ladies who take up such positions. Doing so doesna mean ye have to give up who ye are."

Lady Emilia gave him a puzzling expression and he wished quite emphatically that he could read her thoughts. Alas, he was not gifted with the talent and she quickly masked her expression, leaving him to guess at what she was feeling.

"Does dining with us make ye uncomfortable?" he asked, indicating the room full of men.

"What?" She glanced up at him sharply, once more striking him with the beauty and rareness of her amber eyes.

Ian cleared his throat and offered her a dish of suckling pig. "Does dining with the men make ye uncomfortable? Given there are no other ladies present."

Emilia glanced about the room, perhaps only realizing then that she was the only female present. "Oh, nay. That is not the reason." She blushed. "Or, rather I should say, I am quite comfortable. Thank ye. I apologize if ye think me ungrateful."

So there was something bothering her, but she didn't feel comfortable enough to share it with him and he didn't blame her. They were basically strangers to one another. "I dinna think ye ungrateful. I understand."

"Do ye?" She cocked her head in challenge.

Ian kept his gaze serious, not taking the bait. He had a feeling she was in the mood for a fight. "Ye're not the only one to think ye dinna belong, lass."

She sat up a little taller. "Is that what ye think I think?"

Heaven help him, what chord had he struck? "Is it not?"

Long, slender arms folded over her chest, pressing her breasts up higher—a delight he tried hard to keep from his line of vision. "What would ye know of not belonging? Ye're the laird. Afore that, ye were the laird's son."

He narrowed his eyes. Och, but it was a lot more complicated than that. Now she was pushing his buttons. "I am more than simply the product of my parentage."

"That is truer than ye know, though I have heard many people say the apple doesna fall far from the tree."

A flash of anger seared across his middle. Whatever control he'd hoped to maintain while speaking with her evaporated. "What do ye mean by that?" *Spiteful, angry wench.*

The lass looked taken aback. A look he recognized. She'd spoken before thinking, wanted to tug her words back, but she couldn't. "I dinna mean to offend, sir. I was not speaking of ye."

Ian set his fork down, turning fully sideways in his chair so he could face her more directly. "Then who were ye speaking of?"

Her gaze fell to her elbow. "I'd rather not say."

"Yourself?" he prodded.

She pursed her lips. "Nay."

"I am not my father's son," he said in a low tone, bordering on a growl.

When her eyes widened, he felt a twinge of guilt at his anger, but he was tired of everyone comparing him. His father was a good man. Brought his clan prosperity. Kept them safe. Who could blame the man for slaking his needs or for attempting to retrieve his manhood when he couldn't get his wife with child? None of the women had gone to his bed unwilling. Aye, their bairns had been taken, but many of them were glad to give them up, at least that was what they'd told him. They wanted the pleasure without the hassle. None had ever been turned away. All were treated well.

And he, himself, did not have any bastards. He'd been careful of that since his very first woman.

The problem was, women were not supposed to take lovers. And men, if they had bastards, were supposed to secret them away.

And sons, oh sons, they were not supposed to open their doors wide and call in all of their father's bastards as he'd done.

Emilia carefully placed her eating knife on the table. "I, in no way, meant to offend ye. I was simply speaking. Not thinking."

Ian blew out a breath, the anger in him deflating. She'd pricked the boar and he'd let it loose. "I must offer ye my apology, my lady. I havena slept well. I admit the topic of my father and his preferences has been at the forefront of my mind of late. I overreacted."

"I accept your apology." She unfolded her arms and lightly touched his hand where it lay on the table. "I hope ye accept mine."

Ian didn't move. He liked the look of her hand on his.

Perhaps, if he stayed very still, she'd not move and just keep it there. The pang of longing in his chest was for something more than bedding her, but of comfort, of sweetness and... Och, what a fool he was. He moved then, pulling his hand out from under hers, patting her hand, and then running his hand through his hair.

"If ye would excuse me," she said. "I am quite tired and I should like to get some rest before tomorrow. I expect to be up with the children not long after dawn."

"Aye," he said regrettably. He hated to end their evening on a sour note. "I bid ye goodnight and good luck."

She offered only a tight smile and a curt nod before walking away. He'd have to make it up to her somehow. A cake, mayhap, would be good. Did she like sweets?

As soon as she was out of earshot, Ian sought his king's attention. "My lord, I beg a boon of ye. What is the lady's story?"

Robert the Bruce sat back heavily in his chair. "She's had it tough of late."

"I gathered. She is running from something or someone. Is that why she needs my protection?"

"Aye."

The Bruce did not continue. He took sudden interest in his food, wolfing it down with an urgency that only made Ian more curious.

"From who?"

"Ina Ross."

"Ah." Ian watched until Emilia disappeared through the door, wishing he could call her back. Smooth over the rough patches from before. If she was going to live in his household, help raise his brothers and sisters, they needed to get along quite well. "How were she and Ina acquainted?"

The Bruce tapped his fingers on the table and leaned

close, his voice hushed. "Ye must swear to keep her story to yourself. I placed her here with a tale we created, naming her my cousin, having her seeking employment. 'Twas the best distraction I could think of on short notice. The only reason I'm telling ye is because being here with the children may trigger some of her trauma."

"Trauma?"

"The lass was married to Padrig Ross."

Padrig Ross, the infamous cousin to Ina Ross. Before Ina, there was her father, a hellion of a man, causing one battle after another. He'd betrayed Robert the Bruce to Long-shanks, terrorizing his own people. His daughter inherited his penchant for meanness and continued on, only ceasing when her favorite cousin, Padrig, was taken hostage. He was to be held for a period of five years, the length of the peace treaty. But the lad had escaped and, not a day later, Ina was back to business as usual, terrorizing anyone and everyone. And her Sassenach husband... He'd do anything for his wife.

Sweet Emilia had been married to Padrig? Och, but what horrors had she seen? Just the thought of what Ina was capable of was enough to make a grown man shudder.

Now it was Ian's turn to sit back heavily in his chair. "How is that even possible?"

The Bruce shook his head. "I hadn't the heart to ask her."

"I see." So, she'd had to carry the burden of whatever horrors she'd witnessed on her own.

Ian felt all the more like a prig. He'd goaded her in conversation and come to find out, she'd likely been referring to the Ross Clan all along. And he'd taken it personally. He'd been spending so much time wallowing in his own self-pity lately that he'd forgotten what it was like to really see another person for what they were.

"She's been through much." Robert patted the table.

"Barely fled with her life. Padrig arranged her escape and sent her to me along with a map of every hidden entrance in to the castle."

"And your siege, 'tis partly for her. Allow me to join ye. Allow me to help exact vengeance."

The Bruce shook his head. "Partly for her. But also for every injustice the Ross Clan has put on anyone else. For their treasonous actions. It is time, once and for all, they were wiped away. I know ye love a good battle and your skills are valuable to me, but so is her life. She has given us this gift and I dinna want to see it wasted." He hooked his thumb toward Magnus. "When he left to do battle, Ina snuck into his castle and stole his wife and his sister-by-marriage."

"Damn."

"Aye. Treat her with kid gloves, Matheson," the Bruce said.

"Ye have my word, my lord. I will make certain she is treated well by all. And no one will get to her unless over my dead body."

"Ye shall be rewarded for it."

Ian waved away the offer. "I seek no reward, my lord."

The Bruce winged a questioning brow. "What do ye seek?"

"I find it changes daily."

The Bruce laughed. "Aye, we all have that. But what remains constant?"

Ah, the deep heart of his inner self. The dark truth that he never spoke of. He'd not give that away. So, instead, Ian laughed. "I want the name Papa Matheson vanquished from the land."

"Good luck with that," the Bruce said. "Half the land thinks ye're as virile as a bull."

"And the other half?"

"They're wondering if they can send ye their troublesome bairns."

The two men roared with laughter and raised their glasses. To have the regard of his king, Ian felt he'd won a great battle already.

CHAPTER 7

Emilia could not escape the great hall fast enough.

Bile rose in her throat along with the few bits of bread she'd managed to swallow down. Her fingers were clenched so tight she was getting cramps. She wanted nothing more than to rush up the stairs and into her new chamber where she could bar the door and pretend that no one would ever bother her again.

She had one foot on the stair before someone whispered her name from behind. Nearly falling backward as she gasped and clutched at her chest, she leapt off the stairs, whirling around at the same time.

Ahlrid materialized as if from nowhere.

"Ye scared the wits out of me. Dinna go sneaking up on people. What are ye doing here?" she whispered angrily, glancing from side to side. If he were caught... "They will see ye."

"Many have already." He looked at her confused. "Are ye well, my lady?"

She pressed her fingers to her temples, rubbing. That was a loaded question. A searing pain had taken up residence behind her eyes. Physically, emotionally, she was not feeling at all well. "Forgive me," she said in an effort to deflect him, and perhaps herself, away from her own feelings. "I simply forgot ye were one of the Bruce's guard."

He regarded her with narrowed eyes. "All right, as ye say. I but wanted ye to know that I am here if ye were needing anything."

Emilia studied the oversized man. He was at least seven feet tall and wide as a gate. Scars marred his face and while she used to find him terrifying, he'd made her feel safe when she'd fled Ross Castle. Forced to trust him then, she'd not lost that trust upon parting at the Bruce's camp. Still, she couldn't help but question him. "Ye once told me ye'd leave me to die if I fell behind, and now ye're asking if I need anything?"

He grunted. "Necessary, my lady. I had to see if ye were worthy of taking Padrig's place. He was a good friend of mine."

Emilia nodded, understanding what it felt like to lose a friend. Her sister, Ayne, had been a good friend to her. "I know ye miss him. I am sorry for your loss." While she was sorry for him having lost a friend, she would never feel anything but great glee at having finally gotten free of the Ross Clan.

Though she wasn't completely free, yet. Ina Ross had vowed to find her. And if anyone were to whisper of Emilia not being loyal to the Bruce, she'd likely be handed back over into Purgatory.

"We all miss somebody, my lady." Ahlrid shrugged, looking completely disinterested, though she didn't hold that against him. Most men tried to hide their true feelings. 'Twas unmanly to have any sort of affection toward another.

Ahlrid spoke the truth. Despite shoving her into enemy hands, she missed her parents. Though, she wasn't certain she could ever face them again. When she'd first been delivered to the Bruce, he had offered to send her home and she'd refused. The king never asked her any questions, but his quiet respect of her wishes told her he could guess at her reasons. Mostly, she missed her sister, Ayne. Once at Nèamh Abbey, Ayne rarely wrote, on account of being a novice and teased much by her homesickness by the other young women there. They'd been close growing up, only a couple of years apart and the dearest of friends. Emilia had written her sister every day, imparting comfort, until she'd been sent to Ross Castle.

Her time at Ross Castle had, not surprisingly, produced zero confidantes. And though Padrig had saved her, she preferred to forget about him, too.

In fact, she'd like to leave her entire past behind and start anew. This time, here at Balmacara would be a time of healing. And once she felt whole, she thought she might like to join Nèamh Abbey along with her sister. To spend the rest of her life in quiet solitude, serving those in need.

Once this business with the Ross Clan was over with, she would ask the king's permission to go to Skye. She was so close. Just a short boat trip across the loch, followed by a day or two's ride, and she would be there. Theoretically, now that she was a widow, she should go back to her parents and wait like a dutiful daughter to be married off again. But since the Bruce had taken her in and decided to give her a secret identity for the time being, she hoped to convince him to give his blessing in regards to her joining the church. There could be no other way. How could she marry after what she'd been through? In her mind, she knew that her marriage to Padrig had been a sham, that it was not the way for men and women. But, still, it had been enough of a torment that she was certain she'd rather keep her virginity for eternity than be stripped bare again.

Emilia shook herself from her thoughts, brushing away the cobwebs of her mind. "We do, Ahlrid. And time will heal us both."

"Aye." Ahlrid ducked his head and took a step away from her. "I'll be off then."

"Be safe."

He grunted his reply. Then he muttered, "My lady," before disappearing through the archway.

Emilia sank against the wall, her heart still pounding, head splitting. The coolness of the stone sank into her bones, giving her a few moments reprieve.

Why could she not go back to the days at Terrel Tower? The only things she worried over were whether her tutor would realize she'd only skimmed her verses because she'd stayed up all night knife-sharpening and tossing her blades, or if Cook would let her help make the mincemeat pie and knead the dough for the day's bread. Why did growing up mean losing all the things she'd once found joy in?

Well, at least tonight she had a few things to be grateful for. What she needed to do, instead of focusing on anything negative, was to count her blessings. She was safe. There was a roof over her head. She'd escaped Ross Castle. Magnus Sutherland had not recognized her—this was, perhaps, the most exciting thing to be grateful for of all.

His eldest daughter, Belle, was betrothed to Emilia's brother, Dirk. An alliance that would not come to fruition for another ten years, at least. She'd only ever met Magnus once and it was several years ago, before she'd been anything other than a flighty adolescent.

Thank goodness the Bruce had kept her secret, claiming her to be his cousin to one and all, including Magnus, whom she'd not seen face to face until this very night.

If he recognized her, he would demand to know why she

was masquerading as the Bruce's cousin, and then he would find out what her parents had done out of desperation. He'd break off the betrothal if she weren't careful. Oh, she couldn't risk such a thing happening. Her parents would never forgive her. And her brother, his life would be ruined. The Sutherlands were the most powerful family in the north. If her clan were to be shunned by them, they would be ruined forever. Dirk would never be able to find a bride.

If the Bruce was sincere in his decision to pardon her parents, then all she had to do was lay low until that time came. No more feasts in the great hall, especially if the Sutherlands were present. She just couldn't risk being recognized. Also, if she were recognized, rumors could spread, and Ina would know where she was hiding.

How sad it was. Any other time and place, she might have gushed at meeting the infamous Earl of Sutherland. Magnus's wife, Arbella, was the sister to Aliah de Mowbray, Emilia's idol. Ronan, who was also present, was married to the Bruce's half-sister, Julianna. She was the very definition of a female warrior. Those two women, Aliah and Julianna, had shown her that she could do more with her talents than stab thread through a needle. They had shown her what an exhilaration it was to throw knives.

If only she'd not met Magnus and his brother, Ronan, under such circumstances, things could have been different and she might have been able to meet Aliah and Julianna. Ever since she was a girl, it had been a dream to stand in a line with them, face off with the targets, and throw their knives.

Zounds, but why was she still lurking at the bottom of the stairs daydreaming about childhood fantasies? She needed to get some sleep. She'd barely had any since she'd escaped Ross Castle, and tomorrow would prove most challenging. Though she'd played with her younger siblings, she'd never been in charge of them, let alone twelve... Luckily four of them were too young for much of the activities they'd be taking part in.

Making certain there was no one else lurking in the shadows to nearly cause her a tumble down the stairs, she trudged up the winding steps, trailing her fingers along the cool stones of the wall. The stairs themselves were worn slick in the center where hundreds of boots had stepped. She imagined on particularly wet days they'd be slick and terrifying. At Terrel Tower, when she was about eight years of age, she'd taken quite a tumble down the stairs in her haste to join the other children in a May Day celebration. She'd broken her leg and fell ill with a fever. Her parents had counted her blessed when she healed quickly. From that time forward, she'd made certain to take the stairs as slow as she could, even if meant being late.

When she arrived at her bedchamber, there was a maid waiting for her to help her undress. She did need help getting out of her dress. But Emilia dismissed the maid when she asked to brush out her hair. If she was going to play a governess, then she should probably act the part. A governess did not need the same care that a lady did. Right? She should be acting more the part of a servant and not that of a lady.

Emilia climbed into bed, but sleep did not come. She stared wide-eyed at the canopy over her bed, shadows bouncing hither and yon. Overhead was strangely quiet. Perhaps her baiting the children with the impending loss of treats had truly gotten to their hearts. She smiled into the dark at the remembrance of Laird Matheson's decree that he would have a massive cake made for them. He was a proud warrior. A man of skill. The Bruce had told her of Laird Matheson's impressive rescue of the queen when a band of Scottish outlaws ambushed them on the road. He'd taken on six of them by himself and been victorious. She found it extremely endearing that a man with that much ferocity could also decree a cake be baked for a horde of children that any other man might have shunned.

Laird Matheson had a kind heart. Perhaps, that was why the Bruce had taken it upon himself to take her from the north all way to the western coast near Skye. Despite the fact that Matheson was in huge need of help with his new wards, he'd fiercely protect her and be kind to her at the same time. Kindness was something that Emilia desperately needed to remember.

At some point, she did fall asleep. When she woke in the morn, it was to the sound of children shouting in the corridor outside her room, their tiny knuckles rapping against the wood. There was a joy and excitement in their voices that tugged at her heart and put a smile on her face—a reaction she wouldn't have considered possible.

She threw back her covers and slid from the bed, pulling on a wrap to cover her nightrail. The floor of her chamber was freezing and she hobbled toward the door, lifting the bar and opening it up to find eight smiling faces staring back at her, Alice in the front of them all.

"Pleasure to see ye this morning, my lady," she said, the rest of them following somewhere around the *morning* part.

They curtsied and bowed respectively.

"And a pleasure to see your bright and smiling faces," she replied. She touched one of the lad's cheeks. "I see the lot of ye have already washed your faces, too."

They all nodded eagerly. "Aye, Nurse said ye'd like that."

"She was right." Emilia tapped Alice on the tip of the nose.

"We're ready for our lessons," one of the boys said. "I want to learn to read today."

Emilia chuckled. Their enthusiasm was refreshing. "Well, let me dress. Have ye broken your fast yet?"

"Nay, my lady, we were waiting on ye."

As if in answer, Alice's belly grumbled. They all had a good laugh about that, then Emilia ushered them along.

"I shall be up right away, so ye dinna have to wait much longer."

Emilia returned to her chamber, pulling out the simpler gown of dull gray, which was more suitable to teaching lessons. It had belonged to one of the Bruce's children's governesses and it didn't require the help of a maid, but would hide any stains she gained while working with the children.

She tugged the gown over her head, laced it up the front, and smoothed out the rough wool of the skirt. 'Twas surprising how freeing it was to wear a gown that was not meant to impress anyone. Emilia ran a comb through her long, unruly locks, then wove her hair into a plait down her back. She washed her hands and face in the basin provided and rinsed her mouth with the tonic she'd been using since she was a lass, making sure to scrub it over her teeth.

With her boots laced and her dagger strapped to her thigh, she felt ready to take on the world—or at least twelve little urchins.

She climbed the stairs, surprised to see that the nursery appeared to be in good order. The older children stood in a line waiting. The bairns were either playing softly on the floor or being fed by a nursemaid. A long trestle table was pushed against the left wall, laid out with bowls of porridge and hunks of bread and cups of milk.

"Good morning to ye, again, my dears," she said. "Who is hungry?"

They all shouted at once and clambered for the table.

Emilia would wait until they were seated and had said their prayers to tell them that when it came time for the nooning, they weren't to repeat that again.

This morning there was only one nursemaid in the room, the tall one, Mary she thought, who scowled fiercely. The dark circles under her eyes gave Emilia the impression she'd not slept in days. Her gown was wrinkled and stained. Right now, she was nursing one infant while another sucked on a rag at her feet.

"Good morning, Mary." Emilia scooped up a crawling bairn and set him near a carved wooden horse, which he immediately picked up to chew.

"Morning," Mary said, her tone begrudging.

"Have ye eaten?"

"Aye."

Mary didn't seem in a very talkative mood, which was fine by Emilia. She wouldn't force her to speak, though she would continue to be kind to her every morning.

She took her place between four children on one side of the table, facing four other smiling faces.

The children must have learned some manners wherever they'd been, for they didn't slurp or slouch, but ate politely. When she instructed, they kept their voices low. While they ate, she asked them each to tell her one thing they liked to do for fun. When it came time for her turn, rather than tell them she liked to throw knives, she simply told them she enjoyed sketching.

That was about the moment that Laird Matheson entered the room. The children all looked at him with admiring eyes. Emilia kept her gaze firmly on her porridge, afraid her gaze would also mirror their admiration. But she had to look at him, acknowledge him, or else she'd be labeled rude and disrespectful.

The benches wiggled as the children stood. "Good morning, my laird," they chimed.

Emilia took a deep breath, stood from the table and offered a curtsy. "Good morning, my laird."

The laird smiled at her, sending a current of warmth rushing through her veins. He stepped closer, his eyes riveted on her. "My lady, I give ye leave to call me Ian."

Ian. She hadn't known what his name was before and she found she rather liked it. Ian.

"I couldna, my laird." She blushed at being singled out.

He chuckled. "Laird Ian, then. I insist."

Emilia gave a tentative nod, studying him as he turned excitedly toward his much younger siblings.

"So, Lady Emilia likes to sketch," he was saying. "Shall we see what she can draw?"

"Oh yes," all chimed with exceptional volume. Thank goodness for the noise, for it covered up the groan coming from Emilia.

Sketch. Out of everything, why had she mentioned that? She couldn't draw a straight line with a ruler to guide her. This was not going to go well. Emilia ground her teeth and sent up a prayer to the heavens that they did something, though nothing that would harm anyone, to stop this from happening. When nothing happened, she tried to make an excuse, instead.

"We havena finished our meal," she said as politely as she could. "And we've lessons to do."

"Och, they can wait. We want to see ye draw something." There was a sparkle of amusement in Ian's expression. He was having fun. He had no idea that she couldn't draw or the humiliation she was about to feel when he saw just what her skill level could produce. She'd be dismissed and sent out into the wilds of the Highlands to fend for herself.

Magically, a stone tablet and chalky rock was placed into her trembling hands. She sat down with it, to hide her swaying.

"What shall she draw?" Ian asked the children.

They must have shouted out a thousand things, each more complicated than the last. A chicken, a loch, a bird's nest, a tower, the Matheson crest... Emilia grew speechless, feeling like all the blood in her body pooled somewhere around her feet. If she even attempted to draw one of the things they wanted, she'd be labeled a liar, a fool, and a fraud.

Ian, possibly sensing her panic, sat down on the bench beside her. He smiled at her softly and pulled the tablet toward himself. "On second thought," he said, "I'm feeling a hankering to draw something... Tell me what ye think, children."

They moved to sit by his feet, completely enthralled, their breakfast forgotten.

A rush of relief flooded her, only to be replaced by more panic. Though he'd saved her, he would have questions, she was certain of it. The porridge and milk curdled in her belly. She smiled at the children, trying to pretend she didn't feel like tossing up her accounts.

Ian furiously scribbled on the tablet, and then exclaimed, "A masterpiece," as he turned it around for them to see. He'd drawn an apple, perfectly shaped, and even shadowed to make it look glossy.

Emilia narrowed her eyes. Was it possible, Ian had a hidden talent for art?

"Another," the children cried.

He used his sleeve to wipe the slate clean and then began to scribble, once more. This time, his hand moved a little bit slower as he glanced up at her again and again. Was he drawing her? Emilia felt her face heat at her suspicions. Saints, but she hoped he wasn't.

When he was done this time, he turned the slate toward the children, but not her, so she couldn't see.

"An angel," several of them whispered.

But it was Alice, the most of astute of them all, who looked right at Emilia and said, "Ye've drawn Lady Emilia."

"Ah-ha! And ye shall win the prize." Ian set down the tablet and chalk on the table and lifted Alice up off the ground to swing her around, before placing her on his shoulders and galloping about the room like a horse.

Emilia's mouth went dry. 'Twas a rough sketch, but all the same, she could see the same features she often met in the looking glass. A hint of sadness around the eyes. It was nerve-wracking how he'd been able to so swiftly capture her and a part of herself she didn't want to face—melancholy.

Who was this man?

Laird Ian Matheson had a reputation for prowess on the battlefield as well as the bedchamber. A man's man, a warrior, a heartthrob.

Yet, he had a nursery full of bastards by his father and hidden talent for art.

He was a man that women dreamed of. A warrior to protect them. A lover to woo them. A kind heart to take care of those both close and far.

Emilia swallowed hard. She was not unaffected by him and all of what he stood for. Her heart did a little pitter-pat behind her ribs.

Saints, but she was in danger of losing herself...

Why couldn't her father have made an alliance with the Matheson Clan, instead?

CHAPTER 8

The next afternoon, while the children were at rest, Emilia took to the outdoors for some fresh air. After yesterday morn, she'd done a good job of ignoring Laird Ian. Afraid that the already growing tenderness she had would increase. And that was the last thing she needed.

Nay, she had a plan. Remain as a governess only until the Bruce had finally rid the land of Ina Ross.

She bent to pick a sprig of rosemary in the herb garden, spying the willowy figure of a maid who trailed far behind. She wasn't quite certain what her purpose was, perhaps as a spy or maybe it was because Laird Ian didn't want her to be alone. The maid could have turned around for all the difference she'd make in Emilia's afternoon walk. She wasn't speaking to anyone or doing anything particularly interesting. Simply breathing in the fresh, crisp autumn air.

'Twas the same with this lass as with every other one of them in the castle. None would get too close. Either because they'd been ordered not to or out of loyalty to the nursemaids who, while courteous on the outside, made it a point to snub her in front of their friends.

She feared her time here would be very lonely, but hopefully limited.

Emilia stopped, turned on her heel and walked toward the maid. The lass faltered in her steps, her face showing panic. She looked side to side and backed up three steps before Emilia had gotten close enough that, to back up any further, would be extremely noticeable, not to mention awkward. It would be completely obvious that the maid was trying to get away from her.

"Ye dinna have to follow me," Emilia said. Her chin rose a notch, challenging the young maid to argue with her. "I'll be fine on my own."

Her eyes widened with panic. "But—"

Emilia cut her off, not afraid to be blunt. "Are ye enjoying following me around?"

The maid cocked her head in confusion, wrinkling up her nose.

"Well, are ye?" Emilia put her hands on her hips and tapped her foot. "We dinna talk and I dinna even know if ye enjoy the out of doors."

"I do. Mostly," she said softly.

Emilia waved away her answer. "In any case, ye dinna need to follow me about like a puppy." She chewed her lip realizing that what she said was probably offensive. "I apologize, I didna mean to suggest..."

The maid shifted uncomfortably on her feet and crossed her arms over her chest. "'Tis no bother at all, my lady. The laird asked me to join ye. I but do his bidding."

Emilia leaned forward, coming within half a foot of the maid's face. Conspiratorially, she whispered, "I willna tell if ye dinna tell."

"What?" She tugged at her ear.

"I promise. We can even decide on a meeting place and time." She shrugged and looked around the empty orchard. "How about right here, in an hour."

Oh, to have an hour of solitude to herself... It had been months since she'd felt so free.

The maid looked from side to side, brow puckered, worrying her lower lip and wringing her hands.

Emilia ignored the lass's obvious signs of distress. "All right, it's all settled then." She turned on her heel, confident the lass would not follow her.

She listened keenly for the sounds of steps behind her, but heard not even the shift of a blade of grass. *Good.* Emilia picked up her pace. She wove between the trees to keep the maid from following or, at the very least, from seeing where she was. The orchard was not the largest she'd seen. Quite modest to be truthful, but lush enough, even without its apples, to keep her hidden from view.

She walked through the orchard, the scents of fruit following behind. Most of the apples had already been picked, even the ones that had fallen rotten to the ground had been gathered up to be used in applesauce, apple butter, and cider. But still, at the very top, she could see a few plump, red pieces of fruit glistened in the sunlight.

Suddenly her mouth was watering for an apple. She ducked under the branch and reached up to grab hold of the base of the limb with a cluster of apples at its very tip. She shook it, but not one of the apples budged. Putting a bit more *oomph* into it, she jiggled harder, until one of the apples finally dislodged and fell to the ground.

Emilia picked up the apple, rubbed it against her bodice and then took a hearty bite. Sweet juice dribbled over her tongue and chin, and she closed her eyes in a moment of pure pleasure. With a sigh, she continued on to the end of the orchard. By the time she got there, she'd eaten all the way to the core.

Her eye caught on an old tree, its limbs, devoid of leaves or apples, hung limp. An idea came to mind. How long had it been since she'd been able to throw a dagger?

Giving herself a little twirl to make certain no one was there, she tossed the apple core far behind her and then lifted her skirts enough to grab her dagger. She curled her fingers around the hilt, taking its weight and measure, as she'd done a thousand times before. She closed her eyes a moment, listening for the wind, feeling the light breeze on her face.

When she opened her eyes, she focused on a particular knot that protruded from the tree. Bringing her arm back slowly, she awakened muscles that had been hibernating for months.

"One," she breathed out. "Two... Loose!" She let her dagger fly, catching the knotted wood on the right side.

Emilia marched toward the tree, a sense of glee filling her, thrumming through her blood. She plucked out the dagger and then returned to the spot a dozen paces away. She needed to aim more toward the left this time.

Again, she brought her arm back. Counted. Let it fly.

Victory! She'd hit her mark squarely in the center. With a triumphant laugh, she marched forward and tugged her dagger free.

"Impressive."

Emilia jumped, whirled, and held back at the very last second before her knife flew from her hand.

Ian Matheson stood before her, tall, dramatic in his dark, brooding way. A slashing brow lifted as he perused her in what she thought must be a new light. "I'd not have known where ye went, save for an apple core hit me on the head. And to think I could have missed out on seeing your talent first hand."

Emilia's chin rose a notch in pride and defiance. She crossed her arms over her chest, tucking the dagger beneath her armpit. "I nearly gutted ye just now," she said, not holding back any of the irritation she felt at being interrupted. She was trying to hide not only the fear she felt for nearly having killed him, but the slight twinge of humor at having hit him on the head with her apple core.

He wiggled his brows, taunting her. "I'd have dodged it."

"Ye're that fast?" Emilia couldn't help the way her eyes rolled heavenward.

"I am." He grinned, a wide, confident smile.

The one she found irresistible and made her want to gut herself at the same time. There had to be a way to resist that smile. How could one turn of a man's lip make her weak in the knees—and the head?

"If ye think ye're so fast, then stand still and I'll toss my knife at ye."

Ian laughed. "I have a better idea. I saw the way ye hit the mark. Why dinna I hold an apple in my hands and ye spear it?"

Her stomach did a little flip of both excitement and nerves. He couldn't be serious. Just the slightest switch in the wind could send her dagger in the wrong direction. "I wish to accept your challenge, but not at the cost if I miss."

"Ye willna miss." He sounded much more confident than she felt.

She brushed a stray lock of hair away from her eyes. "Ye were not here a second ago when I was off my mark, then."

"On the contrary, I was, and ye were off by less than an inch. I'll find a big apple."

Despite her interest in the wager, Emilia shook her head. This was a bad idea. "I canna."

"Aye. Ye can." Ian winked at her before disappearing behind a cluster of trees.

Through the branches, she spied him reaching up and plucking an apple from near the top of the tree that had taken her twenty shakes of a branch to get.

He swaggered back toward her, confidence oozing from his every pore. At least one of them felt certain this would work.

He held the apple on the flat of his palm just before his heart. "Go on then. Take aim."

The man was mad. "Nay!" She shook her head and pointed at him. "At least hold it to the side so if I miss I dinna stab ye in the heart." Oh saints, but was she really going to go through with this?

"As ye wish, my lady." Holding the apple in his right hand, he extended his arm out. "I'm ready when ye are."

Ready? She was not ready at all. Why did he have to interrupt her? Why did he have to challenge her? Sweat trickled down her back. She'd never shared her knife throwing with anyone and, now, here she was with a handsome warrior goading her into hurling her dagger toward him. 'Twas kind of a dream come true and, if she weren't so nervous about it, she might have laughed with joy at the irony of it.

How was she going to go through with this? She shook her head. "Nay, my laird—"

"Lady Emilia, I beg ye, call me Ian. I've not been laird long. The last thing I want is for a bonny lass to think me in such a position of power as to not have a name."

She'd never thought about it like that. Put that way, she

could do no less than call him as he wished. But that didn't mean she could go through with his plan. "Ian... I canna."

He waved the apple toward her. "Ye're overthinking it. I watched ye throw your dagger before. Be one with the hilt. Dinna doubt yourself."

He was right. She had to stop doubting herself and just throw the damned thing. If she hit him instead of the apple, she would apologize profusely and remind him of this very conversation.

"If I hit ye, ye canna blame me for it."

"I will endeavor not to." Again with that infectious curl of his lip...

She closed her eyes, let out a deep breath, and felt for the wind. She was really going to do this. Go through with it. She'd never thrown a knife at another person. No one had ever been willing. Her arm came back, fingers wrapped just so around the hilt.

Emilia opened her eyes, kept them level on the apple, letting the rest of him fade out... and let her dagger loose. In slow motion, it went round and round, through the air. Her teeth were clenched, jaw tight. She watched as it whirled closer and closer to its mark. Inch by painful inch. Finally, she winced when it pierced the skin of the apple, taking it flying off of Ian's hand and at least a dozen paces behind him, landing with a thud on the ground.

Ian whooped a cheer and rushed forward, stopping at the last minute before her. Oh, how she wished he hadn't stopped. She thought he might have lifted her up. Swung her around in a joyful dance of victory.

Instead, he bowed. "Well done, my lady!"

Emilia's chest swelled with pride and she bobbed a curtsy. "Thank ye."

"Again?" He wiggled a brow.

She had to hold back a snort. "I dinna want to jinx myself."

Ian chuckled and tapped the tip of her nose. "One more time. If ye only do it once, it could have just been luck. Succeed twice and it is skill."

Why did he have to make so much sense? And why, oh why, did throwing a knife at a handsome laird sound so appealing? Emilia couldn't back down from his challenge. "All right. One more time."

Ian grinned and jogged to grab the apple with her dagger still protruding from it.

He slid her knife from the fruit and took a bite. She couldn't take her eyes off him. So much so, that he offered the fruit out to her.

"A taste, my lady?"

To take the attention off her own stare, she took the apple. Ian stared at her a breath or two more, before striding to the tree to retrieve a fresh apple. When he returned to her, once more, he stood still, arm out to the side with the apple sitting pretty on his wide palm.

Emilia sucked in a lengthy, cleansing breath, her hands at her sides, fingers flexing around the hilt. Once was luck. Twice was skill.

Her heartbeat kicked up a notch. Ian could have no idea how much this meant to her. To share her love and thrill of blades. To be appreciated rather than admonished for her interest in what was typically deemed an activity meant only for the male sex.

Again she was struck by how unique he was. How much she *liked* him. This was not good. Nay, she couldn't be thinking of him in such a way.

Blade. Apple. Wind. Emilia cleared her mind and worked to concentrate on the task at hand.

Breathe. Just breathe.

She brought her arm back. *One. Two... Loose!*

Again her dagger hurtled in slow motion toward the apple. But just before it landed, Ian twitched. The apple flew up into the air and her dagger sailed right past, stabbing into the earth behind him.

Emilia's mouth dropped open and she stomped her foot. He'd deliberately moved so she couldn't hit her target. "Why did ye do that?" she demanded.

His eyes sparkled with humor and a bit of satisfaction. "Ye were going to hit the mark and I wanted to prove I was as fast as ye were skilled. Call it a bit of friendly competition."

Emilia smirked and stalked toward her blade. "Ye might be careful walking back to the castle. I might decide to throw one at your head to see just how fast ye are."

"Then I will be certain to see ye walk in front of me." He swaggered forward, following her. He stopped beside her, his masculine scent enveloping her. She swore she could feel the heat of his body sinking into hers. "Admit what ye want."

Emilia's mouth went dry and she gazed into his eyes—she could have been falling for all she knew. 'Twas hard to make her tongue move to form words, but she did manage one syllable. "What?"

His gaze was fastened hard to hers, pinning her in place, demanding she open up to him. "Tell me what ye want."

She clamped up, breathing in deep the scents of him: spicy, earthy, masculine, a mingling of apples. An intoxicating combination that held her prisoner, motionless. What was happening to her? "I dinna know what ye mean." She clenched her toes in her boots, afraid she might lose her footing.

"Ah," he murmured, his eyes sliding over her lips. "I think ye do, but ye dinna want to admit it."

Could he see? Could he tell by her expression that she wanted... Oh, saints, but could she even admit it to herself? She *wanted* him to kiss her. Aye. She wanted him to ravish her mouth the way he'd ravished that apple. The thought frightened her. She'd made a vow to herself that she would never marry again. That she would go to Nèamh Abbey and devote herself to God's work.

And now this...

Now him...

Now these other thoughts and desires...

"I should go back inside," she whispered. "The children..."

"Dinna make excuses, lass." He slid his fingers from her elbow down her hand where she held her dagger in a tight fist. "All ye have to say is aye and I will grant your desire."

Heat flushed up over her chest and neck, fanning over her face. Could she? They were here in the orchard alone. No one was about. Perhaps it would not hurt to... Her grip on her dagger loosened. Her gaze slid to his mouth, then back up to his enticing eyes. 'Twas no wonder women fell at his feet. A few whispered words, smiles, and she was pudding.

"Aye," she murmured.

"I knew it!" Ian leapt backward, jerking her from whatever heady haze she'd been immersed in.

He lifted up another apple and held it in front of himself, centered in the square of his broad chest. "Look at us. We have shared fruit. I have put my life in your hands and ye havena taken it." He backed up a dozen or more paces. "And now, I am seeing that your deepest desire is realized—to throw your dagger at me and not miss."

Emilia's mouth fell open. What an utter fool she'd been! Her deepest desire? Oh, she could slap him. She could throw her dagger and miss!

This time, she didn't wait for the wind, she channeled her

anger, took aim and, let the dagger loose. Ian concentrated on her throw, both of them watching the sharpened tip hurtle toward his middle. Her mind switched from *Zounds!* to *He deserves it!* to *What in the bloody hell am I thinking?* to *This is, indeed, a dream come true!*

And then the wait was over. Into the apple it sank.

"I knew ye could do it," he beamed.

Emilia grunted, exhaling the long breath she'd been holding. Then she smirked at him. "I was aiming for your heart."

"Liar." He grinned and bit into the other side of the apple, her dagger wobbling.

"Ye'll never know." She stalked forward, tugging her dagger from the apple as she gazed into the whirling, taunting blue of his eyes. She paused, curiosity bidding her speak when she should have walked away. "Now that ye think ye know my deepest desire, what is yours?"

Ian's gaze dipped to her lips and she sucked in a breath, held it. "Mayhap, it was to be saved by a golden-haired pixie." His voice was deep, strained. "And maybe it was this."

He leaned closer, inch by aching inch. He was going to kiss her. And she was too paralyzed with curiosity and desire to move away from him.

Soft warm lips brushed over hers, flooding her with tingles, and taking away all sense. She closed her eyes, sinking against him, pressing her lips firmly back to his. If he'd not slid his arm around her middle, holding her taut against him, she'd have dropped to the ground from her knees buckling.

But his mouth was gone all too quickly when the sound of nearly a dozen children sing-songing their way through the orchard reached their ears.

"I shouldna have done that," he murmured against her cheek. His gaze had darkened, filled with a hunger that touched some place deep inside her. "Please accept my apologies."

Emilia nodded. Unable to find her voice and certain her face was as red as the apples they'd just shared, she tucked her dagger up her sleeve and rushed in the opposite direction to pull herself together before the children found her and asked just what she'd been doing in the orchard.

CHAPTER 9

Ian hunkered down in the woods, his face covered in mud, his bow drawn tight, and his arrow aimed toward the large stag that stood still, more so than the trees surrounding them. 'Twas late afternoon and he'd been hunting since before dawn.

After over a fortnight of being in his castle surrounded by children and the scent of Lady Emilia, he'd had to escape. Had to do something masculine. A good hunt could always do that. Remind him that he was a hunter, a man, a warrior.

But if the truth were to be told, what he most had to escape was his desire. Ever since he'd kissed Emilia in the orchard, he'd thought of little else. Over a week had gone by. Every ledger had been pored over. Every log investigated. Every sack of grain and head of sheep, counted. The wall fortification project had begun. And Ian's muscles screamed from the rigorous training he'd put his men through.

Ian worked himself to the bone. And still, every time he caught a glimpse of her or the scent of wildflowers, his blood surged hot, his nostrils flared, and he sought her out.

She'd given him shy, coy looks as she rushed in the opposite direction or hid behind a child.

The lass was playing hard to get. And it was working.

With the castle secure, Ian had determined it was best if he left before dawn with Alistair. In fact, he'd packed enough provisions that they could stay out in the woods a night or two. Their horses were tethered in a nearby glen, as he preferred to hunt on foot.

They'd already gathered a dozen rabbits or more for a stew, but a stag like this would be a prize to any man's prowess. With the king returning soon, they'd have roasted venison pies. He could almost taste it. Would Emilia enjoy a venison pie?

Och, but nay! He could not think of trying to please her. She was the reason he was out here to begin with. Hiding. Escaping. Longing...

The stag twitched its ears, sensing that it was being watched. Ian remained still, waiting for the right time to let the arrow fly. Flashes of Emilia's closed eyes, pursed lips as she felt for the wind before she threw her dagger assaulted him.

Blast it! He gritted his teeth, worked to stare down the stag without seeing her beautiful face.

One... Two...

Now!

He aimed and let loose, the arrow finding its mark in the stag's heart. The great animal fell without a sound. Since he was a lad, Ian had trained himself to shoot only once and fell an animal. He despised when they suffered needlessly from a man's sloppy work.

"Excellent, my laird," Alistair said with a nod.

They approached the animal, preparing its body for when they'd bring it back to the castle. They found a thick branch to hold its weight and tied its hooves to it, along with the strings of rabbits. By now, the sun was beginning to descend, and they were at least two hours away from the castle. Though he'd planned on staying the night in the woods, his gut bade him return. If he couldn't resist her while away, then he was doomed. Maybe the best thing would be to kiss her once more and put himself out of his misery. Aye, that was it. He'd not been able to give her a proper kiss before. And Ian never liked to leave a lass unsatisfied.

Shouldering their catches, they gathered their horses and made their way back to Balmacara Castle.

"What are ye going to do about the lady?" Alistair asked, shifting the weight of the branch on his shoulders and startling Ian from his own disturbing thoughts.

Ian readjusted his side of the branch. Ballocks, but was he that obvious about her? "I dinna know your meaning." He tried to play at indifference.

Alistair chuckled. "Truly? The governess."

"Aye, I knew to whom ye were referring. What do ye mean what am I going to do about her?"

Alistair blew out a low whistle. "She's awfully bonny."

A feeling, much like jealousy churned in Ian's belly. He had to shove off the quick reaction of tossing their catches aside and demanding Alistair fight him right then and there. He settled for squeezing the branch tight enough to hear the wood creak. "She is."

"I might have had the wrong of it, but I thought, perhaps, ye might... be interested in pursuing her."

Ian scoffed. "I've no time for a wife."

Alistair grunted. "Then ye'll not be upset if I pursue her?"

Och, but jealousy was a hot-tempered demon and it reared its ugly head, once more. Ian held back a negative snarl and, instead, said, "If ye're so inclined." The words were painful to speak and even more so to bear when he caught flashes of an imaginary Alistair gathering Emilia up in his arms and ravishing her in front of all the Highlands.

Ballocks, why did he say that? There was no doubt that he was attracted to the lass. None whatsoever. And, aye, he wanted her for himself. He didn't want Alistair to pursue her. He'd rather let her throw her daggers at Alistair's head with no apples between, then ever see them gaze into each other's eyes or share a sweet kiss.

Saying such was unfair of him. Why couldn't the two people he cared most about find comfort with each other?

The very idea left a bitter taste in his mouth. While Ian couldn't have her, he didn't want Alistair to either.

He'd spoken the truth about not having time for a wife. He still needed to establish himself as laird. To gain the respect of his people. To mark his place in the world and with his king. If he were to lose sight of that in his wooing of a woman, no one would believe he could be a good laird. Besides all that, the king would never grant his cousin to be Ian's wife.

"Dinna get your hopes too high," Ian added, hoping to dissuade his friend. "She is the Bruce's kin."

"Aye, but she's in need of protection." Alistair's tone was filled with a determination Ian had not heard before. "And, mayhap, if her circumstances were different, she'd not need to play governess."

Ian frowned. "Ye'd steal away my governess? I ought to have ye lashed. I've a dozen little devils residing at the top of my tower. I'll not have ye take away the only thing that's kept them from destroying the lot of it."

Alistair was quick to respond. "Och, nay, my laird, I'd make certain to find ye a replacement." Why did it sound as though he were being overly generous, gloating almost?

"And what would ye know of governesses? If ye had one in mind, why let me suffer for a fortnight before Lady Emilia arrived?"

"Before, ye said ye were looking for a wife. Now that ye've changed your mind, that changes everything."

"I hardly see how it changes much," Ian grumbled. "Besides, how am I supposed to find a wife when none will have me?"

Alistair was silent for several moments. He'd been present in Ian's study when he'd received the many rejecting letters. Witnessed Ian's temperament, too, when the most recent one had topped the list of damning complaints.

"They're all fools," Alistair said.

"I dinna blame them." He'd been the fool for even thinking a good marriage was something he could ever have.

They gathered their horses and walked the rest of the way in silence. As they marched through the village and up to the castle gate, the people cheered their catch. Ian worked hard to smile at them. At least it appeared that the majority of his clan accepted him. Had pride in his ability to provide.

The children greeted them in the bailey, touching the fur of the rabbits and deer and giggling between exclaiming their aversion. Ian patted their little heads and smiled, but his gaze was drawn to Emilia who stood off to the side.

A slight smile curved her lips. She stood rigid, unmoving, and he couldn't tell if she wanted to run away or stay. She wore the same gray gown she wore most days. He knew for a fact she had it cleaned more than once already. His father's children had fallen in love with her. Even in just these few days' time, he could see a remarkable difference in their behavior. She'd been able to work a miracle with them. He'd be forever grateful to her for transitioning his brothers and sisters from one life into another.

Two men came to take the branch from Ian and Alistair's shoulders. They'd take the meat to the butcher to be prepared for cooking. He gave them the instructions for the cook to make the meat pies for the king, but kept his eyes on Emilia the entire time.

Aye, he was certain he was right. He needed to simply kiss her properly and then push her from his thoughts. As if she agreed, she slicked her tongue over her lower lip before biting it.

Lady Emilia curtsied to him and he nodded, about to offer her his arm to walk her inside when Alistair beat him to the chase.

"My lady?" Alistair said, offering his elbow.

Saints, but Ian had forgotten all about Alistair's blasted vow to court Emilia.

She cocked her head, a spark of curiosity in her eyes as she shifted her gaze to his friend. That made Ian's insides clench.

Please, dinna be interested in Alistair.

'Twas unfair of him to think such things. He only wanted happiness for his closest friend, but Lady Emilia? Of all women, Alistair had to want the one he desired?

Though Ian was certain the Bruce would deny him, that didn't mean that some deeper part of him didn't wish she was on *his* arm. Och, but who was he kidding? Alistair's prospects were even lower than his own. The lad had washed up on the shore and though he'd been taken in by the laird, he'd not been adopted as the man's son and left as the only heir.

Ian ushered them in front, wanting to see just how interested Lady Emilia was in his friend. When she turned around to speak to him over her shoulder, he was certain he'd won.

But the words that came out of her mouth were the last he wanted to hear.

"There is a woman here to see ye."

There was a twinkle of mirth in her eye. He could only imagine her recalling the very first words he'd said upon greeting her in the great hall.

He grimaced. Another of his father's lovers?

But then, she put him out of his misery—only to set him on edge again.

"She says she is your mother."

Ian's heart skipped a beat. Emilia could not know that such a phrase had two meanings for him. He shook off the cobwebs of his past and gave her a curt nod, walking into the castle. He'd not made it up the first three steps of the interior spiral staircase before his mother called out behind him.

"Ian, my dear." Standing in the nun's habit, she looked tinier than he remembered. It had only been a couple of months since she'd gone to Skye, but still, he thought she looked different.

"Mother." He shifted uncomfortably on his feet, wanting to reach out and hug her, but at the same time uncertain if that was proper given her new station in life.

"Come, give me a hug. Dinna dally."

He breathed a sigh of relief and reached for her. She might have looked different, but she felt and smelled the same—like comfort, home, and warm summer days.

"I have missed ye," he said, his chest swelling with emotion.

"And I ye, my boy." She stroked his shoulders and then patted his cheeks. "No matter how big and gruff ye get, ye're still the little lad I love." Her face turned serious. "But I didna come to talk nonsense."

Ian nodded, feeling the pit of his belly drop. "I wondered when ye'd come."

"Then ye know why I'm here."

Ballocks, but this was going to be painful. "Mother, I have loved ye from the moment we first met eyes, but I canna send the bairns away. I know how they must shame ye, but they have nowhere else to go. Mathesons take care of their own."

A soft smile touched her lips and she shook her head, reaching out to pat his chest. "Ye've always had a good heart. But that is not why I've come. Let us go to your study where we might have more privacy and, perhaps, a wee nip of whisky which I've been sorely missing."

Ian chuckled. "Same old mother."

She sniffed, though her eyes sparkled with humor. "Some things never change."

He took her by the elbow and led her up the stairs, past the great hall and to his study. Anticipating his return, one of the servants had already lit a small blaze in the hearth, as well as the torches that hung on either side of the wall and the two windows against the far wall.

His mother took up the chair by the hearth, sitting on a cushion she'd embroidered with thistles some years before. This was the same chair she'd normally sat on when his father occupied the study. It brought back a rush of memories. Ian headed to the sideboard to pour her a wee nip and himself a larger serving.

"Do they have whisky at Nèamh Abbey, Mother?"

Her laughter filled the dim chamber. "Not to drink. Though there is a stockpile in the infirmary. We sometimes get patients with wounds that need cleaning and it helps. But, I suspect a few of our heavenly sisters might imbibe a nip or two here and there."

He laughed and handed her a small cup. Ian stood beside her with his hand on her shoulder, needing that subtle, reliable contact of his solid mother. She held her cup to his, clinking them together.

As they sipped, her smile faded. "Sit with me a spell."

Ian took a seat opposite her, swallowing his whisky slow enough that it burned his tongue. He should have brought the jug over to refill. He wasn't sure he wanted to hear what she had to say while sober.

"I did come because of the bairns, my son. But not for the reason ye would believe."

He drained the rest of his cup.

"I wanted ye to know that I admire what ye're doing. That I am proud of ye."

"Ye're proud?" Ian frowned. "But——" He cut himself off before he could say what he truly wanted to, that his actions of bringing the children in were disrespectful to her, to her name and place.

"I know ye must be verra confused. That ye have a lot of questions and, most of them, I probably canna answer. But there is something I must share with ye and I think it best ye hear of it coming from me. 'Tis the reason I was allowed leave to come here. I will also help arrange the baptisms of the children with Father Locke. Even if it was done previously, before they arrived, the children will be given the Matheson name, with your permission of course."

"Ye have it. Ye dinna need to ask."

She waved away his comment. "I do. Ye're the new laird. If your mother dinna seek the laird's approval, it would give any dissenters cause to rise up." She regarded him a moment. "Have there been any dissenters?"

"None so far, but I expect to have at least one before the year is out. Now especially, with having welcomed my father's..." Again he trailed off, uncertain how to phrase it without upsetting her.

She lowered her gaze to the cup in her hands, blinking rapidly before looking up at him again. The moment of sentiment passed, and her gaze was, once more, virtuous and resilient. "I am just going to say what I came to say so that we can move on. That way, I can stop feeling on edge and ye can stop feeling uncomfortable." She drained her whisky, pursing her lips, squeezing her eyes shut, and giving her head a little shake. At once, she blew out a breath and spoke quickly. "I gave your father permission to take lovers." She paused, letting that bit of news sink in.

Ian didn't move. Didn't blink. He was stunned.

"When the first of his illegitimate children came, he was so ecstatic. He could have children, he exclaimed to all. But at that same moment, we both knew the fault of our empty cradle lay with me. I gave him permission to ask for an annulment, that I would let him go though I loved him, so he could find a wife to produce his heirs." A nostalgic smile touched her lips and she shook her head slowly at the memories. "But your father, he denied me. He said he loved me too much to set me aside, that though I couldna have his children, he still wanted me by his side, to rule with him. When ye came along, I wanted to keep ye, and he was more than happy to oblige me." She frowned. "I'm rambling, I know, but ye must understand, I was aware of the children. I wanted him to have them. I dinna want them sent away, but your father thought it would be too painful for the many of them to be kept near. So he found the older couple and their daughter to help raise them." Her hands pressed in prayer over her heart. "I couldna watch him suffer with his frustration at not being able to fix me, to get me with child when I was broken."

Ian sat forward, and grabbed hold of her hands. "Ye're not broken, Mother. There are many women who canna have children. It doesna mean ye're not whole. Or unworthy."

She smiled and patted his hands. "Ye've always been a sweet lad. And now a man grown. A man with a clan behind him. I dinna think myself unworthy, but perhaps meant for something else. And now I am seeing that through at Nèamh Abbey."

Ian scrubbed a hand over his face, the information she'd offered sinking in. "So ye knew of them all along. Why dinna ye tell me afore ye left?"

"I wasna certain ye were ready." She reached for his arm when he moved to rise, her eyes pleading. "I am sorry, Ian. Ye'd just lost your father and were in such turmoil about being named laird. I thought it would be best for ye to gain your footing before telling ye about them." She shook her head. "I had no cause to know that they would bring the children back."

"Father gave them your jewels."

She pressed her lips together and shook her head in denial. "Nay. I did."

"Ye? Why?" This time he did shake free of her hold and go to the sideboard for another dram.

"Raising children takes coin and they clearly dinna have enough, even with your father's generous gifts and granting them to live without tax or rent. I couldna let your father's children suffer."

"Och, Mother, ye're too good." He slugged back his cup.

"I am not too good." She walked toward him, holding out her own cup for a refill. "Any decent person would do the same. Look at ye, ye've gone from bachelor to ward of a dozen children all on your own."

"Not all on my own." He glanced at her sideways, completely touched by her acceptance and pride in him. "They've a governess."

Interest sparked in her eyes. "Tell me about her. Is she bonny?"

"Aye."

The huge smile that filled her face all the way to the creases of her eyes had him groaning. "She is bonny, Mother, that doesna mean anything other than what it is."

"Hmm..." She stood up and grabbed the jug of whisky pouring him another dram.

Hmm, indeed. While on hunt, he'd had a hard time pushing the feel of her lips from his mind, the look of determination in her eyes when she'd tossed her dagger, the scent of flowers when she'd been so close. And then when he'd finally seen her again, it had almost undone him not to wrap her up in his embrace and claim her mouth for his own.

Seeing her on the arm of Alistair, his closest friend and ally, and knowing that his mate had an interest in her, burned him up. Saints, but Ian couldn't be possessive of her. She wasn't his. Never would be.

As if hearing his own thoughts, his mother asked, "Why not, Ian?"

Why the hell not, indeed?

CHAPTER 10

Emilia stared, perplexed, at the door of her chamber. After welcoming Ian home, she'd settled the children in their nursery for their afternoon rest. Already, she'd settled for a quick nap herself. She was thoroughly exhausted from not getting enough sleep the last few days, thoughts of her handsome protector constantly running rampant through her mind.

And now it would appear she had another suitor. Sir Alistair had shown a sudden interest and been very charming. He'd offered her a beautiful falcon feather that he said would bring her good luck and he'd followed her all the way up the nursery.

'Twas a bit overwhelming and she really could have used at least an hour to herself. What would happen if she pretended she wasn't in her chamber?

"Who is it?" she hesitantly asked.

"The laird wishes to speak with ye in his study, my lady."

Emilia sighed and climbed out of bed. By the time she opened the door, whoever had been on the other side was gone. She gave one last longing look at her bed. She could always pretend she'd never gotten the message...

Nay, 'twas best to get it over with. He may have something important to discuss in regards to the children, and she'd rather know it before heading up to sup with them as she'd promised.

But, on her way down the stairs, she ran into Alistair.

His dark, wavy hair fell in reckless waves over his forehead. He smiled up at her, his blue eyes welcoming. "My lady." He bowed. "I was just coming up to the nursery to see if ye..." He flicked his gaze around as if he'd not gotten that far in his thought process. "To see ye."

"About?" she asked with a raised brow.

He chuckled, a boyishness about him that made her smile in turn. "I'll be honest, lass, I hadna thought so far ahead."

"Ye're funny, sir. But I am on my way to the laird's study."

He bowed again and stepped aside. "Shall I escort ye?"

"If ye like."

He nodded and offered her his solid arm. By the time they reached the study, they were laughing and were met by the thunderous glare of Ian who stood with his hands on his hips in the corridor.

"What in the blazes is going on?" His voice was clipped and filled with disapproval.

Emilia stopped laughing immediately, her eyes widened. Why did she feel guilty for having done nothing wrong?

"Naught but a wee laugh, my laird. I passed the lady on the stair and she was headed this way."

"What were ye doing on the stair?"

Alistair gave her a pleading look and Emilia jumped to help. "I asked him to come to the nursery to discuss... archery with the children."

"Archery?"

"Aye. They were excited about the hunt and had many questions," she said.

"Why did ye not ask me?"

Emilia chewed her lip, sensing there was more than bluster to Ian's irritation—jealousy.

"I thought ye might have been busy with your mother," she offered.

He grunted, leveling his irritated gaze on Alistair who grinned wide at his laird. Alistair then offered Emilia a conspiratorial wink. Suddenly, Emilia thought she might be missing some important piece of an unknown puzzle.

"Go on, then," Ian said. "She's found her way here."

Alistair bowed, took her hand, and kissed the back of her knuckles.

"So chivalrous, ye are," she teased Alistair, certain there was a disgusted growl from Ian.

What on earth? Why did she suddenly feel like the two men were vying for her attention? Or rather, why did she feel as though Alistair were goading a reaction out of Ian?

Interesting. She'd have to think on this further.

"Come in," Ian ordered.

She rolled her eyes, feeling like the bone a big dog had fought for and won.

Ian closed the door behind them both. When he walked past her, he brushed his arms over hers in a way that sent shivers racing down her back. No matter how many days she'd avoided him, after that kiss, she still felt the heat of his lips on hers.

"Have a seat." He indicated a seat by the hearth and when she'd sat down, he took the one opposite of her.

Their eyes met, the space between them charged with a palpable tension that made her squirm in her seat. No one had ever made her feel this way. As though he could see deep inside her soul. That he knew her. And yet, he didn't really know her, did he? They'd only just met a couple of weeks before. They'd had that one incredible afternoon in the orchard, and, now, just sitting across from him she wanted to leap up and—

And what?

She wasn't certain. But she knew she wanted *something* to ease the ache that had settled all over her entire body.

"Ye're probably wondering why I asked ye to come here," he said, his voice low, gravelly.

Emilia cleared her throat. "Aye." She searched his blue eyes, watching him rake his large, masculine hands through his locks, the color of burnished, fiery embers.

"I was curious to see how ye're getting on... with the children." He steepled his hands in front of him, leaning back in the chair, his long, muscular legs spread out before him.

'Twas a testament to her fortitude that she was able to keep her gaze somewhere above his neck. Curiosity taunted her with the strength of his knees, the sprinkle of hair on that tiny sliver of his thighs that was exposed.

Heaven help her.

"Verra well, my laird."

He leaned forward, elbows on his knees, hands still steepled, and the muscles of his upper arms bulging from the white of his shirt. "I asked ye to call me Ian."

She swallowed. "Apologies."

"Ye needna apologize." His lips curved into a flirtatious grin. "I like the way ye say my name."

"If I am to call ye by your name, then ye must call me Emilia."

"If ye insist, Emilia." Suddenly he was standing and walking away from her.

She stared after him, admiring the length and breadth and

strength of him, and feeling that oddly delicious itch inside her grow. A trickle of fear slid up her spine. She sensed that she should leave his study now. Sensed that there was something changing between them, though she couldn't name it specifically.

Emilia stood, prepared to excuse herself. But the moment she stood, Ian turned around and stalked back toward her.

Before she could blink, he'd seized her hands and tugged her close, pressing her palms to his chest.

"Ian," she breathed out, eyes wide. "What are ye doing?"

Feather light, he slid his hands over her arms to her elbows, over her ribs and grasped her waist.

"Finishing what we started."

"What did we start?" she squeaked.

"A kiss."

"I thought we quite finished it."

He slowly shook his head. "That was not a proper kiss, lass."

"A proper kiss..."

"Aye. A lass as bonny as ye has probably had plenty of proper kisses and I canna allow your memory of me to be so fleeting."

Emilia chewed her lower lip. She'd never been *properly* kissed. Nor ravished in the way she desired to be ravished right then and there. Every inch of her skin tingled. Her hands trembled against his chest.

"Aye," she lied. "Ye'd best see that I dinna find ye lacking." Zounds, but where had that come from!

Ian grinned. His coarse palm slid over the side of her neck, his thumb stroking her cheekbone. "That thought shall never cross your mind."

He dipped his head toward hers. Her eyes fluttered closed just as his warm mouth brushed over hers, softly at first. Teasing. He slid it back and forth, his nose grazing hers. Emilia slid her hand from his chest up toward his neck, scraping her palm over his stubbled cheek and then to the back of his neck where she feathered her fingers in the hair at his nape.

Ian groaned softly, pulled back to look at her, a hunger blazing in his eyes, before he closed them and kissed her again. Angling his head to the side, he claimed her mouth once more, only this time in a deeper kiss. He nibbled her mouth and swept his tongue along the seam. Emilia parted her lips, recalling the careless invasion of the stable lad she'd kissed in her youth, and admiring Ian for his talent... This was, indeed, a proper kiss.

Emilia was swept up by him. By the taste of whisky on his tongue as he slid it over hers. The soft velvet caress, saints, but she felt it all the way to her toes and then back up to the top of her head. Her heart pulsed a rapid beat and she had to remind herself to breathe. Desire unfurled in her middle, spreading its wings outward. If he didn't hold her grounded to the floor, she might simply fly away.

But she couldn't. In fact, she shouldn't have let her curiosity get away with her. 'Twas all fine and dandy when she was a lass and the lad she was kissing was her father's stable hand. But now, she was a woman grown and the lips she was kissing belonged to a man, a warrior. Desire flooded her, and him, too, judging by the hard length that pressed to her hip.

Suddenly, she was full of fear. All the warmth left her, replaced by an icy chill that sank all the way to her bones. Flashes of Ina, Padrig, Marmaduke making her pull back and shudder. Fear outweighed all the tantalizing feelings Ian had brought out.

"I have to go." She couldn't look at him. Her face flamed hot. She started for the door.

"Wait," he said.

Emilia stopped in her tracks, facing away from him.

"What just happened?" he asked.

"Ye kissed me. And I let ye." She wasn't afraid to acknowledge that.

"After," he said. "Ye seemed... scared. Ye know I'd never hurt ye or pressure ye..."

"I know." Emilia swallowed hard. "Ye're a good man."

"I'm a good listener, too."

She squeezed her eyes shut. "There is nothing I have to tell."

"We all have something to tell."

"Ye first." Why didn't she just leave?

"I'm afraid of what people will think of me. I've not done a proper thing."

"The children?" she asked.

"Aye."

"They all love ye. The young and the old."

"Now it's your turn."

"I was... married before," she said. "It was unpleasant."

Ian let out a sigh and softly approached her. She didn't want to turn and face him, but he didn't make her. Instead, he came to stand in front of her and slowly threaded his fingers through hers. "I wish I could erase those memories for ye, lass. But I canna. And mayhap ye canna either. But, never let those unpleasantries be who ye are. They are shadows, passing in the night. And your soul, the candle flame that guides ye away from them."

Emilia let out the breath she was holding. "I will try to remember that."

He lifted her fingers toward his lips and gently kissed her. "If ye ever wish to talk, I will be glad to listen."

"I thank ye for that, Ian." She smiled up at him, suddenly

warm again. "For what it's worth, ye did kiss me verra properly."

Ian chuckled, a satisfied grin on his face. "Aye, 'twas a proper kiss, wasn't it?"

The man had no idea how he was changing her. How his kiss twisted her up inside with hopes and dreams and desires she'd pushed away the moment she'd found out she was to wed into the Ross Clan.

Nay, nay, nay. His kisses would ruin her, for she knew they couldn't go any further than that. Besides, he'd just wanted to finish what they'd started. And even if he had swept her off her feet, that was all there was to it. A one time (or two times split in half) event.

Emilia cleared her throat. "Well, now that we've finished what we started, I must really be going." She smoothed her hair, certain that anyone who saw her when she left his study would know exactly what was happening behind closed doors.

Ian locked his gaze on hers. "Lass, I confess, I'm not certain if we've finished or only begun."

At that, Emilia did sway on her feet. And she fled.

Fled from the need to kiss him again to find out. Fled from dreams she was certain couldn't come true. Fled because Ian didn't know who she really was and, once she told him, he would shun her. But mostly, she fled for fear of a broken heart. She was only just starting to pick up the pieces of herself. Now was not the time to get lost again.

Emilia ran out to the back gardens, the orchard where she had found solace. Just when she was ready to turn around—because now it also brought memories of Ian. She spotted his mother sitting on a stone bench, fingering her rosary beads.

Sister Meredith was at the same abbey as Ayne.

The older woman looked up and beckoned her closer.

"What is it, child? I can tell ye have something ye wish to discuss with me."

Emilia nodded, wringing her hands in front of her. She'd been itching to get Sister Meredith alone ever since she'd introduced herself. But now, she felt awkward having most likely just committed a sin. Was kissing a sin? She cleared her throat and took a few tentative steps forward. "Aye, I must ask after my dear sister, Ayne. Do ye know of her? She is a novice at Nèamh Abbey, same as ye."

The lady's smile broadened. "I should have known ye were sisters. Ye've the same golden mane." She reached out to touch a curl on Emilia's shoulder. "But, she didna mention being a cousin of the Bruce."

Emilia ducked her chin, sweeping her eyes over the mostly picked herbs in the garden. "Is she well?" she asked, ignoring the implied question.

Sister Meredith took mercy on her. "Sister Ayne is doing wonderfully well. She belongs to our choir and performs for us on Sundays after the nooning. Her voice is like angels coming down to bless us."

Emilia broke out into a joyous smile. "That pleases me so much. Her voice was the purest I've ever heard. Beautiful." She stared off wistfully, recalling how Ayne used to sing about everything from the milk swirled in their porridge to a raven flying high in the sky.

"But, she does miss ye." Sister Meredith patted the bench beside her and Emilia took a seat.

"I miss her, too."

"If ye like, when I return, ye can give me a letter and I will see it brought to her."

Emilia clutched her hands to her heart. "I should like that verra much."

"There is just one question I have."

Emilia swallowed at the way Sister Meredith's face had grown strained.

"Ayne comes from, I believe, the MacCulloch Clan," she said.

Zounds, had the canny woman heard of her father's treachery? Was she about to be discovered?

Emilia cocked her head to the side, silent, neither responding in agreement nor dispute.

That didn't stop the canny woman from continuing. "The MacCulloch Clan is aligned with the Ross Clan, aye?"

Emilia ground her teeth, searching for just the right words and finding none.

Sister Meredith looked off toward the castle. "Sometimes clans align for reasons unknown. And it doesna necessarily mean that everyone within the clan agrees." She searched Emilia's eyes. "Allow me to be blunt. If ye are aligned with the enemy, I willna sit idle while ye hurt my son or this clan. I brought many resources and coin to Nèamh Abbey. I have influence there. I can make your sister's life verra... difficult."

Emilia swallowed hard, panic rising, burning the back of her throat. Poor Ayne had nothing to do with any of this. She should have kept her mouth shut. Now she'd put her sister's happiness at risk. "I am loyal to Robert the Bruce and a Scottish independence from the English. I have never harmed anyone in my life. And I take offense to your threat against my sister." Och! Why couldn't she keep that last part to herself? Now, Sister Meredith would for certain see Ayne crushed.

But instead of responding to Emilia's outburst, Sister Meredith inclined her head and asked, "And the Ross Clan?"

"My mortal enemies."

"So ye are *she*?" Meredith tapped her chin, and Emilia could only guess at what that meant.

'Twas obvious that now the lady knew who she was without question. She'd let her desire to find out how her sister was doing get in the way of her better judgment. The Bruce had told her to keep her secret safe until he'd had a chance to deal with the Ross Clan.

Emilia forced herself not to drop to her knees and beg the woman to keep her secret.

"I am Lady Emilia. As far as anyone knows, by the king's decree, I am his cousin, nothing more or less. There are lives at stake, Sister, and I humbly beg your agreement to keeping my secret safe."

"I understand." Meredith nodded. "Swear to me and before God that ye willna harm my son."

"I would never harm him or anyone in your family, nor this clan. I am here..." She trailed off, not wanting to divulge anything else to Sister Meredith, for fear she would take the information and give it away. Laird Matheson, Ian, may become angry at not knowing who she was before. She'd already told him too much when she mentioned being married before. "I am here to help him. To help the children."

"I believe ye."

"I willna be here long," Emilia said as an afterthought.

"We can never know for sure how long we will be any one place. 'Tis not our choice as women."

"Did ye choose to go to the abbey?"

"I did."

"Then, perhaps, I, too, will get the chance to choose a similar path."

"I'm certain the Mother Abbess would accept any sister of Ayne's." Meredith swiped her hands down the front of her dull gray habit. "But, ye may find ye are happier here with my son."

"Ye mean the children."

She only smiled. "I must be moving along now. I told Father Locke I would meet him at the kirk this morn."

"Sister—" Emilia reached out to touch the older woman's arm. "What we've said here..."

"'Tis just between us." She licked her lower lip and steadied her wise gaze on Emilia. "Unless ye give me cause to divulge the information."

CHAPTER 11

Most afternoons, the nursery was quiet. A small blaze lit the hearth on the opposite end of the room. By the fire one nursemaid fed a baby, while another lass changed the soaked linen of two others.

Sitting at the table, a small body huddled up on either side of her, Emilia had each child practicing their letters. She was surprised at how much the older children knew. At least six of them could write their own name, as well as sound out a few basic words and formulate a pattern of letters representative of the actual word.

"All right, now erase your boards. We're going to do a fun exercise." They used the little rags she'd brought up to wipe their slates clean. "Are ye ready? This is called blind writing. Let's see how steady your hands are. Write your names with your eyes closed and no peeking!"

Emilia used to love it when her instructor brought fresh games to the mix.

Through the window, whistled a shout from the guards at the gate tower. A call of greeting. Emilia and the children cocked their ears to listen and she thought she heard the chink of metal and the thunder of hoof beats.

The commotion below had the children up in arms. They leapt from the table with as much impulse control as flies, rushing to the thin window, shoving each other out of the way for space.

The shortest and plumpest of the nursemaids frowned from where she rocked a sleeping bairn. The child woke and squalled as though a mighty stone had crashed through the wall.

"Children," she cautioned. "Settle down. Ye've woken your brother."

"The king! The king is back!" they cheered, not hearing the nurse at all. "Will ye let us go down and greet him, Lady Emilia? Please, oh, please."

Urgent curiosity filled her, too. When the king had left, it had been to ride on the Ross Clan. Whatever news he brought would be the deciding factor in her future. But still, Nurse was rising from her rocker, and Emilia feared her retaliation would be swift.

"Aye, but only if ye are quiet. Anyone who makes a fuss," she glanced at the nurse who glared daggers at her, "will be sent to bed without supper," she warned.

"Aye, my lady." They all dipped and bobbed and then lined up at the door, silent as the grave.

"Apologize to Nurse for waking the bairn."

"We're so sorry, please forgive us."

Nurse nodded curtly and settled the bairn back into her plump arms.

"Your hands," Emilia reminded them when they rushed toward the door. They swiftly turned, running amok to the water basins before Alice, smart wee lass, cautioned them all to go one at a time else they not be allowed down.

Emilia tapped her foot, forcing herself not to run from the nursery. *Zounds!* She wanted to know right *now* what had happened. Her hands were shaking with nerves and she had to force herself to blink, to breathe.

Finally, the children finished washing and were ready to descend. Emilia led them quietly, down the long spiral stairs to the great hall where the king and his men gathered with Ian near the hearth. She was very pleased with their polite behavior.

Unfortunately, they were silent enough that the men did not hear them approach, so she heard every word they said.

"Your men did well for themselves," the king said, patting Ian on the shoulder. "Took out many a Ross."

That was good news! Ina Ross must have been captured! However, Ian looked somber, despite the news. Why did he look so upset?

"Damn shame we weren't able to detain Ina Ross and her husband," the Bruce continued. "They fled. The Sutherlands fear it was northward. They've gone to protect their lands and will send word if they find them."

That was why Ian looked that way. He must have already known. That meant that Ina Ross was still out there. Could still come for her. Still demand she return to Ross lands. Emilia gasped, her hands coming to her face. She wavered on her feet, fearing she'd faint. Fear, unbidden, clawed its way up her body, gripping her throat. The men turned to see that she and the children stood in the opening. Their discussion ceased, faces turned placid.

"My lady?" Sweet Alice tugged on Emilia's skirt, her eyes filled with concern.

Tears of frustration gathered in Emilia's eyes, stinging, but not nearly as hard as the news that Ina had not been defeated. Somehow, she must have caught wind that the

Bruce's army was closing in on them or she'd had help, somehow, to get away. He'd brought so many men with him. How was it possible?

Was she forever going to be haunted by the likes of that woman?

She tried to force her tears at bay, to keep the children from seeing how upset she was.

"All will be well," she whispered to Alice.

"Cousin," the Bruce drawled out, taking several steps toward her.

Emilia worked to clear the emotion from her face. She grasped her hands together to keep them from shaking. Straightened her shoulders and faced the king with a curtsy and a bowing of her head.

Ian snapped his fingers at the children and ushered them out of the great hall amidst a promise of a sweet treat. He flashed a concerned glance her way before he disappeared through the arch. Since their kiss several days before, he'd begun joining her and the children every morning for their prayers and breakfast before rushing off to do whatever it was a laird did. In the afternoon, after the children rested, he took the older boys out to the field to work with them on sword play and archery, while Emilia attempted to teach the lassies how to wield a needle and thread. More often than not, she let the girls pretend to sword fight with their needles, using their thimbles as shields.

Emilia didn't want Ian to leave, but it was best that the children not be here. She should have known better. Should have come down and asked permission for them to be presented instead of just bringing them down.

Her mind had been such a jumble of nerves at wanting to know the news of Ina Ross that she'd not been thinking straight.

"I gather ye heard," the Bruce said.

Stunned silent, Emilia nodded. "I've written your parents, to warn them of the risk of the Ross army likely advancing on them in retaliation, if they haven't already gone in search of ye there."

Emilia nodded, her head feeling heavy and her neck weak. Saints, but she prayed her clan was safe. That they were prepared for the onslaught. They had to be. Had to have heard the news of her disappearance after Padrig's death. And then Ina Ross would come for her. She'd never stop until she had Emilia locked in a tower, forced to do her every bidding...

Emilia's chest tightened. She couldn't breathe. Felt like someone was choking her. Ina Ross from afar.

Her knees buckled, her vision went blurry. Nay! She couldn't faint. Couldn't let that woman torment her when she wasn't even in front of her. But it was too late. She started to fall back, but strong arms caught her from behind. *Ian.*

With his arms around her waist, he straightened her up, holding her in place. He kept his arms around her. A strong comfort. Kept her steady as she tried to find her footing.

Oh, Ian.

And then it hit her. She'd never told him about her past. About her relationship with the Ross Clan. How could she face him when he must think her a liar? A withholder of information? The whole reason she was here was because of the Ross Clan. Certainly, he would see it as some form of trickery, wouldn't he?

Well, she'd have to face that at some point. She didn't stray from his arms, but met the king's gaze.

"I have to go to them," she murmured. "My parents... I need to make certain they are all right." Her lower lip trembled. "Mayhap, I should never have run. If I'd simply stayed, endured, then all these lives wouldna be in danger."

"Nay, lass. Ye must stay here, where Laird Matheson can guard ye. He's your protector. Ye know that." The Bruce's eyes were filled with sympathy, pity.

Emilia shook her head, not daring to meet Ian's gaze behind her. He remained there, steady, strong, holding her up when her own body refused. Accepting. Protecting. It was almost too much to bear. Hadn't he heard? She was married to the enemy. She was the reason they were all at war.

"But who is to protect them?" She pleaded with the king. "They are beaten already. Let me go. Let me save them."

The Bruce shook his head slowly, sliding his long fingers over his trim beard. "Nay, my lady. We sent men. This is not women's work. They've got their own warriors and we've helped bolster them in case Ina Ross and Marmaduke seek them out. Trust me, lass, we want them detained as much as ye do. The Ross Clan has been a blight on the Scots for many years now. 'Tis not your fault. This battle began when ye were but a wee lass."

Ian's arms tightened around her, steadying her. She let him hold her up, let him be her source of strength when her legs felt too frail to do the job. When she felt too weak to do so herself. From the beginning, he'd protected her. Made her feel safe. Showed her that there was more to warriors and power than feeding off the vulnerable. She had great respect for him. Trusted him implicitly.

Emilia turned in his arms and pressed her face to his chest. She started to shake with fear for her family. For herself.

If Ina Ross and Marmaduke Stewart were able to outsmart Robert the Bruce not once, but for nearly a decade, then what made him so certain they would be caught now?

She clutched Ian's shirt, breathing in his scent and closing her eyes. His arms wound around her, hands splayed firmly on her spine.

"I'll not let anyone hurt ye, lass. I swear it," he whispered against her ear. "I will guard ye with my life."

His words filled her chest with warmth and a tumult of emotion that she couldn't grasp. She clung to him all the more and sobbed. "Ye know, then, who I am?" Her words were garbled in tears against his shirt.

"Aye. I've known all along."

She didn't know why, but that revelation made her cry all the more. He'd known her truth, her secrets since the very beginning, and he'd not judged her for them. He'd only sought to make her stay at his castle more inviting... And his intoxicating kisses... Those had been given knowing full well that she'd been married to his enemy.

Knowing who she was, where she'd come from, he'd even entrusted her with the care of his dozen siblings. Aye, the king had vouched for her, but he'd accepted her nonetheless. Without question. He'd made her feel welcome. Wanted. Protected. Cared for.

"It matters not to me," he whispered against her ear. Words meant only for her to hear. "We all have our secrets, our darkness. Dinna let your enemies define ye."

Wise words that left her trembling. The last few months she'd forgotten who she was and she wasn't certain she'd ever get herself back again. And right now, all she wanted to do was stay right there in his warm embrace forever.

As soon as his mother guided Emilia upstairs for a warm bath and an herbal tisane, Ian braced for more of what the Bruce would tell him. Only this time, they moved to his study where they couldn't be overheard by anyone. Namely, Emilia.

Och, but it had torn him up inside to see her tears. To hold her trembling body as she lost herself to fear and grief. Her anguish had been intense, and he'd found himself gritting his teeth against his own emotional response. His heart had swelled, and he'd wanted to beat every last Ross into a bloody pulp for giving her such pain.

The door closed, whisky poured, Ian gave his king his full attention.

The king tossed his weapons aside and sat heavily in a chair. He gulped his whisky and rubbed the crease of his brow. "The Ross army was cut down by a third, I'm guessing. They are losing men and ranks as the hours pass. We are closing in on them. They willna last the winter. I vow it."

"What can I do?" Ian asked, taking the seat opposite his king. On the wall opposite him was a tapestry of a great ancestor of his past on a horse, his sword raised, mouth open in a battle cry. "Take my archers. Do ye need more footmen? Horses? Provisions?"

The Bruce templed his fingers at the bridge of his nose. "We need mostly everything and anything ye're willing to give."

"I would come and fight beside ye."

The Bruce nodded. "Come the spring, if we've not rendered them to dust, then I may ask that of ye. But right now, what I need most is your support. And I need something else." The king sat up straighter, regarding Ian intently.

"Name it."

"Lady Emilia... She mentioned to me before we arrived that when the Ross Clan is finally eliminated she would join her sister at Nèamh Abbey."

Ian gritted his teeth at the sudden pang that caught him

in the belly. The more he tried to shove away the feeling, the more harshly it ached. "She wishes to take her vows?"

Heaven help him... He'd kissed a woman who wished to spend her life devoted to the lord. Was that a sin?

"I like to think I'm a man of action. A man who pulls his clans together," the Bruce started.

Ian cocked his head, trying to concentrate on what his king was saying. But he was unable to do anything except remember the feel of her in his arms, the way her gaze held his, filled with trust and emotion.

Would he ever find another woman as fascinating as her? A woman who could laugh while throwing a dagger at him? A woman who could kiss with as much enthusiasm as she? A woman who he *felt* so many different emotions for? He'd had liaisons, countless lovers, but none of them had moved him as Emilia did. 'Twas as if a piece of her soul spoke to his. An instant connection that sizzled between them.

And he couldn't have her.

"What I'm trying to say, Matheson," the Bruce continued, "is that I have a challenge for ye. It is one I'd not normally make."

"Aye, my king. Whatever your pleasure, I am up for the challenge." He braced himself for what his king could want. To train an army. Assemble one? Gather taxes, mayhap. Fashion weapons?

"I want ye to woo the lass. Lure her away from the church and marry her. Make an alliance."

For a split second, Ian waited for his laird to laugh. To say he was jesting. Then his ears started to ring. His king was looking at him with all seriousness, not even a hint of a smile wrinkle anywhere on his face. "What?" he choked out.

The Bruce sat back in his chair, stroking the bridge of his

nose. "I know, 'tis a lot to ask of ye. But ye're not wed and ye're in need of a wife."

Ian blinked, too stunned to answer.

"Lady Emilia's parents were too easily swayed by coin when it came to their daughter's marriage the first time. Taking vows willna stop them from trying again. There is also her brother, Dirk. The lad is betrothed to the Sutherland's eldest daughter, but the marriage willna take place for another decade or so. The Sutherlands want the alliance. The MacCulloch lands to the east rule the entrance to Dornoch Firth. Across the firth, the land is ruled by Sutherlands. To the west, the Ross Clan. Sutherland doesna want the firth controlled by the Ross Clan, which is what will happen. The Ross' will sell their lands or rent them, and then the English will have full access to the Highlands by sea. They can come in by the hordes. We need to make alliances now that can bolster the MacCulloch Clan into staying one with Scotland."

Ian couldn't help the flash of anger he felt at hearing his king's explanation. His loyalty to his sovereign didn't stop him from saying so. "So, she is to be sold again? Only this time, 'tis all right because I am on the suitable side?"

The Bruce let out a harsh laugh. "Matheson, where have ye been living? Under a rock? This is how alliances are formed. I'm headed to Urquhart come morning and I want to know by Samhain that ye've wed the lass. Ye can argue all ye like, but that is a direct order."

Samhain. The celebration of the end of the harvest. The night those made of flesh mingled with those made of something else entirely. The dead. The living. The otherworldly. And that was only a few weeks away.

Ian gave his king a curt nod. How could he refuse his king? The man had given him a direct order and he needed to follow it. Truthfully, doing so wouldn't be hard. He wanted

Emilia for his own. He just wanted her to want him, too, not to force her into a union when she'd already lived that.

The Bruce had said woo her. So woo her, he would. And he only had a couple weeks to do it. "Ye have my word."

The Bruce lifted his empty cup to be refilled. "Good."

LATE INTO THE EVENING, Alistair knocked at the study door.

"Enter," Ian growled. He'd been brooding for most of the night, trying to figure out just how he could make Emilia fall in love with him. He needed her to love him so that when he mentioned marriage, she didn't run like she had when he'd kissed her before with nearly every ounce of passion he possessed.

"Ye look like hell, my laird." Alistair snickered.

Ian grunted. "I have some disappointing news for ye." Ballocks, but he didn't want to have to tell his friend. What a wound to his pride. The man had confessed he wanted Emilia for his own, and now Ian would have to yank away his desire. And worse still, he wasn't that upset about it.

Alistair frowned. "The Bruce said we'd not be joining the fight?"

Ian chuckled, though only half-heartedly. "That is not the news, but ye're right. I willna be joining the fight this time. But if ye insist, I can send ye with the others."

Alistair rubbed his hands together. "Ye just want me to leave so ye can keep on kissing the bonny lass."

Ian flicked his gaze away. "That is part of it."

Alistair laughed out loud this time and thwacked Ian on the back. "About damn time."

Ian regarded his mate with confusion. "What?"

"I was never going to go after the lass. I could tell how

much ye wanted her. I simply wanted *ye* to realize how much ye wanted her. Nothing like a little friendly competition to get a man's heart in the right place."

Ian rolled his eyes. "Ye're an arse."

"But I was right, wasna I?"

"Aye. The king demands we wed. But I want to try to get her agreement afore I tell her the news."

"I heartily support your mission."

Ian chuckled, his chest filling with pride. Lady Emilia would be his.

CHAPTER 12

The bath that Sister Meredith had drawn for Emilia was filled with the scents of rose water and jasmine. After soaking for nearly an hour, completely relaxed by the warm water, the tisane of chamomile and something sweeter, the soft chatter of Sister Meredith and her prayers for the safety of all, Emilia wanted to climb into bed and sleep for hours. But instead, she'd refused a quiet supper in her room and went upstairs to dine with the children.

They were naturally concerned for her as Alice told them all that she'd been upset. But she reassured them she was well and thanked them profusely for their lovely gifts of interestingly shaped rocks, acorn collections, and a grassy bouquet.

After supping with the children, Emilia helped to tuck them into bed. She then rushed back to her chamber to pen a letter of warning to her parents and to let them know that she was well. She must have started and restarted her letter a hundred times for the single sheet of parchment she'd been writing on was covered in slashes and ugly, inky blots. If it weren't such a commodity, she would have gladly burned it to start over fresh. She just wanted so badly for it to be the perfect missive.

If she couldn't visit with them, which she accepted given the danger, at least she wanted some contact.

Aye, she'd had much anger with her parents. Many regrets over their parting. She wished they'd not done what they did, but all the same, she could understand why—even if she didn't agree with it. They'd felt backed into a corner. They'd felt there was no other choice. Starvation, death, seemed a harsher choice compared to giving one child to an enemy when they had two others.

She sat back in her small chair, biting her lip. When she thought about it like that, feelings of jealousy and anger reared their heads, and she couldn't let them. She couldn't let those emotions eat away at her.

After having been at Balmacara Castle for nearly a month, she'd decided to forgive them. Forgiveness was a sign of grace and if the Lord could forgive sinners, she could, too. It was just another way in which she could heal. Already she'd found herself recovering from the suffering she'd endured at the hands of Ina Ross and her clan. Now, that wasn't to say she was ready to forgive Ina Ross and Marmaduke. That was an evil she wasn't certain deserved anything other than a long journey to hell.

Emilia rolled the parchment up and, with a dagger strapped under each sleeve, slipped out of her chamber.

There was almost a certainty that Ian and the Bruce would not allow her to actually send her letter, for then her parents would know where she was. And perhaps she might not have given them the Matheson name, but she hoped they would write her back in secret. And, so, she needed to find the one man who had helped her before and hope that he would help her again, though she'd not be able to pay him as Padrig had.

Getting out of the castle was easy.

Finding Ahlrid was going to be a different matter.

Night had fallen, leaving everywhere cast in shadows save for the few feet surrounding every torch. She'd snuck out the kitchen door and made her way around the side of the tower toward the bailey. It was teeming with not only the Bruce's army, but Matheson's as well. In the dim light, their plaids blended together. If she'd not recognized the men from various clans, she wouldn't have been any the wiser. They were all terrifying in the dark. Brutal men of all sizes assessed her with leering stares, while others ignored her completely.

She slipped in and out of the throngs, ignoring overwhelming scents of ale and whisky, studying men's faces, in search of the scarred one she was familiar with. When a kind man stopped her, which some did every so often, she would ask after Ahlrid and be pointed in another direction. She was spinning in circles just trying to locate the man.

Just when she thought it was a lost cause and she was ready to give up in frustration, the man finally found her.

He grabbed her elbow and tugged her close to him, his face coming within inches, wafts of stale breath washing over her face. "What are ye doing out here all alone?"

Emilia blinked, trying to get the taste of his breath out of her mouth. "I was looking for ye."

He jerked a little in surprise. "Why? Ye are well, are ye not?"

"I am." She thrust the rolled parchment toward him, wishing she could better see his facial expression in the dim light to ascertain how he felt about this. "I hoped ye might get this to my parents at Terrel Tower."

"And how might I do that?" His tone was close to an angry snarl.

"'Tis a day's ride or so from Urquhart where the king is going in the morn. Mayhap less if ye ride hard."

"Or more should I run into any Ross maggots along the way. I might never reach there. And then your missive will be lost in the wrong hands."

She chewed her lip feeling despair curdle the milk she'd had with her supper.

"Och, lass," he chuckled. "I'm jesting with ye. I'd never let one of them slimy bastards catch me." He slipped her missive up his sleeve. "The Bruce has already asked me to scout the area around Terrel. I'll deliver your message."

Emilia clasped her hands to her chest and breathed out a sigh of relief. She wanted to grab the overlarge warrior in a hug, but knew that would be taking it a step too far. Besides, he smelled about as ripe as a pig in a sty.

"Get ye back into the castle, lass. The sun has set and the men will be looking for..." He flicked his glare around toward a few men who'd been closing in on them. "Never ye mind. Come now. I'll escort ye back." He grasped her by the elbow and led her back through the throngs of men toward the keep stairs.

"Thank ye, Ahlrid. I dinna know how I can repay ye for the kindness ye've shown me."

"There is no need, my lady. Padrig paid me enough."

"In any case, I am grateful." She patted his arm and bid him goodnight, feeling much relieved that her family would soon get her message.

WHAT IN BLOODY hell was Emilia doing outside with all the men?

Ian watched her, guided on the arm of some ogre-sized buffoon, as she made her way back to the castle, weaving through the throngs of men who elbowed each other as she passed. No doubt taking bets on who could bed her first. Nasty whoresons.

What disturbed him more, however, was that even in the dim light of the fires and torches lighting the courtyard, he could see she felt comfortable with the fiend. How long had she been outside? And why? A pang of jealousy struck him in his middle.

Who was the boor?

Ian watched Emilia smile, pat the troll on the arm.

She seemed perfectly at ease with the Bruce's warrior.

Was her hesitation in kissing Ian not truly a product of a miserable Ross marriage but, in fact, because she'd already found another lover? This bastard?

Whether she had a lover or nay, did not change the fact that the Bruce wanted Ian to wed her. But it would make his wooing of her that much more difficult. And he'd not be able to get the image of the two of them together out of his mind.

Helping her heal from her past seemed infinitely more surmountable than competing with an overgrown boil of a man.

Ian studied the moving tree trunk. He turned his back to Emilia as she walked inside—not at all what a chivalrous man would do—and then pulled something from his sleeve. A missive perhaps? The toad unrolled the missive, reading whatever it was and then stuffed it back in his sleeve.

Gut instinct told Ian that whatever was in that missive had to do with Emilia. Maybe even written in her hand. He wanted to read it. Right now. Blast it, could he use his authority as Laird Matheson to go and take the missive from the brute?

Did he want to know the contents? What if it was a love letter?

He wasn't sure his pride could take that.

Something in the man's countenance made Ian weary. He was too rigid. Too distant. Ian had concentrated so much on Emilia' reaction to the man that he'd failed to recognize that the bastard hadn't even returned her smile. A curt nod was what he'd given her. More stern than affectionate.

Who was he? Why did she seek him out? For certainly she had. They were outside and the man could not have come into the castle searching for her, could he? Bloody hell, if that whoreson even tried to walk into his castle, Ian would have him tossed in the dungeon. Let the rats at him.

Perhaps the best thing to do was have the man followed. Ease his worries about what he was up to and be certain that Emilia was safe. Pray that it was innocent. That perhaps he was also her cousin, or some such nonsense, that left the lout a far cry from a lover.

Ian left the battlements in search of one of his archers. Richard, he thought might be best. The man was an excellent hunter. Never heard in the woods by his prey. He could sneak up so close to a stag, he could ride it if he wanted. No one would know he was following, including that ogre. Besides that, Richard had always given his loyalty and support to Ian without question. He'd known him since they were both just learning to handle a bow.

"My laird." Richard leapt up from the stump he'd been sitting on, fashioning a new arrow.

"Walk with me."

Richard nodded, following Ian.

Keeping his voice low Ian said, "When ye leave in the

morn with the Bruce and his army, I have a mission for ye that is to be kept quiet. Between ye, me, and your commander."

"Aye, my laird."

"There is a man, larger than the rest, dark hair, scars on his face. Do ye know him?"

Richard nodded. "Aye. That is Ahlrid."

"What do ye know of him?"

"He is one of the Bruce's scouts. The best. He can take on eight men at a time, which is why he does the scouting, in case of an ambush. He is fierce. Deadly. He used to have a partner, Padrig Ross, but the man has died."

Padrig Ross.

Emilia's dead husband.

So she did know this man. He was the only connection to her old life. If she truly wanted to forget about it, then why talk to him?

"The Bruce trusts a Ross man?"

"Seems odd, aye, but he does. The man has acted as a kind of spy in the past. Same as Padrig. They worked against their clan."

A spy. A double agent. The missive up the man's sleeve... Warning bells went off in Ian's head. If she knew the warrior was a double-agent, then she could have used him to send out a missive if she didn't want anyone else to know about it.

"I'm not certain he can be completely trusted," Ian said. "I witnessed something a few moments ago that gave me pause. This man, Ahlrid, he's got a missive tucked in his sleeve. I want ye to follow him. Keep an eye out for who he gives that missive to. If ye get a chance, read it."

"Aye, my laird."

"If he sneaks off or goes scouting, follow him. But keep your distance. If my instincts are right, your life could be in danger. Your life and that of everyone else in the camp." Ian paused to study Richard. "Are ye certain ye can do this? If not, I will think no less of ye."

"Aye, my laird. I can do this."

"I will be counting on ye then, to be my eyes and ears. Report back to me. I will let your commander know ye are on a private mission, that if ye disappear it is only because ye're gathering information for me, and that ye are to report news back to me. He'll give ye no trouble and will see to it that no one else does either."

Richard pressed his hand over his heart. "I willna fail."

Ian squeezed Richard's shoulder. "I have every faith that ye will succeed."

CHAPTER 13

"**M**y laird, there is a woman here to see ye. She says ye requested her presence." Alistair raised his brow.

"For the love of all that's holy, I didna request the presence of any lass." Ian stared pointedly at Alistair. "Ye of all people should know that, man. Did we not just have the discussion regarding my wooing into marriage a certain governess? Or, perhaps, I could point out the many exchanges in which I have emphatically stated I havena my father's penchant for...female companions?"

Alistair smirked, obviously trying to keep himself from laughing. He crossed his arms behind his back, standing at ease. "Just making certain, my laird, that we are both still of the same mind. But, most earnestly, she did say ye requested her."

Ian threw his hands up in the air. "Oh, for the love of all that's holy, send her in." He pointed at Alistair. "And ye stay, else anyone get the wrong idea."

Alistair chuckled on his way out to retrieve her. And for

the briefest of minutes, Ian considered tossing his best mate out the window.

Instead, he took the time to set aside the papers he was working on, hiding all pertinent information and setting his cup of whisky back on the sideboard so he didn't seem too casual with his unwanted guest. He remained standing behind his large desk, arms crossed over his chest, wanting to look the part of intimidating laird. All business, no pleasure, *thank ye verra much*.

Alistair returned shortly with a plump lass, brown hair pulled into a tight bun and a few streaks of gray at the temples. Not uncommon for a crofter in which every day could be filled with hardship. Her brown gown was worn but clean, and she had a Matheson plaid sash across her middle.

"My laird," she said, dipping into an awkward curtsy. Her face was smooth. She was younger than her graying hair portrayed.

"Rise," Ian said gruffly, raising his hand at her. "Tell me why ye're here."

The woman wrung her hands in front of her threadbare gown and glanced back toward the door. He understood that feeling of wanting to run quite well. He felt like doing so right at that moment precisely.

"Aye, well, ye told my da that I should come, my laird."

Ian narrowed his eyes. "Did I?"

"Aye. They said after they dropped off the bairns that ye demanded my appearance, so I've come. Just as *ye asked*." She harped on that last part to a point that Ian wondered at her thinking.

Was she trying to convince him that he had or herself? Never mind that, as soon as she'd mentioned her parents and the bairns, he knew who she was. His siblings' old nursemaid.

"And did they tell ye why?" he asked.

She nodded slowly, though her hands were now wringing with renewed frenzy. "Could I see the bairns? I miss them so."

Ian nodded, his tone softening. "Aye, ye can. When we're finished here. Take a seat." He pointed at one of the oak chairs in front of his desk.

She hurried to take the seat.

"What is your name, lass?"

She blushed clear from her chest to the line of her hair and ducked her gaze. "Jean."

"Jean, first I must thank ye for helping care for the wee ones. 'Tis a fact that without good care they all could have perished."

"Children are a miracle, my laird. I but did my duty as a good Christian and loyal clanswoman."

"Ye're to be praised for it."

"Thank ye, my laird," she whispered, her cheeks now as red as a rose.

"I hate to discuss business with a lass, but if ye want to be seeing the bairns, we'd best get on with it. All right?"

"Aye, my laird."

"Did ye bring me the tax money?"

She nodded, digging through the folds of her skirt. She pulled a leather pouch from the small purse attached to her belt. "'Tis only the coin my da owes for the last year. He asked that I beg your pardon as he works on gathering the rest."

Ian hefted the bag, testing its weight and hearing the clink of coins. "This will suffice." He was feeling merciful. Grateful. For he'd meant everything he said to her. Seeing how well his siblings had been raised, that was the sort of burden that shouldn't be punished. "I willna demand any further back payment. Your father kept his word and that means a lot to me. Just be certain he pays on time in the future."

Jean looked up at him sharply, her hands coming into prayer position before her chest. "Oh, thank ye, my laird. Thank ye, thank ye. That is ever so kind of ye. My ma and da are getting on with age now, and it would be so hard for them to pay. As it is, my own husband and me helped fill that back."

Ian grunted. "I am not kind, but fair."

"Aye, fair, sir." She nodded emphatically.

He walked around the front of his desk and leaned against it. "Ye should also have two lists for me."

"Right. I do." She tapped her head. "I have them up here."

"All right. However ye have them is fine."

She smoothed her hands over her skirts, closed her eyes a minute, and then spoke. "Father always sold the jewels to the same place, Nèamh Abbey. He traded them for prayers for the bairns and for the laird that he might keep on blessing us with his kindness. And also, so that the children might learn a thing or two from the nuns."

Ian stared hard at Jean. Was she trying to pull the wool over his eyes? To trick him with pretty words? "Ye know what they do with liars, do ye not?"

She nodded, her hair coming loose from her bun. "I swear it, my laird, that is what he told me. I can attest to it, too, for I've gone with him on his missions to the abbey."

"Let's say ye speak the truth. Where do ye think he got the idea to trade the jewels for prayers and education?"

At this, she dropped her eyes to her worn shoes. "From Lady Matheson. She said a laird's children, be they bastards or not, deserved a good education and prayers."

"I see." And he did. How clever of *Sister* Meredith, she'd tricked them all. Ian had to bite his cheek to keep from laughing. His mother was most assuredly having a good laugh at her deception. But she wouldn't see it that way. She likely had a much more elaborate way of explaining how she'd duped them all. He wouldn't be surprised if every jewel was displayed in her modest rooms at the abbey. Not once had she lost a thing, but had gained so much from everyone.

But it did explain how his siblings, children raised by crofters, were already so well-mannered and educated.

"Perhaps, ye can answer something else for me. Why did your parents decide they could no longer keep the children?"

"'Tis my fault." Tears sparked her eyes. "Ye see, when the bairns first came, I was young myself and my mother acted as the nursemaid. As I grew, I married a lad and we lived with my parents. When my mother's milk dried up, I was already having bairns of my own, so I stepped in. My husband died of a fever. But I recently married again and my new husband's family wanted us to live with them. Which was fine at first, but traveling so many times throughout the day to feed the bairns, well, it became too much so I had to tell them I couldna help anymore." Her knuckles whitened as she gripped the sides of the chair. "'Twas my husband who suggested their days as caretakers had come to an end. And I must humbly beg your pardon for it. I did love them all, just like they were my own."

"Nay, lass, dinna apologize. I am glad of his suggestion. I want ye to know that."

The tears that had welled in her eyes spilled down her cheeks. "But I am not. I miss them every day. All day."

"I understand." He awkwardly patted her on the shoulder. "Ye're more than welcome to visit them anytime."

She wiped at her eyes with her plaid sash. "That means so much to me, my laird. Thank ye, thank ye so verra much."

"Now, what about the other children who were grown and moved away?"

"There are four others that survived. Two lads and two lasses. One lad went to Melrose as a choirboy. He has a fine voice as I recall. So fine that when he sang at Nèamh Abbey one Sunday, the visiting Abbott from Melrose wouldn't leave without him. And the other? He was a mighty large lad. Good with a sword and a bow. Proved himself to a laird and went off with him that same year."

"Who?"

"He's dead now. Dinna know where the lad is, but he'd be about your age."

Ian frowned. "Who was the laird?"

"Laird Ross." She waved her hands. "But that was afore he went mad. Harild was a good lad."

He was afraid that was who she meant when she wouldn't answer for who it was. "The old man might be dead, but his daughter and son-by-marriage are not."

Jean shrugged. "That's true, but I dinna see Harild working for the enemy. He was a lad filled with a moral code. Saved me more than once from men whose advances I didna care for. Every once in a while, he stays at the White Fir Tavern, not too far from here. I can leave a message with them to give him, if ye like."

"Aye, that would be most helpful. Perhaps someone there will know where he's gone off to. And the lasses?"

"The two of them married local crofters. I see them quite often at market. I can also give them a message for ye."

"Good. Why dinna ye go to the kitchens for a good meal while I write up the missives welcoming them all for a visit to Balmacara? After, please, go up to the nursery to visit with the children. Alistair will accompany ye to deliver my messages to the local lasses. I'll send someone else to Melrose and in search of Harild."

"Oh, thank ye, my laird." Jean rose, a full smile on her face and backed out of the room then paused. "I almost forgot. My husband..." She coughed and wrung her hands again.

Ian waited patiently for her to catch her bearings. "My husband was wondering if he might be compensated for the loss of my working time today on account of all the coins we added to the satchel for my parents. Ye see, he had to hire someone to fill in at the field as we're harvesting the last of the cabbage... and then there are all the bairns that need watching..."

"Aye." Ian opened the bag and pulled out six coins. He walked over and handed them to her. "Tell your husband I'll be expecting his tax payment on time, as well."

"Aye, my laird, I will. He always pays."

Ian grunted, opening the door and ushering her out. "I thank ye for coming here today, Jean. And for your loyalty."

She curtsied, and then hurried off toward the kitchens.

"What do ye make of all that?" Ian asked Alistair when they were alone.

"Your mother has quite a hand up her sleeve."

"I'll say." Ian poured them each a dram of whisky. "I sincerely hope there aren't any more surprises."

"WHAT IS ONE AND TWO?" Emilia asked, using chestnuts that the children had gathered outside as an example.

"Three!"

"And five take away two?"

"Three!"

"Verra good. Ye're all brilliant with arithmetic."

A noise from behind startled her from their afternoon lesson. Standing in the doorway to the nursery was Ian. His arms were crossed over his chest, the breadth of his shoulders taking up the entire expanse of the frame. He was smiling down at them all.

"Afternoon," he drawled.

"My laird!" The children leapt to their feet and crowded around him, hugging his legs, tugging his arms. "We want to show ye how to count chestnuts."

Ian allowed himself to be pulled into the room. He dropped to his knees on the floor and pretended not to know what four plus four was or five take away three. And then miraculously, after they showed him how to count the chestnuts, he was just as brilliant as they were.

"Now, do ye mind if I take Lady Emilia away for a few moments?"

They balked, but only slightly, for they mostly wanted the extra time to play.

Emilia followed Ian who stepped into the small corridor beyond the nursery door, shutting it behind them. Before she could even ask what he needed, Ian's eyes blazed into hers. There was a storm raging in his blue eyes that set her nerves to zinging up and down her arms and centering somewhere in the pit of her stomach.

"Who is Ahlrid to ye?"

Emilia swallowed, immediately on the defense. Had Ahlrid gone straight to the Bruce and Ian about her wish for him to get a letter to her family? If he hadn't, she didn't want to give that information away herself.

What exactly was she on the defensive from?

Vagueness might be her ally in this. "He is the warrior who aided me in escaping the Ross Clan." She kept her voice level, her eyes on his.

Ian took one step, then two, closer. She edged backward until her bottom hit the stone of the corridor wall. She pressed her hands to the stone, hoping the coolness of their hard surface would cease her trembling and give her strength.

Why did it feel as though he were stalking her? Why did she feel duly trapped? Why did he look so full of jealousy over Ahlrid? Was he mad she hadn't trusted him, instead?

"I saw the two of ye."

She swallowed. *Saw what?* "I know not what ye speak."

Ian pressed his hands to the stones beside her shoulders, caging her in. She should push him away. Make him leave and let her get back to her lessons, but the truth was, she liked being caged in by him. Liked the way his scent surrounded her. Liked that she could feel the heat of his body massaging over hers. Liked that she felt safe, as though he created a bubble that only the two of them resided in.

Just for a few seconds like this, she could imagine she was somewhere else. That her past didn't include being tormented by Ina Ross or sold by her parents. She was someone else. She was carefree, desirable, and confident.

This close, she could imagine him kissing her. His lips sliding over hers. Their breaths mingling. The way he'd tasted her tongue. Threaded his fingers in her hair. His hard body pressed to hers.

Heat filled her cheeks and she worked to clear her throat from how tight it suddenly felt. As she gazed into his eyes, her eyelids grew heavy, dipping low, languid. Her heart pounded against her ribs. Heaven help her...

"Ye were on his arm," Ian murmured. "Walking through hundreds of men in my bailey. Hundreds of dangerous, hungry men. Yet ye smiled like a lass taking a pass through a garden."

Her lip curled, a tiny boost of confidence surging through

her. That spark of defiance that she used to embrace but had buried these past few months, coming out to do battle with this man. To taunt him. "Ye sound jealous, Laird Ian."

His nostrils flared, pupils dilated. "Maybe I am, Lady Emilia."

"Whatever for? Ye've nothing to be concerned over." There was a vein in his neck that pulsed, and she wanted to touch it. To run her finger along the length of it to see how that pulse felt against her fingertip.

He pressed two fingers to her chin and gently lifted her face so she could look at him. "But ye see, lass, I do."

"What?" Her voice sounded hushed. She'd lost her train of thought with this conversation. What did he do?

Ian's face came closer to hers by a fraction of an inch, but enough so that she breathed in deep of his scent. Forced herself not to arch her body into his, just to feel his heat and strength. So different than anything she'd ever experienced. Safe and yet so very exciting. "Emilia... I want to be the only man ye're kissing."

Her heart leapt into her throat. "I've kissed no one. And..." She cleared her throat. "I thought we were clear there would be no more kissing?" Could she take that back? Could she say, mayhap one more wouldn't hurt?

If she was going to spend the rest of her days in virtuous undertakings, then aye, one more kiss seemed to be exactly what she needed. What they both needed. And completely acceptable.

Ian shrugged one shoulder nonchalantly. "I dinna remember saying that."

A thrill rushed through her, sending gooseflesh over her body.

"Does that mean ye want..." Her words trailed off. And good thing, for she was about to ask him if he wanted to kiss her again. *Nay, nay, nay. Come to your senses!* They couldn't! She had told him no more kissing. She had decided what she wanted out of her future. He couldn't just come along and keep making her change her mind!

"I canna kiss ye anymore, Ian. I want to join the church. I want to leave with your mother when she goes back to Nèamh Abbey. To take my vows."

He furrowed his brow, but not in anger, more like she'd injured him somehow. "How can ye go? How can ye leave Balmacara? The children?"

Beneath his words she heard him loud and clear—how could she leave *him*?

Well, she would have to and it would be the hardest thing she'd ever done.

But until then... One parting kiss. For, his proximity grew to be too much. Her desire, yearning for one last embrace took hold, and, this time, it was she who reached up to press her lips to his.

Ian sucked in a breath through his nose, the sudden rush of air tickling her cheek. She reached for him, wrapping her arms around his waist, tentatively touching his back. Muscles bunched beneath her fingertips. He leaned into her, his hips grazing hers. Shockwaves rippled through her limbs at the sensual contact. Hard against soft. Male against female.

Frissons of delicious sensation shot from her fingertips, up her arms, and into her chest, pebbling her nipples and sliding right down her belly to the apex of her thighs. She clung tighter to him, sighing with pleasure.

Emilia deepened the kiss, wanting the thrill of his touch to never end. Ian took what she offered, feasting on her lips, her tongue. His hands captured her face, his solid body pinning her against the wall. He threaded his fingers through her hair and claimed her with the exact urgency careening through her entire being.

Just when she thought she would melt into a pool of desire, he gently tugged back. Ian stared deep into her eyes and said, "Dinna leave."

He backed away slowly, his gaze never leaving hers. Every fiber within her reached out for him, begging him silently to come back to her. *Dinna leave. Dinna leave.*

His feet hit the steps. He disappeared down the long spiral stairs, leaving her trembling, tangled, and filled with a longing she couldn't comprehend.

CHAPTER 14

Somehow Emilia managed to make it through the afternoon and evening with the children only asking a few times if she was well. After the visit from the laird, she'd been walking around in a fever, her face flushed and her mind completely not on task.

She was pretty certain the nursemaids knew exactly what was going on. Now, she lay in bed, wide-eyed, staring at the shadows passing over her ceiling.

Her entire body felt alive with fever—but not the ill kind. Nay, this was a fever of desire, need, excitement, hope.

And she knew who was at fault for it. A certain tall, ruggedly handsome, charismatic warrior.

All the man had to do was look at her and she melted for him.

His kiss... Oh, merciful heavens, his kiss was a heady magic she couldn't escape, even when he was far from her. Every glance. Every touch. Every smile.

Her heart kicked up a notch, and suddenly her blankets felt too constricting. She kicked them off, hoping for some relief from the heat of the room. But it wasn't the room. It was *her*. It was *him*.

He was ruining her future plans. There was no way she could go to Nèamh Abbey. No way she could take vows. She could barely look at Father Locke. Not with her thoughts running rampant in the carnal direction. Every gentle blow of the wind reminded her of his breath on her neck. The warmth of the sun awakened memories of the heat of his body. Confession would only make her think about it more, for she'd have to put a voice to all the thoughts flourishing throughout her body, her mind. Besides that, there was also no way she could go speak to Father Locke about her desires, unless she wanted to be labeled a harlot. Nay, her sin of wickedness was her secret. A secret that was likely to make her go mad.

Dinna leave.

What did Ian want of her? To make her his mistress. Nay. She would refuse. Her body might be yearning hotly for the man and she might crave to spend every moment of every day with him, but not at the cost of her reputation, her self-respect.

Theirs was a desire that was leading nowhere. A need and a want that had to be dismissed. A fire that needed to be put out. A hunger that could not be fed. Saints, but she could go on all day comparing it to every other basic human need, and she'd still be in the same position.

'Haps she should claim to be sick on the morrow. Lay in bed all day working out a plan to get him out of her mind.

There was nothing else she could do. There could be no more kisses. No more heated looks, else she might find the resolve she had now shrinking and somehow convince herself that being his mistress was worth the loss of respect.

He'd previously said he wanted no wife.

And marriage...well, she'd already taken a broken wagon down that rut-riddled road.

The only thing was, her marriage to Padrig was not a *true* marriage. They'd never consummated the union. She was still as much a virgin now as she was the day she was born, even if her innocence had been taken away.

If she wanted, she could probably seek an annulment even now after his death. Wipe the marriage from her life forever.

Emilia sat up in bed. Aye, that was what she'd do. To help erase those few horrible months from her mind, she would have the church erase it from record. But that would mean her family had to pay back the money Ina Ross had given them. That might be a hardship they could not withstand.

She flopped back down on the bed and rubbed at her eyes, hoping that the simple sleepy act would make her tired. No such luck.

Emilia wanted to choose her own path, or at least manipulate the road ahead, but the problem was, she wasn't even certain *what* she wanted. Did she want to go to Nèamh Abbey? Aye, but only because she missed her sister desperately, and because she didn't want her parents to use her in another marriage.

She wasn't entirely convinced that a life within the church was her calling. Spending time with the children had made her crave a child of her own. Spending time with Ian had made her crave a man who respected her for who she was—and his ardent kisses... She could welcome them all the days of her life.

He accepted her. Embraced her talent and passion for knife throwing. That was a skill and passion she'd have to give up if she went into the church. The nuns would shun it as shameful. As a masculine pursuit, not appropriate for a lady.

Emilia measured the pros and cons of choosing a life at

Nèamh Abbey. Her sister, Ayne, had always been much more virtuous. Her passion for singing had been embraced by her fellow sisters.

If Emilia took her vows, there was no coming back from that. Down the line, if she decided she wanted to marry, she couldn't simply tell the nuns that she wished to go find a husband. And she certainly couldn't count on her family doing right by her desires.

She curled up onto her side, hugging the extra pillow to her chest, pressing her face into its fluffiness. For a brief second, Emilia pretended it was Ian's chest, though there was nothing fluffy about him.

What did she want? What did she truly want? Her deepest desire? What could she live with for the rest of her life and never regret?

The questions rang out in her mind—the resounding answer to all the questions clattering over and over: *Ian, Ian, Ian.*

Her protector. Her companion. Her conspirator in spearing apples. The only confidant she'd had since her sister left years before.

Emilia was no expert on men or relationships. But she had to think that the way he kept kissing her, the way he'd trusted her to throw her dagger and not kill him in the process, meant something. Men didn't simply go around kissing women. Or did they?

She frowned.

His father *was* known to be a huge philanderer. Maybe Ian didn't know any better. Maybe he thought it was appropriate to kiss women whenever he wanted. To flirt with them mercilessly. To woo her where it counted—her mind, her heart.

But those lines of thought brought her back to the very first night she'd met him. How she'd said the apple didn't fall far from the tree. Though she'd been talking about her own situation and not his, he'd taken it the wrong way.

I am not my father's son.

He'd been so adamant about it. So furious that she even intoned such a thing.

And she'd not seen him flirting or kissing anyone else. In fact, how many times had he adamantly said he was not looking for any woman? And yet, he continued to seek her out.

Maybe, just maybe, the thing to do was show him that he needed her, wanted her, to be his wife. Convince him that a life with her was the right path to choose. Or the one he truly wanted. Mayhap, he didn't even realize it.

Wife. Husband.

The very words themselves brought with them a flood of anxiety and memories.

She flopped onto her back, kicked her feet, and slammed her hands against the mattress. Flailing like a child having a tantrum.

She glared up at the rafters. "I *wasna* Padrig's wife." Saying the words aloud felt good, so she said them again. Louder this time.

Then she peered at the door, hoping no one who might be happening by could hear her yelling like a loon. She sincerely hoped no one was lurking about, given it was the middle of the night.

And then she giggled. Partly mad from relief at finally voicing that she was not Padrig's wife and partly exhilarated by the idea of becoming Ian's.

Zounds, but the Bruce was leaving in the morning. As far as he knew, she still wanted to go to Nèamh Abbey. If she woke before dawn, that was if she ever fell asleep, she might get the chance to stop him before he left and tell him that she'd changed her mind. But then again, she'd have to tell him why she'd changed her mind, and she didn't really want to do that. Not yet. If she told the Bruce she wanted to marry Ian but Ian didn't really want to marry her, then she'd be mortified.

Perhaps it was best to keep it to herself. As well as keep all of her options open. That way, if Ian did reject her, she always had the abbey and no one would ever be the wiser.

Her stomach soured. It had taken a lot of thinking tonight, but she'd finally realized that a life of virtuous solitude was not what she wanted. Emilia wanted love. A family.

And Ian was the man she wanted all of that with.

She just had to prove it to him. Without him realizing what she was doing.

EMILIA JERKED awake at the sound of scratching on her door. She bounded out of bed, seeing the sun fully shining through the window, leaving slashes of yellow-gold across her blankets. Well, if she happened to have changed her mind about wanting to talk to the Bruce, that chance was thoroughly squashed. It had to be half past nine in the morning.

She opened the door to see what was doing the scratching. Emilia was certain it wasn't the children, because they would have just banged the door down. A hound maybe? But there was no one there.

Lying on the floor of the corridor, just outside of her chamber, was a tray full of boiled eggs, honey cakes, and a tall cup of milk. But what struck her most, was a beautiful, perfectly round, shiny red apple.

Emilia bent to pick up the tray and bring it into her room.

Beneath the tray, a note fell. After setting the tray on her table, she scooped it up and unfolded it.

After ye break your fast, come to the orchard.

What was this? She had work to do. There was no time for a scavenger hunt. She had children to tend. She couldn't enjoy a delicious, quiet meal in her chamber and then go amble about the orchard, as heavenly as that sounded.

Ian would be angry that she was taking her position for granted. He'd agreed to protect her, but also for her to help him. How could she help him if she was up in her chamber relaxing? Shirking her duties?

She bit into a honey cake as she contemplated that thought.

Dear heavens, it was sinful... The cake melted like butter against her tongue, tasting of sweet honey with a hint of almonds and cinnamon. She closed her eyes, scarfing the rest of the cake and washing it down with milk.

At least she was still standing. That didn't count as relaxing, did it?

Emilia stared at the note beside the cakes. Who had written it?

One of the nursemaids, hoping to get her in trouble?

She didn't recognize the handwriting, but then again, she'd not ever had the chance to read anyone's hand within the castle.

Emilia picked up the apple, ready to bite into it, when she spied on the side of the fruit, a perfectly carved rendition of her dagger cut through the skin.

At once she knew who had left her the tray of breakfast— and the note. The last person she would have thought. Ian.

He was the only artist she knew within the castle.

But why would he encourage her to ignore her duties? Well, she was going to find out. And she wasn't going to eat his artwork, either.

She carefully set the apple on the table beside her bed. That way, she could look at it at least for a few days, before the skin wrinkled and the dagger curled in on itself.

Emilia dressed quickly, laced up her boots, plaited her hair, and rushed out of the room only to come face to face with wee Alice.

"My lady! Finally!" She clapped her tiny hands, her pretty face filled with a sweet smile. "We thought ye'd never wake."

Emilia couldn't help but laugh. "Have ye come to escort me then?"

"Aye. To the orchard."

"And who shall we be greeting?"

"Why, all of us—and Laird Ian."

Emilia had guessed as much before she opened her door. But still, hearing the truth of it sent her belly aflutter. He really had orchestrated this? Who was wooing who?

Well, she wasn't opposed to questioning the child in order to get any pertinent information.

"What is the occasion?" Emilia asked.

Alice slipped her tiny hand into Emilia's, tugging her out of her chamber door.

"Oh, my lady, did ye truly forget?"

"Forget what?"

Alice looked at her as though she truly weren't feeling well. "Today is the anniversary of your birth. Ye must remember that."

Emilia's eyes widened. Was it? She'd lost track of the days while she was here and, besides, no one had ever shown any great interest in celebrating her birthday before now.

Wait, it couldn't be. How would Ian know when her birthday was?

Nay, nay, nay. Samhain had not yet come to pass and her birthday was on the first day of November. Still, she smiled, not wanting to disappoint the child. What did Ian have up his sleeve? A little leap of excitement twitched in her belly.

"Did ye like the honey cakes for breakfast? Those were my idea. Sister Meredith says that a lady should be able to eat whatever she likes on her birthday, and honey cakes have always been my favorite." Alice scrunched up her little forehead. "Wait, on second thought, if ye dinna like honey cakes, then they were Adam's idea."

Emilia chuckled at Alice tossing the blame on the youngest of all the bairns, a babe still in swaddling who'd not be able to argue that point.

"I loved them. They were the most delicious cakes I've ever tasted."

"Truly?" Alice's face lit up at the approval.

"Truly. I would eat them every day if I could."

Alice led her into the kitchen. "Now ye must close your eyes. Cook is going to put a blindfold on ye, but dinna be scared. I will help ye outside."

The thought of being blindfolded, even if it were only temporary, was terrifying. But she didn't want to ruin the children's excitement. And truth be told, she couldn't wait to find out what was happening in the orchard.

Hoodwinked, she was led outside, the sun warming her face even as a crisp breeze ruffled her hair.

Alice let go of her hand, tapped her on the belly, and said, "Ye're it, my lady. Come and find us!"

"Oh!" Emilia cried with joy. She'd not played hide and seek since she was a wee lass.

Stretching her arms out, she took tentative steps forward,

hearing the children's giggles float on the air. Her slippers crunched over the grass, and her fingers brushed the branches of the trees as she went deeper into the orchard.

A swift wind blew past her on the right—someone running.

She caught the spicy scent of Ian. Large hands wrapped around her waist and tugged her backward off balance, catching her in his arms.

Her back was crushed to his chest and he whispered in her ear, "See, if ye left us, ye'd miss out on all the fun games we could play."

Then he set her on her feet, his scent fading as he rushed off.

A child ran up and tickled her from behind, and she whirled to tap them but they leapt out of her reach. Emilia laughed out loud, sucking in huge gulps of fresh autumn air and happiness filled her.

She scuffled through the orchard, hands keeping branches from hitting her in the face, a smile on her lips and joy in her heart.

Once more, she caught the scent of Ian, but this time he was right in front of her. Her hands glanced over his chest, the sloping ridges of his shoulders. She bit her lip.

"I got ye," she said. "Now, ye're it."

"I was hoping ye'd say that," he whispered and then his lips were on hers.

Emilia melted into him, wrapping her arms around his neck, tunneling her fingers into the hair at the base of his skull. And just when his tongue slid against hers, the sound of giggling children getting closer brought her back to reality.

She tugged away, laughing, and yanked off the tie from around her head.

"Happy birthday." He flashed her an infectious grin.

"Ye're verra thoughtful, Laird Ian, but today isna my birthday."

"Well, I had a one in three hundred sixty-five day chance. So a happy un-birthday 'twill be."

Emilia giggled, her lashes lowering. "Ye know ye're verra charming."

He nodded, playing serious. "Ye're the first to tell me so."

"Nay, I'm not." She playfully slapped his arm.

Ian chuckled and picked her up, twirling her in a circle. "Nay. But I believe ye when I've believed no other. When is your birthday?"

"The first of November."

"Ah! Then I was close."

He set her down, his arms still circling her middle. She was not willing to tell him to leave off.

"Verra."

He wiggled his brows. "Do I win another kiss?"

Emilia raised a brow, about to lecture him on the impropriety of kissing a lass whenever he wished, but then she remembered her purpose. *To woo him.*

So, instead of giving him the lecture, she lifted the linen tie from where it had fallen on the ground and wrapped it around his head, shielding his eyes.

"Ye can kiss me if ye can catch me." Then she took off running.

CHAPTER 15

Emilia could not remember a time she had been happier. She ran through the orchard, a smile splitting her face. How was it that a simple game of chase could make her feel so free and like her old self again? The shadows of what happened at Ina Ross' were passing with every day.

When Robert the Bruce had first suggested she come to Balmacara, Emilia had dreaded it. Children made her nervous. Men made her nervous. Strangers made her nervous. In fact, simple human interaction made her uncomfortable, but only since she'd been held at Ross Castle.

From the moment she'd stepped foot into this castle, she'd been made to feel comfortable, welcome. And now today. A day proclaimed in her honor. A game organized just for her. Surrounded by people who wanted to celebrate with her.

Ian whooped behind her. "I've almost got ye."

She couldn't help but look over her shoulder to see that Ian gained on her. Arms outstretched, a wide grin creasing his handsome face. The man ran with a dexterity while blindfolded that was wholly God-like. She took only a breath to admire it before picking up her speed.

"Ye only want a kiss!" she called.

"Of course! I've been wanting one since the day I met ye!"

Her heart skipped a beat at his confession.

What had gotten into her? The thrill of the moment? The excitement of his kiss? The possibility that while she was wooing him he was also pursuing her?

The gap between them grew smaller. She lifted the hem of her skirts higher in order to gain more ground. The children caught up to them, cheering them on with hoots, hollers, and claps.

Emilia was no match for Ian's stamina, his long stride. For every step he took, she had to take two or three. Her breath caught, and she stumbled over a root, an apple, or just a clump of grass. Laughing as she pitched forward, she found herself suddenly caught from behind, Ian's fingers seizing her hips to keep her from falling.

She whirled around in his embrace. "Ye caught me."

Ian lifted the blindfold, piercing eyes gazing into hers. "Do ye remember what ye promised?"

She licked her lips nervously and looked around them. The children waited with gleeful eyes. "I do... but we've an audience."

Ian dropped to his knees, an enticing grin curling his lips. Emilia stepped back in shock. Her heart, which had lodged somewhere in her throat, took a dive toward her toes. He grasped her hand in his and brought her knuckles near to his lips. She shivered, biting her lip.

"My lady! Ye have caught me and I have caught ye. What better way to settle *this* than with a kiss on your..."

"Lips!" the children shouted, jumping up and down.

Ian wiggled his brows, a teasing grin curling his mouth.

Emilia laughed, trying for a stern frown. "Ye set that up. Ye wanted them to rhyme."

"And are ye not proud?" He swept his hand out toward the children. "I am. Isna rhyming one of the games ye play with them?"

She pursed her lips, gave him a playful look, and then glanced at the wee ones. "Children, I think Laird Ian was going to kiss my knuckles."

"Aw..." was their resounding whine of disagreement.

"Ye see, my lady? They want me to kiss ye." He stood and tapped her lips, "Right here."

The children whispered behind their hands, giggling and dancing, while Emilia's face flamed with color.

"Ian..." But before she could complain about it further, he swooped down and planted a quick kiss on her lips, then raised his hands in triumph.

The children cheered and she grasped her heated face.

"Another!" they called.

Emilia shook her head and clapped her hands. "Enough of this kissing stuff. Ye have lessons today. I have had the most wonderful of days and I canna thank ye enough for it. Ye've all made me verra happy. But if we were to dally all day, we'd fall far behind."

"Och, not today, my lady, for we are celebrating your un-birthday." He smiled at the wee ones. "And that means ye get to go for your riding lesson. The men are waiting for ye in the stable. Go on now." He ruffled his hands through their hair.

As children do, they broke out into a chaos of eight excitedly shouting voices, disbursing in a herd, leaving Emilia and Ian quite alone. The only sounds left were those of the blowing wind and the fading joyous calls of the children.

Ian's gaze caught hers and, for several breaths, they were locked in a stare-down. He inched closer and she fretted that he might dip to kiss her when she wanted to get a handle on the emotions already swirling inside. So far, today represented everything she wanted. A family. Love. Connection. Bonding. Joy.

"Ye have outdone yourself, my laird. This is by far the verra best un-birthday I've ever had. I thank ye verra much for making it so special to me."

The grin spreading over his sensual lips was boyish and adorable. She wanted to reach out and touch his face, slide her fingertips along his jaw. To *feel* his happiness. She kept her hands folded at her sides. He was satisfied with himself, that much she could see.

"But I must know something. How did ye ever run through the orchard, blindfolded, without falling or running into a tree?"

He chuckled, looking out over the landscape. "I used to play that game in the orchard as a lad. And, knowing the value of it, my men and I often train blindfolded. Ye never know when ye'll come upon an enemy in the dark. Using your senses is important."

Emilia was impressed. There was so much more that went into protecting one's land and castle than she would have thought. When she threw her daggers, she never considered throwing them in the dark. She used her eyes as much as any other skill. Perhaps she should take a chance on the dark. "Brilliant. I hadna thought of that. Well done, sir."

"Ye flatter me, lass. Any intelligent warrior would do the same." He tucked his thumbs in his belt and rocked on his feet. "Are ye ready for our next activity or would ye rather rest?"

Exhilaration filled her and she wanted to shout, *the next activity, of course!* But she couldn't. This whole day seemed too unreal. She'd woken up certain she would be the one in control, wooing Ian. It had turned out to be the exact opposite. And still, no declarations had passed between them, unless she were to consider his kisses as wordless claims, which they certainly felt like, but she could not assume such.

Even still, he'd kissed her, though briefly and chastely, in front of the children. A sure sign he meant to claim her as his own. He couldn't have the young lads growing up thinking it was all right to kiss any lass they wished after a game of chase. Right?

"I would know something," she murmured, looking up at him through her lashes, feeling heat gather in her face. "Why did ye do this today?"

"'Tis a beautiful day." He held out his arms indicating the sun shining overheard.

Emilia cocked her head to the side, studying him instead of the sky. He was trying to change the subject, to distract her from what she wanted to know. "I think ye know the meaning of my question."

Ian's smile faded, his eyes intense as he locked on to her gaze. "I do."

She blinked rapidly, working not to get her hopes up that her scheme was working. "Please, tell me why." Then her blunt side came out. "No need to chase each other with words, Ian. I want to hear your truth."

Slowly, he nodded, his eyes locking on hers. Though he still smiled, it was different, honest, the playfulness pushed to the edges and his thoughtful side coming out. "The children, Emilia, they adore ye."

She quirked a brow, sensing he was censoring his words. "I adore them."

Ian dragged a hand through his hair. "They need ye."

She worked not to laugh at how everything centered

around the children. It was obvious from his gaze it was himself he was talking about. "They need someone."

"Nay. Not just anyone. *Ye*."

"Why me?" *Why do ye want me?*

Ian didn't hesitate in his answer, giving her the impression he'd thought about his words carefully before she'd even asked.

"Ye're kind, smart. Ye let them be themselves rather than backing them into a corner and forcing them to be all the same. Ye're bonny. Ye like to play games. Ye have a hidden and deadly talent," he winged his brows, his expression rapt, "and that has to count for something, for ye can protect them if need be. Ye've bonded with them. Ye share a special connection. 'Tis hard to do with children, getting them to trust ye, especially when they've lost the only caretakers they've known."

"Ye flatter me, my laird... And I dinna disagree about our bond. I care for them, too." *I care for ye.* "But one day, they will grow up and they will move on. What then?" *Will ye still want me?*

Ian tugged one of her hands into his own, giving her a gentle squeeze. A sadness filled his eyes. "I hadna thought of them leaving..."

An ache built in her chest. He said nothing of the future. He'd only arranged all of this, her un-birthday, these confessions, so she'd stay on as a governess? He wanted all of her but without the commitment.

She tugged her hand away from his and started to back away. To get away from his scent, his heat, the closeness of him that made all of her senses go on high alert. The plans she'd made of wooing him made her feel foolish. Ian wasn't the committing kind. "I'm sorry, Ian, but I canna stay, even though the children adore me and I adore them. I will help ye with the children until ye can find someone else to replace me as governess."

"Wait." He held out his hand, pleading for her not to leave. "There is more."

Oh, what a traitor her own mind was, leaping with hope at those simple words.

"I..." He raked his hands through his hair. "I dinna want to lose ye, Emilia."

"But why, Ian?"

His eyes darkened, mouth set, jaw tight. The man was stubborn to a fault. Had he never expressed his own feelings before? Did he not realize how important it was to do it if he truly wanted her to stay?

"It has to be more than kissing." She tried to hide the frustration in her voice, but was afraid she wasn't doing very well.

A teasing smile curled his mouth. "Do ye like kissing?"

Emilia let out a disappointed laugh. "Aye. But a lass needs more than that." She pressed her hand over her heart. "We are more than lips. We are more than kisses."

Ian dropped his eyes down to their feet. She could see he was still struggling with coming up with words.

"I know that, lass. I confess I wish ye to stay for the same reasons as the children. Mayhap those were my reasons all along, but there is more."

"I am listening." Oh, she was close to getting down on her knees and begging him to open up. To tell her what she needed to hear and to mean it. She could see the struggle in his eyes. She had sensed for days that he felt something for her and she'd been working hard to push it away until she realized she wanted it, too. Maybe that's what made it all the more painful—wanting it and seeing how hard it was for him to say it aloud.

But if he couldn't tell her, then she knew she couldn't stay.

"Growing up, I had one friend who accepted me without caring for my past," Ian said. "That is Alistair. He is my greatest champion. When ye arrived, I was struggling to find my place in the clan as a leader. Ye dinna falter in seeing me as the laird. Ye knew my father's indiscretions and ye accepted them without judgment. No matter that the children are bastards, ye treat them as though they belong. Ye treat *me* as though *I* belong."

"Ye do belong."

He shook his head, a bitter laugh escaping. "Och, lass, if ye only knew. There is much doubt."

He wasn't telling her something. He was still holding back.

Maybe if she opened up to him, showed him her own vulnerability, he would feel comfortable enough to share his secrets with her.

"Can we sit down and talk?"

"Aye." He took her hand in his and led her to a stone bench a bit deeper in the orchard. Shaded by trees, the spot secluded and private.

They sat down beside each other, her thigh brushing his. She could have moved it, but she didn't want to. She liked touching him. Again, his closeness threatened to take her sense and train of thought, but she had a mission and she was going to see it done.

"I must first confess to ye, I am no artist. I canna draw a circle even if the lines are traced out for me. Any of my drawings in the past have always ended up looking like a burning bush—even my attempts to draw my mother."

Ian chuckled. "I gathered that much when ye refused to draw for the children."

"*Phew*. I was afraid ye might have discounted me as a good teacher for them if I couldna draw."

"Nay. There is more to being a governess than knowing how to draw circles."

Emilia folded her hands in her lap, staring at the way her fingers interlocked. "There is something else I want to share with ye. About belonging. About chasing your dreams. About being your true self. When I was a little girl, my father took us all to a tournament. There was a woman there, showing her skills with a blade." She smiled, flicked her gaze at him to see that he was engrossed in what she was saying. "Ye might know of her, Aliah de Mowbray Sutherland."

Ian nodded. "Aye, she's verra skilled."

"She and Julianna de Brus, also now a Sutherland, competed in that tournament."

"Dinna tell me ye'd rather join the Sutherlands?"

She laughed and shook her head. "Nay." Then cocked her shoulder, teasing. "Unless, of course, they've a handsome younger brother who wishes to let me throw knives at him." She gazed into his eyes then, to see his reaction.

He narrowed his brow, puckered his lips, a surge of jealousy evident in his features. "They've none and no sane man would do such a thing."

Her grin widened. "No sane man?"

"Nay." Ian slowly shook his head and leaned close to stare in her eyes. "Only a man besotted."

Emilia opened her mouth, forming an "O" of surprise. Did he just confess he was smitten with her?

"Tell me more of your story," he said before she could say anything more.

Feeling flushed and shaky with nerves, she forced herself to continue her story. "That was where I first fell in love with knives."

"So a man must simply become a blade and he will win all of your affections?"

Emilia laughed. "If possible."

"I think I'm a mite too big to be tossed, but we can try."

"I may give it a go."

"I am yours to command." Ian curled a tendril of her hair that had come loose of her plait around his finger. "Did your da let ye throw knives with Aliah and Julianna?"

Emilia was finding it hard to breathe. Was this really happening? Ian sent her into so many different whirls of emotion. Moments ago, she'd thought her heart would break with disappointment and now she could sing with hope. She licked her lips, working to concentrate on the conversation. To keep him talking. To help him open up to her. "Nay. He told me it was unladylike."

"And ye mastered the skill anyway." He stroked her hair on her own cheek, the softness, light and tickly.

She shivered, keeping her eyes wide when she wanted to close them and lean against him. "Every night. I used my eating knife, tossing it at pillows, the wall, anything, and then I managed to steal a grain sack, fill it thick with hay and shove it into the back of my wardrobe. Long after everyone had gone to bed, I'd open up the wardrobe and work the makeshift quintain until it was spilling straw all over my boots."

"A wee good lady by day and a naughty knife thrower by night." He stroked her hair over her lips. Soft, tickling, she parted her mouth and felt his finger graze just the inside of her lower lip.

For a crisp fall day, she was suddenly quite warm. Heavy on the bench. She could have slid like jelly all the way to the ground and stayed there staring up at the blue of the sky, the trees surrounding them, and staring into the deep pools of Ian's mesmerizing eyes.

"What I'm trying to tell ye, is when ye say that I made ye feel like ye belong, Ian, ye've done the same for me."

"Then say ye'll stay."

"I want to... but..."

He inched closer, the length of his thigh pressed fully to hers. "Stay." He cupped her cheek, slid his thumb over the point over her cheekbone. He gazed intently into her eyes. "Not as a governess, Emilia."

Her heart skipped a beat and she found it hard to draw air. Heat flamed against her face. She wished she was in possession of a fan, else she may soon faint from the heat and inability to breathe. "I canna be your mistress," she whispered.

His jaw was set, determined, eyes locked on hers. "I dinna want a mistress."

She swallowed. "Then what?" she croaked.

Ian swallowed. She detected a slight tremble in his fingers where he touched her face. "I want ye to be my wife."

Pure bliss filled her heart. After her marriage to Padrig, she'd never thought she'd hear those words again nor *want them*. Oh, but she did, she craved them. Coveted them. And now she had them, she clutched them to her heart.

She pressed her hand to his heart, feeling the heavy, erratic beat in his chest. "Aye. I will be your wife."

Ian reached for her then, a hand threading through her hair and cupping the back of her skull, the other sliding over her ribs and toward her spine. His eyes locked on hers. Emotions she'd never thought she'd see were swirling in their blue depths.

"I'm going to kiss ye now, Emilia, but this kiss... It will be different than the others."

"How?" she breathed out, tilting her head back, lips parted.

"Our kisses before were playful discoveries. This... This is the verra first kiss I'm going to give the woman who's agreed to spend her life with me."

She closed her eyes, licked her lips, and waited for the first of many kisses as Ian's woman.

CHAPTER 16

E milia's eyes fluttered closed, her dark lashes fanning out over her flushed cheeks. Ian took a moment to admire her beauty, her grace, and to let the fact that she was going to be his wife sink in.

Her mouth was partially open, lips red and dewy from where she'd licked them. Lips shaped liked a bow on a wrapped gift meant just for him. This woman had agreed to be his, and he'd not even had to tell her the Bruce had demanded it.

She wanted him. She trusted him. She felt comfortable with him.

But he'd not told her the whole truth about his past. She didn't really know who he was.

Guilt riddled his gut, making him flinch. She'd given him her trust. He had to tell her everything. They couldn't begin this union with secrets. Ian touched his fingers to her lips and whispered, "I have something to confess."

Her eyes opened, heady with passion. She nodded, accepting.

"I..." But he found his words faltering, stilling on his tongue, glued down thick in the back of throat.

The way she was looking at him... The desire thrumming through his veins. Maybe his confession could wait. Why ruin this perfect moment? It was a cad thing to do and he knew he was a coward.

Would she truly shun him if she knew the whole truth *after* they were wed?

She'd so easily accepted the children—and him. Ian couldn't believe that she would deny him after she found out the truth. Emilia wasn't that type of lass. Besides, he'd proven himself worthy of her by embracing the things she liked, by embracing her.

Decision made. He'd tell her on the morrow. When they were having breakfast and he could concentrate on the right words rather than wanting to kiss her with every ounce of passion he possessed.

"I find myself much moved by ye," he said, instead. "Whenever I'm around ye, I feel..." His throat swelled. Of all the women he'd ever known, none made him feel the way Emilia did. It was almost like he was... *in love* with her.

Emilia stroked her hand over his shoulder toward his neck, sliding her slender thumb over his jawline. Amazingly, it sent a shiver up his spine.

"It is much the same for me," she murmured.

Ian lifted her onto his lap, wrapping his arms around her waist. She squealed but didn't fight him. Instead, she tightened her hold.

He touched his forehead to hers. "Then it would seem we have each found our perfect match."

"Aye." She tugged the hair at his nape. "Now, are ye going to kiss me as ye promised? I warn ye, I have many expectations for this sweeping touch of your lips."

Ian grinned. He wanted to give her what she wanted. And what she wanted was for him to kiss her. "I'd hate to disappoint ye."

"I dinna think that is possible."

He closed the distance between them, his lips brushing over hers, gently at first and then more demanding. He drew in a deep breath through his nose, smelling her, committing that intoxicating floral scent to memory. With one hand splayed on her back, he ran the other one up her spine to the base of her skull, cupping her, kneading her, letting her silky tresses come fully loose of their plait.

Emilia clung to him, fisting her hand in his shirt near his collarbone. Her other hand crept along his neck, tickling the back of his head, tugging his hair.

He parted her lips with his tongue, diving inside to taste her, devour her, claim her.

Where he'd touched the line of her spine, he caressed toward her hip and then her thigh, massaging. Her legs were longer than he would have imagined and were soft where he was hard. She scooted closer to him on his lap, her breast pressing against his chest. He vaguely sensed her tightened nipple. The knowledge that she was aroused sent his own desire pulsing through him.

He wanted so much more than this kiss. He wanted to make love to her.

Make his claim on her real.

But they were not yet wed... However, she'd been married before. She couldn't be a virgin, so if they continued down this path they were headed on, it wasn't as though he'd be taking her innocence.

Women who'd been married before took lovers.

And he had proposed to her...

Then again, he'd told her he wanted to marry her. That he

didn't want to make her his mistress. He couldn't then treat her as such.

Perhaps if they only kissed for a few more moments...

Ian skimmed his hand toward her knee, feeling her quiver against him. He slid his hand back up to her hip, to her ribs, tickling her, and stopping just to the side of her breast.

He paused there, wanting to touch her with an aching need that made his hand tremble slightly, but not willing to do it without her permission. And then she slid her hand onto his and pushed his palm over the top of the soft globe.

IF SOMEONE HAD ASKED Emilia yesterday if she was willing to let a man touch her this intimately, she would have emphatically said nay. To kiss Ian was one thing, but to let him cup her breast was something quite different. But the moment she'd decided that she wanted to be his wife, the second he'd asked her to be his, she'd given herself over to him wholly.

So when he hesitated at touching her breast, her immediate reaction, without thought, was to pull him past his indecision. She'd sensed that he'd been waiting, wanting her permission or perhaps uncertain how she would feel about it. After all, she had a moment of uncertainty herself when he'd kissed her in his study.

And now, he was touching her. His palm was hot and large over her breast. He kneaded the sensitive skin, this thumb rubbing over her taut nipple. Ripples of heat flushed through her, making her skin tingle, sending tendrils of pulsing need to a place at her core she didn't realize existed except when she was with him.

"Emilia," he murmured against her mouth. "Are ye all right...?"

"I am," she whispered back. "I am *so* all right."

"Ye're perfect." He nuzzled her neck.

"This is perfect."

"God, I want to..." He trailed off, skimming his lips up toward her ear.

She wanted to shout, *What? Tell me what ye want to do?* Instead, she sank against him, kissed him with all the passion she possessed. She caressed his chest, too, exploring the muscles over his heart, the way his nipples grew rigid beneath his shirt as she brushed them.

His hardened arousal pressed to the side of her hip and she had a moment of panic. But it passed, replaced by her itching curiosity and his soft encouraging murmurs.

"I've never wanted a woman more," he was saying against her lips. "Ye have made me the happiest man alive, agreeing to marry me."

"How could I refuse?" she asked, smiling against his mouth. "No other man would put his life in my hands."

"More than my life..."

She wasn't sure if he meant the lives of the children or what she truly hoped—his heart. "I feel safer with ye than I've ever felt in my life. Not just physically, but me, who I am..."

Ian trailed his kisses from her mouth to her chin, over to the side of her neck. Shivers raced all over her, now. She bent her head to the side, allowing him more room to maneuver his mouth over the column of her neck. Soft sighs escaped her. His lips climbed an intoxicating path toward her ear, his teeth teasing the lobe while he murmured, "I want ye... I need ye..."

She shuddered, clinging to him as he continued to explore, his tongue tracing the line of her throat down to the little dip between her collarbones. He skimmed his chin over the contour of her bones. His hand was still kneading her breast. Then his mouth was over top of her nipple, close enough she could feel his breath through her gown. Hot enough that she wanted to know what it would feel like for him to kiss her there.

Gently, and then a little more forcefully, she tugged at his hair, arching her back and silently begging him to put his mouth all the way on her.

She didn't have to wait long. He wrapped his lips around the turgid tip and rubbed them back and forth. She sighed, trembling, and holding on to her senses for she was on the brink of falling off the precipice, tumbling deep into somewhere she'd never been before.

A moan escaped her, startling her, she gasped. "Ian..."

"I love hearing my name on your lips." He moved to pay equal homage to her other breast, leaving a darkening ring on her gray wool gown.

At the same time, his hand roved back down over her thigh, down to her knee where he swirled around the cap, before inching lower toward her ankle. He circled her ankle with his fingers, tickling his way up the back of her calf.

"Ye forgot your hose..." he murmured, his fingers skimming over her bare skin.

She laughed. "I hate hose. I only wear them in the dead of winter."

"A lady after my heart..."

She shivered as he rubbed over her naked knee, then drew the tip of his finger along her inner thigh. Emilia held her breath, biting the tip of her tongue.

He looked up at her from where he nuzzled her nipple, his eyes as glazed as hers felt. "Lass?"

"Dinna stop," she said.

"Saints..." he ground out, reaching up to kiss her as his fingers continued their climb toward the apex of her thighs.

Another gasp escaped her, one of anticipation and intrigue. Before she could steady her breathing, he cupped her sex, the heat of his palm rivaling with the heat at the very center of her.

Ian stopped kissing her, his forehead pressing to hers, his breath hitched against her mouth.

"I might have died and gone to heaven," he whispered.

He slid a finger along the seam of her folds. *Oh!* Sensation like she'd never known rippled through her entire body, concentrating in that scorching, damp part of her.

Emilia fisted her hands against his shoulders, in part to steady herself from falling off his lap but also to keep herself from crying out—a noise that would bring attention to the wickedly delicious things they were doing in the hidden parts of the orchard.

"Ye feel so good," he murmured. "Velvet, heat..."

His tone, his words, they kicked her heart up a notch, and then she was lost when he touched a little knot of flesh that sent jolts of pleasure careening through her body.

"I didna realize..." she croaked.

He skimmed over her folds and toward her entrance. The part of her that no man had ever touched and he slipped a finger inside, hissing against her mouth as he did it.

"Ye're so tight..."

Now was probably a good time to tell him she was a virgin, that she'd never consummated her last marriage. That as many times as she'd been made to attempt a rise out of Padrig, he'd never been instructed to touch her.

Ian inserted another finger and she gasped at the penetration, all thoughts of Padrig instantly wiped from her mind.

"Lass?" He looked at her in question. "Are ye...?"

She blinked, certain that he was asking the very thing she needed to tell him and uncertain how he would take it. Most men would be happy, but he looked so confused, concerned, so that she wasn't certain he would be.

His fingers stilled inside her, filling her, stretching her, making her squirm with want.

"I was married in name only," she managed to say, heat of another kind filling her face. Mortification. "Though not for lack of trying."

He slipped from inside her, sitting up taller. "Ye're a virgin?"

Eyes downcast, she nodded, feeling ashamed all over again.

Ian tipped her chin up, gazing deeply into her eyes with an intensity that had her heart lodging in her throat. "There is nothing wrong with that, love. We will be married in truth. In name *and* in body."

"Aye. A true marriage. Not a sham." Her voice caught on the last word.

Ian looked crushed. He hugged her tight. "I'm sorry that ye were forced into that."

She didn't want his pity. "'Tis not your fault. I am working to forget it ever happened."

"I know, but I swear, I will work the rest of my days to show ye how worthy ye are of happiness. Of respect."

"And I will do the same for ye."

Ian stood and tugged her up into his arms. "I will make love to ye, Emilia, when the time is right, when we are wed. Your first time will be properly done." He gripped her hand in his. "Let us go and find Father Locke."

"To plan the wedding?"

He turned his darkly aroused gaze on her. "Nay, lass. I

would marry ye now. I would have ye in my bed this night. If that is all right with ye, of course?"

A thrilling shiver washed over her. "Let us not dally."

An hour later they stood on the stairs of the kirk, surrounded by the children, his mother and the clan. They proudly declared their vows to each other and anyone who would listen. She didn't care that she wore only her gray gown. Or that her hair was in a simple plait. The children had gathered her a bouquet with the help of a few servants. And when Father Locke pronounced them husband and wife, the thunderous cheer that went up all around them sent the birds rushing from the walls and roof lines.

"Open the wine for the clan!" Ian called. "Celebrate life this night!"

Ian whisked Emilia up in his arms and walked her toward the doors to the keep, the people calling cheers behind them. But Ian and Emilia had eyes only for each other.

She was married. Again.

However, this time, married life promised pleasure, joy, and acceptance. Saints, but she prayed this wasn't a dream from which she'd be cruelly awakened.

CHAPTER 17

I an carried her up the stairs, skipping her chamber and going straight to his own. Once they were through the door, he kicked it closed and transferred her from his arms to the bed. He barred the door and turned to stare at her, eyes dark with desire, his tall, broad body exuding strength.

Emilia shivered, ready and yet a little nervous about continuing what they'd started in the orchard.

She patted the bed. Eager to make this a union that was irreversible, unlike the torment she'd endured before.

"Wait." He walked to the table in his room where a platter of food and a large jug of wine had been placed at his behest. He poured them each a glass of wine and gave one to her. "A toast. To my beautiful, daring bride. May our days together be filled with excitement, adventure, and quiet nights before the fire."

He touched his glass to hers and she smiled. "I will say cheers to that." She paused a minute, tasting the word on her tongue. "*Husband.*"

They each sipped their wine, staring at each other over

the rims. The passion that had been simmering on the surface for days was, finally coming to its reckoning. She handed him back the cup and again patted the bed beside her.

Ian set their wine down and turned back to her. His gaze intense as he tugged at the pin of his plaid. Removed his sporran. Unclipped his belt. His plaid unwound of its own accord, falling inch by inch away from his body, leaving him in his boots, hose, and shirt that came to mid-thigh. He bent, unlaced his boots, kicked them off, and then peeled off his hose, freeing his shapely calves and manly feet.

Where she was feminine, he was utterly masculine. Soft versus hard. Hair versus silken skin. Curves versus rigid dips and planes.

Clad in only his shirt, he came toward the bed. She sat up, unlacing her gown in the front. If he was going to only be in his shirt, then she would be in her chemise, at least.

She glanced up at him as she worked the laces, wanting to thank him for not undressing all the way. For going slow enough that she didn't panic, but still for sensing she didn't want him to stop.

Ian's hands covered hers, taking over the unlacing. She watched as he nimbly tugged at the strings and when he was done, he tipped her chin up so she could look at him. "Are ye all right?"

"Aye."

He traced her collarbones. "Tell me if ye ever become uncomfortable... I dinna want anything we do to make ye nervous or scared."

"Ye're my strength, Ian."

He smiled, shook his head. "Ye've got your own strength, love. I'm just helping ye see it."

Her heart did a little pitter-pat within her chest.

"I'm glad the Bruce suggested ye as my protector."

"And I'm glad he suggested ye as my governess. For my wife. Ye govern all of me."

Emilia pressed her hands to his belly, sliding up towards his heart, thinking how quickly she'd fallen in love with this man. How much he meant to her. Would he ever love her in return?

Ian slid his hands toward her elbows, lifting her gently to her feet as he peeled the gown from her body, leaving her in her chemise and boots. He pushed her gently back down to the bed, deftly lifting one of her legs as he went. He unlaced her boot, tossing it aside, before doing the same to the other.

Then he crawled onto the bed beside her, lengthening himself out along her right side. She shivered and he shifted her into his arms, her head on his shoulder. He had one hand playing with her hair, the other pressed to her hip. Her fingers toyed with the ties of his shirt at his chest.

Ian rubbed his nose over hers, nuzzling her lips. He kissed her tenderly at first, and then with more fervor, sending her right back to where she was in the orchard. Heady, hot, full of passion and desire.

He caressed along her thigh, tugging her leg over his hip and fitting himself closer to her, his arousal pressed to the apex of her thighs. Emilia could barely breathe. Every inhale was a gasp, and every exhale was a sigh. While he touched her legs, her ribs, and her breast, she skimmed her hand over the muscles of his arm, his chest, and his back.

Gently, he started to rock against her, his arousal pressing to that place between her thighs that ached with need. Then he was pulling away and, of their own accord, her hips went chasing after him. Her foot hooked behind his knee, tugging him closer. They swayed, a languid seek and find, and then he touched her rear, hauling her closer to him, massaging her bottom. She found herself dashing after the erotic feelings this rubbing together brought.

Ian glided his lips over her chin, teasing her neck and then flicking his tongue over her nipple. Heaven help her, but the feel of his tongue on her, no gown in the way, only her thin chemise between them, it was wickedly delicious. She arched her back, moaning and rolling her hips even closer to him.

He inched her chemise up over her legs, exposing them to his touch until he had the fabric bunched up around her hips. His hand was splaying over her bottom, gripping her tight.

In one swift move, he rolled onto his back, pulling her over the top of him, her legs spread over his hips, hands resting on his chest. He kept his hand on the back of her head, pulling her to kiss him as his other hand reached between her thighs. The pads of his fingers slid over her folds, stroking against that heated knot of flesh until she writhed on top of him in pleasure. Sparks of awakening fired through her entire body before thrumming back to her center. With each stroke, the sensations heightened until she was rocking over him with burning need. His hardened shaft pressed tight to her body, his fingers, oh, his delicious fingers... His mouth tormenting hers.

Overwhelming. Intoxicating. She wanted more and more and more.

"Ian... this is... oh, it feels so good."

"I want to give ye infinite pleasure." He leaned up on his elbows, scooting back until he was leaning against the head-board, his mouth over hers, tongues twining.

He continued to work her sex with his fingers, stroking, swirling, and sliding inside her tight channel. The sparks that she'd thought were the height of desire only grew until all at once, an intense burst of pleasure struck her at her core. She cried out, arching, head falling back, riding out the waves against Ian's body and fingers.

"Heaven help me... Ye climax beautifully." He shifted his shirt out of the way, gripped his arousal, and slid it where his fingers had been. "Lift up just a little bit, love."

She did as he instructed, feeling the head of his erection at her entrance. He was large, satiny, and hard.

"I'm going to push up, and I want ye to press down. In this position, ye control how much of me goes inside ye." He locked his eyes on hers. "I've never bedded a virgin before, love. But I do know 'twill pinch."

"I have heard that." Her nerves started to get the better of her, and she felt her body tightening, resisting.

Ian must have felt it, too, because he stroked her thighs, smiled up at her. "But it will pass. Quickly. I promise, ye'll like the next part as much as ye liked the first."

She believed him. When he pushed up, she didn't resist, she pressed down, feeling him notch at the entrance, coming into contact with her barrier. There was only one way to get past it. She squeezed her eyes, prepared to impale herself on him.

"Wait," he whispered. "Ye're so tight... And ye're nervous, I can tell. Kiss me, love. Let's do this right."

She smiled down at him and leaned low, pressing her lips to his. Ian possessed her with that one kiss. Taking away her thoughts, her fears, and leaving her with nothing but an intense yearning. They rocked together, the tingling between her thighs growing and thrilling as it had before.

And then he was pushing against her barrier and she was helping, pulsing her hips downward until he crashed right through her maidenhead. She moaned against his lips at the pinch.

"Dinna stiffen," he said. "Ease your muscles. Relax..." He

helped her by caressing her, kissing her, stroking his thumb over her folds and finding her pleasure button. "I'm inside ye," he murmured against her lips, biting her lower lip and sucking gently. "And ye feel better than I imagined. How do ye feel?"

Emilia opened her mouth to answer, but found her voice didn't work. All she could do was moan. His shaft filled her completely, stretching her, claiming her for his own.

He opened his eyes, studying her, surely seeing the pleasure written on her face. He stroked her face, kissed her lips, her eyelids, her cheeks, her lips again. He shifted beneath her, sliding out, then slowing gliding back in. Emilia clutched his chest, trying to move with him, to sync her movements with his pace.

She stared into his eyes as they rocked together, his hands on her hips, her hands on his chest.

"My laird!" Someone banged hard on the door. "Come quick! There's a man here, claims to be the laird's son and he's come to challenge ye."

The heady glaze of their pleasure and desire evaporated immediately.

"Did ye hear that?" she asked, praying it was, perhaps, a hallucination. Hoping he'd say she was hearing things, she continued to move overtop of him.

The banging on the door sounded again. "My laird! Come quick."

"Aye, 'tis real. Bloody hell." He scooted to the edge of the bed with her still straddling his lap, his head falling to her shoulder. He pulsed in and out of her body, neither one of them wanting to stop. But the banging continued.

"Can it hold?" Ian bellowed toward the door.

There was a pause. Then Alistair, sounding as though it pained him immensely, said, "Nay, my laird."

Ian kissed her breast, swirling his tongue around her nipple. "I will see to my father's son and then I shall return to ye."

Regrettably, they disengaged, her entire body still humming with pleasure, but also with the fear of what the man outside could want. He intended to challenge Ian?

"Be careful, Ian. This man can have no claim. Ye are laird."

Ian's lips were pressed together tightly. She knew that look of anxiety well. He nodded curtly at her. Then her husband dressed quickly. When he was done, he kissed her lingeringly on the mouth then swept through the door, leaving her quite alone.

Well, she wasn't going to stay here. Emilia dressed, and plaited her hair, and headed toward the bailey.

"I KNOW YE," Ian said. The man standing in the center of the bailey, madder than a cornered boar was Ahlrid, the same man that had been speaking with Emilia privately, the one he'd had followed. "Ahlrid."

He looked around for Richard, the man he'd had follow Ahlrid, and didn't see him.

Ballocks...

"Ye dinna know me well enough," Ahlrid said. "My name is Harild. Ahlrid is made up, I switched the letters around, ye raging imbecile. I am the blood son of the laird." He sneered. Spit on the ground. "Ye are not."

Ian grimaced. He'd been waiting for just his moment. And what luck that it would happen on his wedding night. His entire body still throbbed for his wife. To be completely honest, his mind was not in this fight at all. He was still upstairs. Kissing. Touching. Bedding.

The clan gathered in a circle around their laird. Half of them were drunk on ale and whisky, celebrating the laird's marriage.

"Where is Richard?" Ian asked.

Ahlrid laughed, ignoring the question. "I've come to challenge ye." He pointed his sword at Ian. "The man who stands in my place."

Ian puffed his chest, squared his shoulders. "I stand where I belong. Where your father put me."

"Ye see," Ahlrid called to the gathering clan, his arms out wide as he turned in a circle, urging them to agree with him. "Even this imposter says *my* father chose him. *My* father didna know I existed. Didna acknowledge me. I was only recognized after his death. Invited here by this imposter."

"I think it best ye leave." Alistair stepped forward, his hand on his sword. "Your invitation is rescinded."

Several warriors joined Alistair, stating their loyalty to Ian. Their fearsome glares would have been enough to scare a lesser man, but Ahlrid didn't seem to care at all for their anger.

Most of the clan remained still. Watching. Not reacting one way or another.

Ian watched, unsure of what to do. Mayhap the people would want a man borne of his father as their laird and not him.

A few other warriors pushed through the crowd to stand behind Ahlrid. "Is it true?" they asked. "Ye are the son of the laird?"

Ahlrid nodded. "The eldest bastard. And your laird invited me home just a few days ago."

"Not to usurp him," Alistair shouted.

"Usurp *him*? He is an imposter!" Ahlrid sneered, his eyes roving with disgust from Ian's head to his toes. "Can your laird not speak for himself? Must he hide behind your skirt? What kind of leader only stands there?" Ahlrid taunted.

These words made the crowd murmur. Their stares intensifying.

What kind of leader, indeed? Ian swallowed hard. His clan was divided. He'd worked hard to try and show them he was the leader they needed. And yet now, without knowing who Ahlrid was, several backed him simply for his blood.

"Challenge me," Ahlrid demanded.

"Challenge him." Alistair nudged him in the shoulder. "Draw your sword. This is your castle, your clan. Your father wanted ye to be laird. Not this overgrown cock-sore."

Ian opened his mouth to say he didn't know his true father, that the laird had accepted him into the fold when he was a wee lad. That the only father he'd known wasn't his true father. That Ahlrid-Harild spoke the truth. That his mother had raised him as her own, but he knew full well, all along, he was not their child.

"Draw your sword," was murmured throughout the crowd until it was a deafening sound. Enough of a demand that Ian knew there were some who wished him to defend his place against this untrustworthy stranger. But there were just as many answering calls to the contrary.

"Give up."

"Surrender."

And those were the responses that resonated most in his mind.

He thought of Emilia, his wife, upstairs, waiting for him. Her sweet body surrendering to him. Her trust-filled eyes staring into his. For her, he would not give up. She'd married Laird Ian. Not Orphan Ian.

Ian drew his sword, leveled his glare on Ahlrid and grinned cruelly, fully prepared to send this ogre back to the dark woods where he belonged. "Ye're a man fully grown. Why wait until now to come home?"

Ahlrid shrugged. "I didna realize what was at stake."

"I dinna believe ye. What's changed?"

Ahlrid chuckled, drawing a line in the dirt with the tip of his sword. "Nothing has changed. I've simply woken up. Realized what I was missing. All this and, of course, the lady."

"The lady is *my wife*," Ian snarled. "And ye'll never have her."

"Oh, on the contrary." Ahlrid jerked forward and then back, clearly attempting to intimidate Ian. "After I gut ye, I will marry her."

Ian had heard enough. He might not be able to wholly defend his place as laird, but he would defend his wife. She'd been through enough already. He would guard her with his life and beyond. Their swords crashed together in grating metal.

Ahlrid was larger by several inches in height and at least two stone, but that didn't scare Ian. He was more skilled, he was certain. He parried, clashed, blocked, parried, leapt out of the way, sliced a long cut along the ogre's shin, and sustained a superficial cut along his forearm.

"What is the meaning of this? Stop this at once!" The shrill call came from Ian's mother.

But Ian couldn't stop, not with Ahlrid set on cutting him to the ground and wanting to take his wife.

"I said stop! For the love of God, cease this at once!" she continued to bellow.

Ahlrid flicked his gaze toward Meredith. "I fight for what is mine!"

"There is nothing here that is yours, save the clothes on

your back," Meredith shouted. "Ye fight against the laird's eldest son."

"*I* am the laird's eldest son," Ahlrid countered.

Meredith shook her head. "Ye're a fool. An imposter for all we know. This lad, Ian Matheson, came to us from Laird Ewan's first mistress. Ian is the firstborn." She pointed to the guards. "Seize that man! He is a traitor! He attempted to kill your laird. Throw him in the dungeon. And the rest of ye— how dare ye not come to your laird's aid. He has, time and again, proven he is worthy of your trust, your respect. Your king has given him his blessing as your laird, arranged for him to be married to Lady Emilia. How can ye turn your backs on your king?"

Ian blinked. He *was* his father's son?

What?

Why had no one ever told him?

He dropped the tip of his sword to the ground, shuffling back a couple of steps. Out of breath. Confused. Angry.

Alistair and several others disarmed Ahlrid and led him away as, one by one, men dropped to their knees placing their daggers over their hearts, calling out their pledges of allegiance.

But he was numb. His entire life, he'd felt like he didn't belong. And one simple word, one uttered confession could have put him out of his misery.

Ian's gaze turned toward the keep where Emilia stood, pain etched in her features. As soon as their eyes locked, she turned around and walked back inside.

Behind him, he was finally getting the respect he wanted and deserved. But in just a few days, his priorities had changed. The one thing he truly desired was her respect. She'd opened up to him, shared secret parts of herself, and when he'd had the chance, he'd choked. He'd not even had the decency to tell her that the king had given them his blessing to marry.

Ian had wanted his honey cake and to eat it, too.

How was he going to make this right for her? Would she ever forgive him?

CHAPTER 18

Emilia slammed through her chamber door.

She had an overwhelming urge to stomp her feet, to pummel anything and everything. She was angry at Ian, but mostly at herself. For, she'd been used enough that she should have known what it felt like.

"I should have known better." She flung open the wardrobe and tugged out her meager belongings, shoving them into the leather satchel she'd brought with her.

The king had already approved their marriage? Why didn't Ian tell her? Was it because he didn't have to? Because she'd already fallen so eagerly into his arms? Because she'd been so obvious in her need for affection? For love? That he'd been able to play along.

One kiss and she'd been his from the start.

What a weakling she'd been. What a fool. Thinking she'd been the one seducing him, and he'd been after her from the moment she set foot on the grounds. The Bruce hadn't been sending her here for protection or simply as a governess. Nay, he'd sent her here as a bride. The price—protection from Ian.

198

From one traumatic experience to the next she'd gone. Only this time, she'd been a willing party.

Och, how unfair it all was. She *liked* Ian. *Loved* him. Had found pleasure in his arms. And she'd thought all of those feelings and sensations were reciprocated. But it would seem she'd been kidding herself. He'd only been agreeable, charming, because he had to, because his king deemed it so.

And what better way to get a skittish doe to accept a stag than to make her feel safe, special, flawless, and accepted? Lord, had she been duped. Ian was a mastermind. A conniving mastermind. When had he and the king hatched the plan to trick her into falling in love with him?

Had they done that through letters before she'd even arrived?

Was it all arranged before she even knew she was to be sent into hiding as a governess, under the guise of being the king's cousin?

She charged toward the little table beside her bed, picked up the apple Ian had carved for her and hurled it at the far wall, watching it explode into dozens of pulpy pieces on the floor. That was how her heart felt. Pulverized into applesauce.

Emilia dropped to her knees on the floor, her stomach clenching painfully tight. This mortification at her stupidity, her desperation for love, hurt more than being forced by Ina Ross.

Well, she would run away. She'd run all the way to Loch Alsh, and then she'd swim across its cold depths to get to the abbey. No one had to convince her. The Lord need not send her any more painful messages. She understood fully well her role in this world.

She couldn't seek an annulment from Ian. Not with them being wed before God and the sheets of his chamber likely showing the small bit of blood she'd left from him taking her virginity. But she could swear to the Mother Abbess that she needed sanctuary. She needed saving from herself.

They couldn't force her to remain at Balmacara, could they?

'Twas ridiculous to even think it. Of course they could. She was a woman and she had no say. She could run away though. Risk the dangers of the loch and the Highlands, the mountains of the isle. She was desperate enough to reach a place where Ian couldn't woo her into betraying herself again.

Another lie. She'd not betrayed herself by falling for him. She wanted to fall for him. What she wanted to escape was the mortification that she'd laid her heart on the line, and he likely laughed his arse all the way to the bedchamber.

Well, she wasn't going to live a lie. She couldn't. She had to respect herself, didn't she?

And then there were the wee ones...

Her heart broke for the children, for she had fallen in love with them and they with her. She was looking forward to mothering them and Ian, the selfish bastard, had ripped that away from her.

She didn't even care that he'd lied to her about his past, about being a bastard himself. That part didn't matter. He'd been accepted by his family and his people. Who was she to say anything negative about that? But to lie to her about his feelings? His reasons for marrying her?

That crushed her and hurt in a place she'd not thought possible.

Shoving aside her pain, she pushed to her feet and grabbed her bag. The corridor was empty as she expected. Ian wouldn't come after her. He'd let her stew, knowing her trapped—and he'd not expect her to run away, either. Well, he didn't know her as well as he thought, for she'd already run from a marriage before. She wasn't opposed to doing it again.

She snuck down the back stairs, hearing a commotion near the bottom. Shouting. Grunts. The sounds of flesh being hit.

Zounds! 'Twas a struggle of some kind.

Her heart stopped, and she pressed herself against the wall, trying not to breathe for fear of being heard.

Voices, those of Alistair and Ahlrid. More gut-wrenching sounds, fists, flesh, bone cracking. They were fighting.

Why had the men not gotten Ahlrid to the dungeon?

She shivered. If he'd only been here for the sake of fighting Ian, had he ever intended to take her letter to her parents to begin with? Or had he betrayed her as well? Did her parents even know she was alive?

What could she do? She didn't want to move for fear of drawing attention to herself. Her palms grew slick as she pressed them to the cool stones.

More commotion sounded from everywhere. Reverberating off the walls as bellows boomed through the windows. What was going on outside? Had the entire castle erupted into chaos? Mayhap escape tonight wasn't the best idea.

"Ye hear that," Ahlrid hissed to Alistair. "That is Ina. She was waiting outside the walls. Hidden in the woods. Suppose she's come to lay a siege now."

Ahlrid's words sent a shiver of terror up her spine. Emilia gasped, her hands fluttering to her neck.

"Is that ye, lass?" Ahlrid called up the stairs. "I can smell ye." He sniffed very loudly. "Been wanting a piece of ye since Padrig introduced me to ye. That bastard went mad in his confinement. It was all I could do to convince him to off himself. To let ye come with me."

Emilia shook her head at no one, disbelieving what she

was hearing. Her throat was thick. She couldn't swallow. Could barely breathe.

"Come on down," he called to her. "I'll get rid of this bloke and take real good care of ye."

"Bloody hell..." There was a loud thwacking sound and then a thump.

Emilia's knees buckled. She dropped her bag and reached out to the walls and stairs to steady herself as she dropped to her bottom on the cold step. She needed to get up. To run. To bar herself in her room. But she couldn't make her body work. Too terrified to move.

"Lass? Are ye still up there?"

Emilia opened her mouth to scream, but clamped it shut when she realized that it was Alistair speaking and not Ahlrid.

"'Tis safe, he is tied up." Then he ordered the other guards to take Ahlrid the rest of the way to the dungeon.

His footsteps came quickly up the stairs and then there he was, standing tall over her.

He held out his hand and she feebly reached up, placing her hand in his. He tugged her to standing, his frown intense.

"What are ye doing here?"

"I was..." Instinctively, she stared down at her bag.

Alistair grunted and let go of her hand. "Ye were running to them, to Ina Ross and Marmaduke," he accused. "Were ye going to free Ahlrid from the dungeon?"

She shook her head vehemently. "I wasna, I swear it. Not to them, not to free him."

He crossed his arms over his chest. His frown cutting. "Then where?"

Emilia dragged in a breath. "To Nèamh."

"The abbey?" He shook his head. "Why should I believe that?"

"My sister is there. Ye can ask Sister Meredith. I made it clear, before, that my intention was to spend my days at the abbey."

"But ye're married to the laird. Ye declared yourself loyal to him and this clan in front of God and all only a few hours ago."

"I did." She looked down at her hands, lying limp in front of her. "Before."

"Before what?"

She chewed her lip, wondering what the consequences would be of not sharing her personal thoughts with her husband's dearest friend.

"Ye've about ten seconds afore I lock ye in your room and go outside to help Ian fight for his castle."

"He doesna want me." Her voice sounded so small. So stupid. "He only married me because the Bruce bid him do it. Because he needed someone to take care of the bairns. And he made it seem as though he... cared for me."

Alistair laughed bitterly. "Begging your pardon, my lady, but ye're a fool. A damned fool."

"What?" Emilia stood still, anger rushing through her. She met the warrior's cold glare. "How dare ye judge me without knowing what I've been through?"

"This is what I know. That my laird has changed since ye've been here. He's been happier. He's been stronger. More confident in his position. He's been a better man. And outside, when that bastard dared challenge him, it wasna losing the clan or the castle that made Ian lift his sword, it was ye. Ye were the reason he went to battle. If that's not showing ye he cares about ye, deeply, then I dinna know what is."

Clangs of metal echoed through the window. They both

stared at the arrow slit, realizing that the battle was raging heavy now.

"I'll leave ye here, my lady. And if ye choose to run away, to not see Ian for who and what he is, that is your choice. I'll not stop ye because I'd rather see him heartbroken over the loss of ye, then heartbroken over your doubt of him." And with that, Alistair drew his sword, ran back down the stairs and disappeared.

Emilia stared down the empty stairwell, realizing that he was right. If she'd only taken a moment to recall the way Ian smiled at her, the things he'd said, the way he touched her, she would have known. He did care for her.

And she loved him.

So, she couldn't leave him. No matter how much it hurt that he'd not told her the truth. She couldn't keep running. Sooner or later, she had to face her problems head on.

Emilia picked up the bag and carried it back up to her room.

CHAPTER 19

Archers rained arrows from the battlements down on the Ross army below. But they were no match for the men swarming over the walls.

"To arms!" Ian shouted.

All thoughts of Harild, the few Matheson men who'd betrayed him, his mother's news, and Emilia's disappointment, all of it, was gone in a heartbeat. The, and warrior in him came full to life, ordering men this way and that.

Ian was a protector. A warrior. A leader. And when his people, his castle, his lands were under threat, he was going to fight back to the death.

He ran up the wooden stairs to the top of the gate tower and crashed over the battlements, cutting men down at the top of their makeshift ladders. His men followed suit but, still, several Ross warriors got over the walls. They crossed swords, axes, maces and every other weapon with his men. Brutal. Bloody. Unrelenting.

Below, Ross warriors slammed against the wooden doors of the castle gate with thick, heavy logs, shuddering the thick planks until they crashed wide and more men poured inside.

The Mathesons had not been prepared for this onslaught. How could the Ross army have known that Emilia was here?

And then, all at once, he knew deep in his gut the answer to that burning question: *Harild*.

He had to be behind it.

And where in bloody hell was Richard?

Ian concentrated on shoving men off a ladder and hacking at those who made it over the walls. He'd have to worry about his scout later. Mayhap, he was still safe and sound with the other archers in Robert the Bruce's army.

Every Matheson man had been summoned to protect the castle. All of the guards were awakened and hauled their arses from the barracks to join the fray. They fought hard to beat off the blasted Ross army. His mother and Father Locke were in charge of getting the women and children to safety. He prayed that one of them had gotten to Emilia, hidden her safely away.

Alistair leapt to the top of the battlements beside him. Soon, they were able to yank the ladder from the men below, tossing it behind them into the bailey, knocking a couple of Ross warriors off balance. But by then, no more men were climbing ladders anyway, preferring to come through the battered gate.

"Archers, the bailey!" Ian ordered.

His archers, whirled, taking their deadly aim toward the bailey now. They fired their arrows, shooting one Ross warrior after another.

Ian and Alistair rushed down the rickety stairs to leap into the skirmish.

Ian barely had a chance to glance around, but from what he could see, they were winning. They were pushing the Ross men back and taking out any of them that wouldn't budge.

His own losses looked to be minimal. Despite Harild's

distraction, every man wearing Matheson colors was with him now, taking the enemy down. Onward they went, until they'd gotten every Ross out of the gates. Matheson warriors were following them out into the fields where they retreated behind their leaders.

Ina Ross and Marmaduke Stewart were there, waiting on their horses, a sword in each hand. Demons in human flesh. Ian was ready to greet the bastards head on. He marched his men within shouting distance of the two of them. The Ross warriors who'd retreated were lining up behind their leaders.

On the horizon, the sun was beginning to set, blotting the line of where the sky met the earth with orange. But that didn't matter to him. He would fight these bastards in the dark. He would fight them blind, until every last one of them had breathed their last.

"We've more warriors," Ina Ross shouted to him. "If we give them the signal, they will advance. Ye dinna want that with your gates crushed, your women and children defenseless."

"We have already beaten your men," Ian replied. "Leave now, else we wipe out your entire army. We've the support of Robert the Bruce, King of Scotland, and ye are nothing but traitors!"

Ina Ross laughed, a sound that grated like a dull blade over his spine. "Give us Lady Emilia and we will retreat. I will even have my men rebuild your gate."

"No deal," Ian bellowed. Rage pummeled his insides. He held his sword to the side, ready to swing if need be. Ross blood ran down the length of steel to the tip, dripping on the ground in a growing circle of red. He was ready to make it rain with their lifeblood.

"Ina Ross!" Echoing over the moors was the voice of Emilia.

Ian reared his head back, catching a glimpse of Emilia walking up behind him, her blonde locks waving around her in the gentle breeze. Damn, but she really did look like an angel. She stood tall, proud, and beautiful. Stunning. Pride swelled his chest. His wife. And then he realized where she was, how exposed she was. Heaven help him, did she want to give him a fit of apoplexy?

But he couldn't shout to her to run, to hide, to find his mother, because he didn't want to draw any more attention to her than was necessary. He didn't want Ina Ross to know how much Emilia meant to him, either, else the woman make it her personal mission to end his wife right before his eyes.

"Ah, there ye are," Ina Ross called in a singsong voice. "Come over here and let us leave. Ye can save all these men's lives by simply returning with us."

"Hold," Ian urged his men who, like him, itched to continue with the battle.

"I'm not going anywhere," Emilia said, her tone full of strength and conviction.

Matheson men whooped and cheered at that, banging their swords against their shields.

Ina Ross looked at her husband and the both of them laughed. "As if ye have a choice, lass. Ye belong to us."

"I belong here. With my husband."

Ina Ross frowned at that, a dark brooding look coming over her. "And who is that?" Her glared turned toward Ian.

It wouldn't have taken much for the woman to deduce that he was married to Emilia.

"Emilia is my wife, and ye'll not be getting anywhere near her."

"We'll see about that!" Ina Ross waved her sword in the air, blowing out a piercing whistle. True to her word, a fresh army of Ross men came from beyond the woods.

Ian looked to Emilia. "Run to the castle, lass, right now. Do it, so I can finish this!"

"Aye, my husband," Emilia said and turned for Balmacara.

Knowing Emilia was safe, Ian then addressed his men. "Hold!" he bellowed. "Formations!"

The men formed a line, their shields up, swords ready.

Ina Ross grinned at him evilly. "She will be ours. And ye will belong to death."

"Like hell," Ian bellowed.

He made his own hand signals into the air. Archers began raining arrows down on the advancing Ross men and, surprisingly, Ina and Marmaduke charged toward him, both of them entering the fight.

Before Ina made it more than a dozen feet, a dagger came whistling through the air, sinking with a sickening sound into the evil woman's eye. Her mouth fell open in shock before she fell from her horse.

Ian knew at once what had happened. Emilia had thrown her dagger. She had taken down her own enemy. She had done so with the aim of saving Ian.

"Emilia. Ye've got to go now!" Ian demanded.

At once, all hell broke loose. Marmaduke leapt from his horse to run to his fallen mate and Ian did not waste time engaging the man. In his grief, Marmaduke was distracted, shouting about Ina Ross' death and death to all Mathesons. Ian took it easy on him at first, but the man became erratic in his movements, hacking and stabbing—and missing, but close enough that Ian wasn't about to risk it any further.

At last, Ian delivered a killing blow and put the man out of his misery.

He turned on the rest of the Ross army. After seeing both of their leaders fall, they were less inclined to fight. Half of them ran off, deserting their comrades, while the others, either too wounded to run or too dedicated to the cause, continued on with the battle.

"Ian!" The piercing scream came from Emilia.

He glanced back in enough time to see that, somehow, Harild had escaped his bonds. His thick arm was holding Emilia captive, a knife at her throat as he dragged her back through the castle gates.

"Harild! Stop!" Ian yelled. He hacked his way back toward the castle. He had to get to her. Had to stop that bastard from harming his love.

Saints, but he was hopelessly in love with the lass.

He wanted her forever and always by his side. And if that bastard harmed one hair on her beautiful head, he was going to gut him alive, toss him to the hounds, and watch his slow, painful death.

❦

HARILD HAD QUICKLY TAKEN her atop the castle battlements, forcing her to look down at the carnage below. "Look at him running toward ye," Harild hissed into Emilia's ear, his arm clutched tight around her middle. "Running through one warrior after another. If I werena convinced the man was a waste of breath, I'd say he probably loves ye. How painful it must be for him to witness ye in such a position."

Emilia gritted her teeth. "Ye're going to die, Harild. I'm sorry that I ever trusted ye."

Harild laughed, a loud, boisterous sound that was wholly out of place with the situation. "Trust? Ye just needed someone to get ye from one place to another and I did that. Nobody had any idea what my plans were. Thanks for killing Ina Ross, by the way. That made everything much easier for me."

"Do ye have any last words?" she taunted, ignoring his disturbing confessions.

The man might have his dagger to her throat, his arm around her middle, but her arms were free. She, too, had daggers up her sleeve. She wasn't jesting when she said he was going to die.

After this night, she was seriously considering giving up daggers altogether. Not once had she ever taken up the sport with the thought of taking human life. And now his would be the second in less than an hour. She didn't regret it. She knew it was something that had to be done. She had to get away from him. And he wasn't going to let her go. With these evil people, it was either kill or be killed. Well, Emilia chose life.

She spied her husband below, slowly making his way through the throngs, Blood on his face, the front of his shirt. Anguish was written all over his face and she could see in his eyes that he loved her. Guilt made her belly churn that she'd once doubted him. Had almost left him. She would never doubt him again.

She gently slid the daggers from the sheaths at her wrists. One hilt in each hand. She let out a deep breath. This was a move she'd practiced for fun, by herself, in her chamber. When she fancied herself a warrior like Julianna de Brus. She had no idea if it would work. Or if she'd end up getting hurt or killed in the process. But she knew one thing—it was the only way. Ian was too far away. The men engaged with the enemy. They'd not be able to save her.

She was her only chance at getting out of this alive.

Emilia closed her eyes. Feeling the weight of the daggers in her hands. Sensing the position of the man behind her.

One...

Two...

Loose!

With her right hand, she slammed her dagger into Harild's right thigh. Too stunned by the pain, he loosened his grip on her, not cutting her neck. Emilia whirled around and jammed her other dagger into his throat. His eyes bulged as he stared at her, blood pouring from both wounds in ribbons of red. She shoved him away from her and stumbled backward, catching herself against the stone ramparts. Harild grappled with the knife in his neck, his fingers slipping. His mouth opened, gurgling out words she couldn't identify. He stumbled forward, one arm outstretched toward her. She slid along the wall to get out of his reach. Emilia was afraid that with this much strength still left in him, he could push her over the ramparts.

Ian was up the stairs then, murder in every angle of his face and body. He swung his sword and lopped off Harild's head in one swipe.

She crumbled to her knees, hands shaking. Ian ran to her, dropping beside her. He gathered her up in his arms, kissing her frantically on her face. She clung to him, shaking uncontrollably.

"Ian…"

He shoved his face into her hair. "Oh, God, love. I thought I'd lost ye. I'm so sorry!"

"Nay, I am sorry, for not trusting ye. For fearing the worst. For wanting to escape."

"Och, but ye're perfect. 'Tis I who am sorry. I should have told ye everything, but I didna want ye to think less of me. I wanted ye to love me, to marry me because ye wanted to and not because the Bruce decreed it. I confess I fell quite in love with ye along the way. I love ye so much, it hurts."

"I love ye, too. So verra much." She shoved her face against his neck, sobbing. "I love ye so much, it hurts."

A shout of victory went up around them. The Ross army had been defeated.

Ian lifted his wife in his arms, nodding to Alistair who'd joined them on the stairs.

"Please tend to the men. The fortifications. I need to take care of my wife."

"Of course, my laird." Alistair immediately started issuing orders.

Emilia clung tight to Ian all the way up to his chamber. Silently, they undressed and washed each other with fresh water in the basin, scrubbing away the blood and muck of the battle with linen cloths. The fire in the hearth warmed them.

Ian laid her down on the bed and hovered over her. "I want to finish what we started, to erase away the ugliness that interrupted us."

"Take me away. Back to that place that is only ye and me."

He wrapped her up in his arms, stroking her body back into flames of passion. Neither of them wanted to wait, to hold out any longer. Ian eased his way inside of her.

"Are ye all right?" he asked.

She threaded her hands through his hair, looked him in the eye and said, "I have never been better."

He claimed her mouth with his, stroking his tongue in and out the same time he plunged within her velvet heat. Wrapped around him, she could think of no other place she wanted to be. He was in her, over her, his scent, taste and skin surrounding her. Body, mind, and spirit. They were one.

Ian brought her to the heights of pleasure she'd never dreamed were possible. What she'd felt with him before, it was only a fraction of what she felt now—now that they'd told each other how they felt. Now that she knew he loved her, and she'd been able to tell him how much she loved him.

Fear of death and loss only brought out more of their emotions, heightening every liquid touch and satiny caress.

Tears of joy spilled from her eyes, and she buried her forehead against his shoulder, clinging to him as he drove her body mad with passion. They murmured of their love until neither of them could speak any longer, until their only utterings were moans of pleasure and gasps for more.

When the waves of decadent bliss rolled over them both, keeping them captive in their embrace, they could have floated off to the heavens for all they knew. All that mattered was they were together.

Forever.

CHAPTER 20

Two weeks later...

The bonfires had been lit.

Great orange flames danced into the blanket of the black and gold sparkled night sky. One of the few times in the year that some believed the Otherworld mingled with that of the living. Spirits and fairies could be dancing in the shadows all around them, and they would never know until they felt the touch of the Otherworld on their skin.

The magic of the night sent shivers of elation skating over Emilia's skin.

The air was crisp, a calm breeze blowing over the moors. The sounds of Loch Alsh lapping at the shore was a gentle backdrop. The scent of the fires, roasting meat and the press of bodies surrounded them.

If she closed her eyes, she could almost envision the fairies dancing. A smile spread on her face. She tucked herself closer to Ian who sat on the log beside her.

Since the battle with the Ross Clan, life at Balmacara

Castle had changed drastically. There was no longer a heavy layer of fear or worry suffocating them all, only hope and eagerness to rebuild, to be stronger.

Tonight was not just about celebrating the end of the harvest, but the defeat of their enemies, and freedom from secrets that had hung openly oppressive among them all.

Ian was free from his troubled thoughts, feeling a greater sense of belonging than he ever had in his life. Everyone had pledged their loyalty to him. Everyone respected him as they should, for he was a great leader and had proven that time and again.

The three missing illegitimate children also came to the celebration. No one needed to break the news about Harild, as they already knew and they made it a point to show Ian their allegiance.

Emilia, too, was finally delivered from her pain. Allowed to be herself. She'd even taken the children out to show them how to throw knives, and no one said that wee lassies couldn't take part. Every Matheson was a warrior, no matter their gender.

With each passing day, at every quiet, intimate moment, and even on the more boisterous occasions, Emilia and Ian had grown closer and more deeply in love.

Together, they'd drafted a letter to the pope asking for an annulment from her first marriage. Though she knew in her heart she'd never been aligned with the Ross Clan, having it on paper meant the rest of the world would agree.

Across the fire, standing in a cluster of men, was Robert the Bruce. His usual intensity alleviated some with the eradication of one of his biggest enemies.

Even the Bruce had returned to congratulate Ian on his victory, but Ian gave all the credit to Emilia who had taken Ina Ross out. And with him, the Bruce had brought back

Richard, the archer of Ian's who'd gone missing. He reported that Harild had outsmarted him, slipping a heavy sleeping draught into his ale that kept him unconscious for the better part of three days. He'd not even noticed the man was gone until too late. And then he'd been ill for nearly a week from the aftereffects.

After Ina Ross' defeat, Sister Meredith had returned to Nèamh Abbey. To Emilia's surprise, Sister Meredith brought her sister, Ayne, back just this morning. Emilia had been so thrilled to see her sister that she'd burst into joyous tears, which, of course, scared her husband. After assuring him profusely that she was fine and simply overjoyed, he relented.

And now, sitting on a log on the moor, just across from the great blaze from Emilia, was her sister, talking with Alistair. The man looked positively besotted, and while her sister tried to remain aloof and pious, it wasn't necessarily working out for her. Emilia wasn't certain if the budding interest between the two of them would ever pan out into anything given that Ayne was devoted to the church, but she'd have to talk to her sister about her options. When she'd thought the church was her only path, Ian had opened her eyes to other things. There were more ways to devote yourself to the Lord than being a nun.

"What are ye thinking about?" Ian asked.

Emilia pressed her head to his shoulder. "Just how blessed I am."

Ian stroked a hand down her back. "Ye're an angel, did ye not know it?" he teased.

"I've been told often enough since I arrived." She smiled softly thinking of sweet Alice. "I hope that tonight, on the moors, I dinna return to the place I belong."

"I will come chasing after ye. No earthly or otherworldly realm could keep me from ye."

"This day couldna be any more perfect. Games. A delicious feast. Wine aplenty." Not to mention a missive had arrived from her parents begging her forgiveness, which she gave, though she was not yet ready to see them in person.

"Och, but I can think of at least two more things I want to do."

Emilia raised a brow. "Is that so?"

Pipers and fiddlers were still playing their sometimes haunting but mostly jovial tunes. Men and women leapt up to dance around the fire and those still seated tapped their feet. The children all ran wild. Ian's younger brother, the one who'd traveled from Melrose, sang at the top of his voice, an enchanting melody.

"My lady wife, may I have this dance?" Ian held out his hand to her and she shot him a radiant smile as she slid her palm over his.

"Always," she answered.

He pulled her toward the dancers and they kicked up their feet, their hands clasped. They laughed and swayed, bumping in to each other, playful. And then Ian was pulling her away from the dancers. Away from the fires.

"And now for the second... Getting my wife alone to make love to her beneath the stars."

"I love the way ye think, husband."

He led her into the shadows where no one else could see them. He tugged her, hand in hand, toward the loch. From beneath his arm, he produced an extra blanket.

"Where did ye get that?" she asked.

"Never ye mind, wife." He spread it out on the shore and sat down, patting the spot beside him. "Come and share my blanket."

She snuggled close to him, his arm around her shoulder. They stared up at the stars that twinkled overhead.

"What are your dreams?" Ian asked.

"My dreams?" She was certain no one had ever asked her that before.

"Aye, we all have them. I wanted to belong, to know who my parents were. To have the respect of my people, to be their true laird." He squeezed her close. "To find a lass who was willing to marry me because she wanted to and not because it was ordered."

"Ye sound like a lass now," she teased, tickling his ribs. "Love, ye wanted love."

Ian tickled her back until she was lying down on the blanket, tears of mirth in her eyes.

"So tell me. Was it to throw your knives at a man ye might one day wed?"

She lowered her eyes, somberness washing over her. What she'd had to do with her knives...with Ina Ross and Harild. She knew he meant their time in the orchard, but she'd never be able to think of knife throwing at a person the same after having to use it as a defense. Even when she'd been showing the children the proper ways, she'd repeated over and over the dangers. She even had their quintains shaped like overlarge turnips instead of a human chest.

"Why did ye get so quiet?" Ian asked, running his finger along her jaw and lying down beside her.

She leaned her head on his shoulder, her arm resting over his heart. "I was thinking about what happened..."

Ian sighed, pulled her closer against him, and stroked his chin over the top of her head. "Ye did the right thing. Dinna ever question it. That woman tortured ye. That man would have tortured ye."

"I was saving ye, too."

"Aye. Ye saved us all. In fact, ye saved a great number of

Scots, for Ina and her husband wouldna have stopped. They fought for the English. They were our enemies."

"When I found a passion for throwing, I never thought that I'd use it to take lives."

"Nay, and ye shouldna think of it that way. Dinna quit your passion because of what happened, else those bastards win."

"Ye're right." And he was. She couldn't let them win.

"Now, about your dreams. Do ye want to tell me?"

"I am living my dream right now." She wrapped her arms around his middle and leaned up to kiss him.

His mouth was warm compared to the chill of the skin on her face. Away from the great Samhain blazes, the air was much chillier, though not uncomfortably so, especially when she had a husband that always seemed to carry a fire beneath his skin that lit her own.

They kissed languidly, as though they had all the time in the world, which truly, they did. Everyone was celebrating. No one would come looking for them. They could make love until dawn broke if they wanted to.

The ground beneath their blanket warmed from the heat of their bodies. As Ian kissed her, he unpinned his plaid, unraveled it, and tucked it around their bodies.

"We'll keep the warmth trapped around us," he murmured, kissing the slope of her neck.

"I want to be skin to skin."

Ian let out a wolfish growl and helped her to disrobe, then finished undressing himself. Fully nude, their bodies sliding warm against one another beneath the plaid, an exhilarating thrill rushed through her blood.

"I dinna think I will ever get used to this," she said, playfully biting his chin. "Every time I lay with ye, my body ignites as though it is the first time. I canna get enough."

"Och, lass," Ian groaned, his arousal thickening against her. "Ye have a way with words. 'Tis the same for me. When I see ye pass, I think of the last time I kissed ye, touched ye. When ye eat your meals, I think of the places your mouth has tasted on my body. And then... then I think of how ye taste, like honey and sweetness and desire."

Emilia shivered, the images he conjured vivid in her mind. "I would taste ye now." She gently pushed him onto his back, climbing over him, keeping the blanket on her back.

"Heaven helped me," he whispered as she trailed her kiss from his neck down the length of his torso.

He sucked in his belly the further she went, gasping as her heated breath fanned over his engorged shaft. Emilia had very much enjoyed the first time he'd shown her this. The taste of him... She licked the tip of his arousal—salty. Wrapping her fingers around his rigid length, she tasted of him. Kissing, licking, sucking. She listened for the sounds of his breathing, his gasps, and enjoyed the power that came from giving her husband pleasure he could not give himself.

Ian let out a loud groan and pulled her away from her task. Gripping her hips, he hauled her up his body until his face was pressed hotly between her thighs.

"Ride me, love," he murmured.

His tongue, hot and wicked soft, flicked over her folds, searching until he found that knot of pleasure. And then he swirled and teased. Emilia moved her hips slowly at first, head back, the blanket falling from her shoulders, immune now to the chill of the night. The more he lavished her flesh, the greater her pleasure grew until her hips swayed back and forth in wild jolts.

"Mmm..." Ian moaned.

He massaged her buttocks, his tongue swept her to paradise.

Emilia answered his moan with many of her own, crying out as his tongue brought her to the height of pleasure. She shuddered as wave after wave crashed over her, through her, all around her. She was drowning in pleasure.

Before she had a chance to recover, he lifted her again, laying her on her back. He settled his hips between her thighs and plunged forward, sinking deep inside her body. Emilia welcomed his invasion, lifting her legs around his hips, tilting her pelvis to meet each and every thrust.

She clung to him, fingers digging into his back, her lips finding his in the dark. They rocked in perfect harmony, pleasure, and love, making them one in body and soul.

"Tell me when ye're close," he breathed against her ear, sliding his tongue along her earlobe.

"I am there."

He surged forward, thrusting with increased vigor, until they were both crying out with release.

Sated, with their hearts still pounding, Ian fell to the side of her and tugged her close. He pulled his plaid overtop of them like a blanket, shrouding them in heat. They stared up at the stars, their hearts starting to quiet their pounding and their breaths became even.

Being in Ian's arms, she felt like she'd finally come home.

EPILOGUE

March, 1309 (four months later...)
St. Andrews Cathedral
Robert Bruce's First Parliament Meeting

Emilia was overjoyed that Ian had brought her with him to the meeting of the clans and Robert the Bruce's first holding of parliament. St. Andrews was filled thick with important clansmen and women. They were even lucky enough to secure lodgings at the castle with the rest of those attending.

They were ushered through the crowded courtyard and great hall, up the stairs to a modest, yet elegant chamber. A lovely oak four-poster bed was to the right and a cushioned bench was placed at the foot of the bed. The wall opposite had a table and two chairs. There was a small alcove with an arrow slit window and a brazier for warmth.

Emilia sank onto the bed, exhausted from their travels. "Would ye mind terribly if I rested?"

"Nay, love. I have a few things to arrange anyway." He kissed her on her forehead, then the lips.

A few hours later, Ian returned, waking her with a gentle stroke on her arm. "I've a surprise for ye."

Emilia sat up, rubbing the sleep from her eyes. "I love surprises."

Ian handed her a narrow oak box, about twelve inches in length.

The wood was smooth and soft to the touch. She unclasped the lock and opened the box to find a beautiful dagger with a silver hilt ornately carved with Celtic knots and her name. The blade was about six or seven inches long, with a blood groove down the center. "Ian! 'Tis gorgeous!" She touched her fingers to the cool metal of the hilt and lifted it up. The light from the sun came through the window and glinted off the surface. "What an amazing surprise. I love it!" She leaned toward him and kissed him. "I love ye."

"I love ye, too, darling. And, that is not the whole surprise."

"What else then?" She peeked behind his back finding nothing but the back of his kilt and, of course, her imaginings of what his naked rear looked like.

"Come with me." A wide grin covered his face and his eyes beamed at her with excitement.

"Are ye certain ye dinna want to stay here?" She slid onto his lap and kissed him until they were both breathing hard.

"Lass, there is nothing I'd love more... But we must go downstairs. I'm afraid that part is out of my control. I promise, however, tonight I will ravish ye until ye canna speak."

Emilia gave a playful pout and climbed off of his lap, swaying slightly on her feet. He steadied her, his hands on her hips.

"As long as that's a promise."

Ian pressed his hand over his heart. "I swear it."

"Then let us go."

He took her hand in his, guided her down the stairs and outside to the bailey where a crowd had gathered.

Holding his arm out wide, Ian said loud enough for the crowd to hear, "Lady Emilia Matheson—your tournament!"

"What?" Her eyes widened, and she exhaled slowly as she stared at the people clapping. Her gaze shifted to the very center of the bailey where Aliah de Mowbray and Julianna de Brus stood, daggers strapped to their hips. Beyond that were three targets set up.

Ian leaned close and whispered. "Ye didna confess to me your dream, but I knew what it was anyway."

Emilia's knees knocked together and she swayed on her feet. "Are ye certain 'tis safe in my condition?" She touched her hand to her growing belly where their bairn kicked constantly, throwing her off balance.

Ian laughed and whispered seductively, "If what we did last night was safe then a healthy competition must be."

She blushed clear to her toes, recalling all the various positions they'd tried in the little inn they'd stayed at. "All right, ye have a point."

"Are ye happy, my love?"

She beamed up at him. "I couldna be happier."

Ian guided her toward her place in the tournament where she greeted Aliah and Julianna. She was a bit lightheaded at the prospect of meeting her idols, but they were both exceedingly gracious and beamed over her swollen belly. A herald blew his horn, then began to regale the crowds with stories of the women's lives. When he got to Emilia, he pronounced that she'd saved the Matheson Clan and taken down one of the Bruce's greatest enemies.

She swelled with pride and could feel Ian's loving eyes on her.

"Throwers take your places!" called the herald.

Emilia steadied her shaking hands, breathing in and out as she'd always done. Before, she was a little girl throwing makeshift wooden knives to a stuffed grain sack. Now, she was a woman fully grown. In love. Happy. A savior of the Scots. And standing on either side of her, were the two women she respected most in the world.

"One!" the herald called.

She gripped her dagger, tested the wind.

"Two!"

A long pause and then she bent her elbow, bringing her dagger to her shoulder.

"Loose!"

At once, the three of them let their daggers fly, sinking them into the targets at nearly the same time.

All three were in the center.

"Again!" They repeated the throws three more times. Every time, each of them hit the center.

"To the right!" They shifted their bodies sideways, all hitting the center.

"To the left!" Again, a dead heat.

"Backwards!"

Emilia smiled. She'd practiced it this way as a child, too. Turning her back on the target, she looked over her shoulder, giving a few practice swings, pointing the tip right at the target.

When the herald called *loose*, she was the only one to hit the center.

"Lady Emilia Matheson is the victor!"

Julianna and Aliah embraced her, congratulating her on a job well done. Ian lifted her into the air, twirling in a circle as the crowd cheered for her victory.

"Ian Matheson," she whispered against his ear. "Ye have made me one of the happiest of lasses in all of Scotland."

"I love ye, Emilia, and I'll see to it that ye remain just as happy, all the rest of your days."

IF YOU ENJOYED **GUARDED BY THE WARRIOR**, *please spread the word by leaving a review on the site where you purchased your copy, or a reader site such as Goodreads or Shelfari! I love to hear from readers too, so drop me a line at* authoreliza-knight@gmail.com *OR visit me on Facebook:* https://www.facebook.com/elizaknightauthor. I'm also on Twitter: @ElizaKnight. If you'd like to receive my occasional newsletter, please sign up at www.elizaknight.com. *Many thanks!*

EXCERPT FROM THE HIGHLANDER'S GIFT

An injured Warrior...

Betrothed to a princess until she declares his battle wound
has incapacitated him as a man, Sir Niall Oliphant is glad to
step aside and let the spoiled royal marry his brother. He's
more than content to fade into the background with his
injuries and remain a bachelor forever, until he meets the Earl
of Sutherland's daughter, a lass more beautiful than any other,
a lass who makes him want to stand up and fight again.

A lady who won't let him fail...

As daughter of one of the most powerful earls and Highland chieftains in Scotland, Bella Sutherland can marry anyone she wants—but she doesn't want a husband. When she spies an injured warrior at the Yule festival who has been shunned by the Bruce's own daughter, she decides a husband in name only might be her best solution.

They both think they're agreeing to a marriage of convenience, but love and fate has other plans...

CHAPTER ONE

Dupplin Castle
Scottish Highlands
Winter, 1318

Sir Niall Oliphant had lost something.

Not a trinket, or a boot. Not a pair of hose, or even his favorite mug. Nothing as trivial as that. In fact, he wished it *was* so minuscule that he could simply replace it. What'd he'd lost was devastating, and yet it felt entirely selfish given some of those closest to him had lost their lives.

He was still here, living and breathing. He was still walking around on his own two feet. Still handsome in the face. Still able to speak coherently, even if he didn't want to.

But he couldn't replace what he'd lost.

What he'd lost would irrevocably change his life, his entire future. It made him want to back into the darkest corner and let his life slip away, to forget about even having a future at all. To give everything he owned to his brother and say goodbye. He was useless now. Unworthy.

Niall cleared the cobwebs that had settled in his throat by slinging back another dram of whisky. The shutters in his darkened bedchamber were closed tight, the fire long ago grown cold. He didn't allow candles in the room, nor visitors. So when a knock sounded at his door, he ignored it, preferring to chug his spirits from the bottle rather than pouring it into a cup.

The knocking grew louder, more insistent.

"Go away," he bellowed, slamming the whisky down on the side table beside where he sat, and hearing the clay jug shatter. A shard slid into his finger, stinging as the liquor splashed over it. But he didn't care.

This pain, pain in his only index finger, he wanted to have. Wanted a reminder there was still some part of him left. Part of him that could still feel and bleed. He tried to ignore that part of him that wanted to be alive, however small it was.

The handle on the door rattled, but Niall had barred it the day before. Refusing anything but whisky. Maybe he could drink himself into an oblivion he'd never wake from. Then all of his worries would be gone forever.

"Niall, open the bloody door."

The sound of his brother's voice through the cracks had Niall's gaze widening slightly. Walter was a year younger than he was. And still whole. Walter had tried to understand Niall's struggle, but what man could who'd not been through it himself?

"I said go away, ye bloody whoreson." His words slurred, and he went to tipple more of the liquor only to recall he'd just shattered it everywhere.

Hell and damnation. The only way to get another bottle would be to open the door.

"I'll pretend I didna hear ye just call our dear mother a whore. Open the damned door, or I'll take an axe to it."

Like hell he would. Walter was the least aggressive one in their family. Sweet as a lad, he'd grown into a strong warrior, but he was also known as the heart of the Oliphant clan. The idea of him chopping down a door was actually funny. Outside, the corridor grew silent, and Niall leaned his head back against the chair, wondering how long he had until his brother returned, and if it was enough time to sneak down to the cellar and get another jug of whisky.

Needless to say, when a steady thwacking sounded at the door—reminding Niall quite a bit like the heavy side of an axe—he sat up straighter and watched in drunken fascination as the door started to splinter. Shards of wood came flying through the air as the hole grew larger and the sound of the axe beating against the surface intensified.

Walter had grown some bloody ballocks.

Incredible.

Didn't matter. What would Walter accomplish by breaking down the door? What could he hope would happen?

Niall wasn't going to leave the room or accept food.

Niall wasn't going to move on with his life.

So he sat back and waited, curious more than anything as to what Walter's plan would be once he'd gained entry.

Just as tall and broad of shoulder as Niall, Walter kicked through the remainder of the door and ducked through the ragged hole.

"That's enough." Walter looked down at Niall, his face fierce, reminding him very much of their father when they were lads.

"That's enough?" Niall asked, trying to keep his eyes wide

but having a hard time. The light from the corridor gave his brother a darkened, shadowy look.

"Ye've sat in this bloody hell hole for the past three days." Walter gestured around the room. "Ye stink of shite. Like a bloody pig has laid waste to your chamber."

"Are ye calling me a shite pig?" Niall thought about standing up, calling his brother out, but that seemed like too much effort.

"Mayhap I am. Will it make ye stand up any faster?"

Niall pursed his lips, giving the impression of actually considering it. "Nay."

"That's what I thought. But I dinna care. Get up."

Niall shook his head slowly. "I'd rather not."

"I'm not asking."

My, my. Walter's ballocks were easily ten times than Niall had expected. The man was bloody testing him to be sure.

"Last time I checked, I was the eldest," Niall said.

"Ye might have been born first, but ye lost your mind some time ago, which makes me the better fit for making decisions."

Niall hiccupped. "And what decisions would ye be making, wee brother?"

"Getting your arse up. Getting ye cleaned up. Airing out the gongheap."

"Doesna smell so bad in here." Niall gave an exaggerated sniff, refusing to admit that Walter was indeed correct. It smelled horrendous.

"I'm gagging, brother. I might die if I have to stay much longer."

"Then by all means, pull up a chair."

"Ye're an arse."

"No more so than ye."

"Not true."

Niall sighed heavily. "What do ye want? Why would ye make me leave? I've nothing to live for anymore."

"Ye've eight-thousand reasons to live, ye blind goat."

"Eight thousand?"

"A random number." Walter waved his hand and kicked at something on the floor. "Ye've the people of your clan, the warriors ye lead, your family. The woman ye're betrothed to marry. Everyone is counting on ye, and ye must come out of here and attend to your duties. Ye've mourned long enough."

"How can ye presume to tell me that I've mourned long enough? Ye know nothing." A slow boiling rage started in Niall's chest. All these men telling him how to feel. All these men thinking they knew better. A bunch of bloody ballocks!

"Aye, I've not lost what ye have, brother. Ye're right. I dinna know what 'tis like to be ye, either. But I know what 'tis like to be the one down in the hall waiting for ye to come and take care of your business. I know what 'tis like to look upon the faces of the clan as they worry about whether they'll be raided or ravaged while their leader sulks in a vat of whisky and does nothing to care for them."

Niall gritted his teeth. No one understood. And he didn't need the reminder of his constant failings.

"Then take care of it," Niall growled, jerking forward fast enough that his vision doubled. "Ye've always wanted to be first. Ye've always wanted what was mine. Go and have it. Have it all."

Walter took a step back as though Niall had hit him. "How can ye say that?" Even in the dim light, Niall could see the pain etched on his brother's features. Aye, what he'd said was a lie, but it had made him feel better all the same.

"Ye heard me. Get the fuck out." Niall moved to push himself from the chair, remembered too late how difficult that would be, and fell back into it. Instead, he let out a string of curses that had Walter shaking his head.

"Ye need to get yourself together, decide whether or not ye are going to turn your back on this clan. Do it for yourself. Dinna go down like this. Ye are still Sir Niall fucking Oliphant. Warrior. Heir to the chiefdom of Oliphant. Hero. Leader. Brother. Soon to be husband and father."

Walter held his gaze unwaveringly. A torrent of emotion jabbed from that dark look into Niall's chest, crushing his heart.

"Get out," he said again through gritted teeth, feeling the pain of rejecting his brother acutely.

They'd always been so close. And even though he was pushing him away, he also desperately wanted to pull him closer.

He wanted to hug him tightly, to tell him not to worry, that soon enough he'd come out of the dark and be the man Walter once knew. But those were all lies, for he would never be the same again, and he couldn't see how he would ever be able to exit this room and attempt a normal life.

"Ye're not the only one who's lost a part of himself," Walter muttered as he ducked beneath the door. "I want my brother back."

"Your brother is dead."

At that, Walter paused. He turned back around, a snarl poised on his lips, and Niall waited longingly for whatever insult would come out. Any chance to engage in a fight, but then Walter's face softened. "Maybe he is."

With those soft words uttered, he disappeared, leaving behind the gaping hole and the shattered wood on the floor, a haunting mirror image to the wide-open wound Niall felt in his soul.

Niall glanced down to his left, at the sleeve that hung

empty at his side, a taunting reminder of his failure in battle. Warrior. Ballocks! Not even close.

When he considered lying down on the ground and licking the whisky from the floor, he knew it was probably time to leave his chamber. But he was no good to anyone outside of his room. Perhaps he could prove that fact once and for all, then Walter would leave him be. And he knew his brother spoke the truth about smelling like a pig. He'd not bathed in days. If he was going to prove he was worthless as a leader now, he would do so smelling decent, so people took him seriously rather than believing him to be mad.

Slipping through the hole in the door, he walked noise-lessly down the corridor to the stairs at the rear used by the servants, tripping only once along the way. He attempted to steal down the winding steps, a feat that nearly had him breaking his neck. In fact, he took the last dozen steps on his arse. Once he reached the entrance to the side of the bailey, he lifted the bar and shoved the door open, the cool wind a welcome blast against his heated skin. With the sun set, no one saw him creep outside and slink along the stone as he made his way to the stables and the massive water trough kept for the horses. He might as well bathe there, like the animal he was.

Trough in sight, he staggered forward and tumbled head-first into the icy water.

Niall woke sometime later, still in the water, but turned over at least. He didn't know whether to be grateful he'd not drowned. His clothes were soaked, and his legs hung out on either side of the wooden trough. It was still dark, so at least he'd not slept through the night in the chilled water.

He leaned his head back, body covered in wrinkled goose-flesh and teeth chattering, and stared up at the sky. Stars dotted the inky-black landscape and swaths of clouds streaked across the moon, as if one of the gods had swiped his hand through it, trying to wipe it away. But the moon was steadfast. Silver and bright and ever present. Returning as it should each night, though hiding its beauty day after day until it was just a sliver that made one wonder if it would return.

What was he doing out here? Not just in the tub freezing his idiot arse off, but here in this world? Why hadn't he been taken? Why had only part of him been stolen? Cut away...

Niall shuddered, more from the memory of that moment when his enemy's sword had cut through his armor, skin, muscle and bone. The crunching sound. The incredible pain.

He squeezed his eyes shut, forcing the memories away.

This is how he'd been for the better part of four months. Stumbling drunk and angry about the castle when he wasn't holed up in his chamber. Yelling at his brother, glowering at his father and mother, snapping at anyone who happened to cross his path. He'd become everything he hated.

There had been times he'd thought about ending it all. He always came back to the simple question that was with him now as he stared up at the large face of the moon.

"Why am I still here?" he murmured.

"Likely because ye havena pulled your arse out of the bloody trough."

Walter.

Niall's gaze slid to the side to see his brother standing there, arms crossed over his chest. "Are ye my bloody shadow? Come to tell me all my sins?"

"When will ye see I'm not the enemy? I want to help."

Niall stared back up at the moon, silently asking what he should do, begging for a sign.

Walter tugged at his arm. "Come on. Get out of the trough. Ye're not a pig as much as ye've been acting the part. Let us get ye some food."

Niall looked over at his little brother, perhaps seeing him for the first time. His throat felt tight, closing in on itself as a well of emotion overflowed from somewhere deep in his gut.

"Why do ye keep trying to help me? All I've done is berate ye for it."

"Aye. That's true, but I know ye speak from pain. Not from your heart."

"I dinna think I have a heart left."

Walter rolled his eyes and gave a swift tug, pulling him halfway from the trough. Though Niall was weak from lack of food and too much whisky, he managed to get himself the rest of the way out. He stood in the moonlight, dripping water around the near frozen ground.

"Ye have a heart. Ye have a soul. One arm. That is all ye've lost. Ye still have your manhood, aye?"

Niall shrugged. Aye, he still had his bloody cock, but what woman wanted a decrepit man heaving overtop of her with his mangled body in full view.

"I know what ye're thinking," Walter said. "And the answer is, every eligible maiden and all her friends. Not to mention the kitchen wenches, the widows in the glen, and their sisters."

"Ballocks," Niall muttered.

"Ye're still handsome. Ye're still heir to a powerful clan. Wake up, man. This is not ye. Ye canna let the loss of your arm be the destruction of your whole life. Ye're not the first man to ever be maimed in battle. Dinna be a martyr."

"Says the man with two arms."

"Ye want me to cut it off? I'll bloody do it." Walter turned in a frantic circle as if looking for the closest thing with a sharp edge.

Niall narrowed his eyes, silent, watching, waiting. When had his wee brother become such an intense force? Walter marched toward the barn, hand on the door, yanked it wide as if to continue the blockhead search. Niall couldn't help following after his brother who marched forward with purpose, disappearing inside the barn.

A flutter of worry dinged in Niall's stomach. Walter wouldn't truly go through with something so stupid, would he?

When he didn't immediately reappear, Niall's pang of worry heightened into dread. Dammit, he just might. With all the changes Walter had made recently, there was every possibility that he'd gone mad. Well, Niall might wish to disappear, but not before he made certain his brother was all right.

With a groan, Niall lurched forward, grabbed the door and yanked it open. The stables were dark and smelled of horses, leather and hay. He could hear a few horses nickering, and the soft snores of the stable hands up on the loft fast asleep.

"Walter," he hissed. "Enough. No more games."

Still, there was silence.

He stepped farther into the barn, and the door closed behind him, blocking out all the light save for a few strips that sank between cracks in the roof.

His feet shuffled silently on the dirt floor. Where the bloody hell had his brother gone?

And why was his heart pounding so fiercely? He trudged toward the first set of stables, touching the wood of the gates. A horse nudged his hand with its soft muzzle, blowing out a soft breath that tickled his palm, and Niall's heart squeezed.

"Prince," he whispered, leaning his forehead down until he felt it connect with the warm, solidness of his warhorse. Prince nickered and blew out another breath.

Niall had not ridden in months. If not for his horse, he might be dead. But rather than be irritated Prince had done his job, he felt nothing but pride that the horse he'd trained from a colt into a mammoth had done his duty.

After Niall's arm had been severed and he was left for dead, Prince had nudged him awake, bent low and nipped at Niall's legs until he'd managed to crawl and heave himself belly first over the saddle. Prince had taken him home like that, a bleeding sack of grain.

Having thought him dead, the clan had been shocked and surprised to see him return, and that's when the true battle for his life had begun. He'd lost so much blood, succumbed to fever, and stopped breathing more than once. Hell, it was a miracle he was still alive.

Which begged the question—*why, why, why…*

"He's missed ye." Walter was beside him, and Niall jerked toward his brother, seeing his outline in the dark.

"Is that why ye brought me in here?"

"Did ye really think I'd cut off my arm?" Walter chuckled. "Ye know I like to fondle a wench and drink at the same time."

Niall snickered. "Ye're an arse."

"Aye, 'haps I am."

They were silent for a few minutes, Niall deep in thought as he stroked Prince's soft muzzle. His mind was a torment of unanswered questions. "Walter, I…I dinna know what to do."

"Take it one day at a time, brother. But do take it. No more being locked in your chamber."

Niall nodded even though his brother couldn't see him. A phantom twinge of pain rippled through the arm that was no longer there, and he stopped himself from moving to rub the spot, not wanting to humiliate himself in front of his brother. When would those pains go away? When would his body realize his arm had long since become bone in the earth?

One day at a time. That was something he might be able to do. "I'll have bad days."

"Aye. And good ones, too."

Niall nodded. He longed to saddle Prince and go for a ride but realized he wasn't even certain how to mount with only one arm to grab hold of the saddle. "I have so much to learn."

"Aye. But as I recall, ye're a fast learner."

"I'll start training again tomorrow."

"Good."

"But I willna be laird. Walter, the right to rule is yours now."

"Ye've time before ye need to make that choice. Da is yet breathing and making a ruckus."

"Aye. But I want ye to know what's coming. No matter what, I canna do that. I have to learn to pull on my bloody shirt first."

Walter slapped him on the back and squeezed his shoulder. "The lairdship is yours, with or without a shirt. Only thing I want is my brother back."

Niall drew in a long, mournful breath. "I'm not sure he's coming back. Ye'll have to learn to deal with me, the new me."

"New ye, old ye, still *ye*."

Want to read the rest of *The Highlander's Gift*?

EXCERPT FROM SAVAGE OF THE SEA

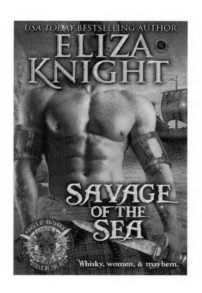

CHAPTER ONE

Edinburgh Castle, Scotland
November 1440

SHAW MACDOUGALL STOOD IN THE GREAT HALL of Edinburgh Castle with dread in the pit of his stomach. He was amongst dozens of other armored knights—though he was no knight. Nay, he was a blackmailed pirate under the guise of a mercenary for the day. And though he'd not known the job he was hired to do until he arrived at the castle, and still didn't really. He'd been told to wait until given an order, and ever since, the leather-studded armor weighed heavily on him, and sweat dripped in a steady line down his spine.

The wee King of Scotland, just ten summers, sat at the dais entertaining his guests, who were but children themselves. William Douglas, Earl of Douglas, was only sixteen, and his brother was only a year or two older than the king himself. Beside the lads was a beautiful young lass, with long golden locks that caught the light of the torches. The lass was perhaps no more than sixteen herself, though she already had a woman's body—a body he should most certainly *not* be looking at. And though he was only a handful of years over twenty, and might be convinced she was of age, he was positive she was far too young for him. Wide blue eyes flashed from her face and held the gaze of everyone in the room just long enough that they were left squirming. And her mouth... God, she had a mouth made to—

Ballocks! It was wrong to look at her in any way that might be construed as...desire.

There was an air of innocence about her that clashed with the cynical look she sometimes cast the earl, whom Shaw had guessed might be her husband. It wasn't hard to spot a woman unhappily married. Hell, it was a skill he'd honed while in port, as he loved to dally with disenchanted wives and leave them quite satisfied.

Unfortunately for him, he was not interested in wee virginal lasses. And so, would not be leaving *that* lass satisfied. Decidedly, he kept his gaze averted from her and eyed the men about the room.

Torches on the perimeter walls lit the great hall, but only dimly. None of the candelabras were burning, leaving many parts of the room cast in shadow—the corners in particular. And for Shaw, this was quite disturbing.

He was no stranger to battle—and not just any type of battle—he was intimately acquainted with guerilla warfare, the *pirate* way. But why the hell would he, the prince of pirates, be hired by a noble lord intimately acquainted with the king?

Shaw glanced sideways at the man who'd hired him. Sir Andrew Livingstone. Shaw's payment wasn't in coin, nay, he'd taken this mission in exchange for several members of his crew being released from the dungeons without a trial. Had he not, they'd likely have hung. Shaw had been more than happy to strike a bargain with Livingstone in exchange for his men's lives.

Now, he dreaded the thought of what that job might be.

This would be the last time he let his men convince him mooring in Blackness Bay for a night of debauchery was a good idea. It was there that two of his crew had decided to act like drunken fools, and it was also there, that half a dozen other pirates jumped in to save them. They'd all been arrested and brought before Livingstone, who'd tossed them in a cell.

And now, here he was, feeling out of place in the presence of the king and the two men, Livingstone and the Lord Chancellor, who had arranged for this oddly dark feast. They kept giving each other strange looks, as though speaking through gestures. Shaw shifted, cracking his neck, and glanced back at the dais table lined with youthful nobles.

Seated beside the young earl, the lass glanced furtively around the room, her eyes jumpy as a rabbit as though she sensed something. She sipped her cup daintily and picked at the food on her plate, peeking nervously about the room. Every once in a while, she'd give her head a little shake as if trying to convince herself that whatever it was she sensed was all in her head.

The air in the room shifted, growing tenser. There was a subtle nod from the Lord Chancellor to a man near the back of the room, who then disappeared. At the same time, a knight approached the lass with a message. She wrinkled her nose, glancing back toward the young lad to her left and shaking her head, dismissing the knight. But a second later, she was escorted, rather unwillingly, from the room.

Shaw tensed at the way the knight gripped her arm and that her idiotic boy husband didn't seem to care at all. What was the meaning of all this?

Perhaps the reason presented itself a moment later. A man dressed in black from head to toe, including a hood covering his face, entered from the rear of the great hall carrying a blackened boar's head on a platter. He walked slowly, and as those sitting at the table turned their gaze toward him, their eyes widened. In what though? Shock? Curiosity? Or was it fear?

Did Livingstone plan to kill the king?

If so, why did none of the guards pull out their swords to stop this messenger of death?

Shaw was finding it difficult to stand by and let this happen.

But the man in black did not stop in front of the king. Instead, he stopped in front of the young earl and his wee brother, placing the boar's head between them. Shaw knew what it meant before either of the victims it was served to did.

"Nay," he growled under his breath.

The two lads looked at the blackened head with disgust, and then the earl seemed to recognize the menacing gesture. Glowering at the servant, he said, "Get that bloody thing out of my sight."

Shaw was taken aback that the young man spoke with such authority, though he supposed at sixteen, he himself had already captained one of MacAlpin's ships and posed that same authority.

At this, Livingstone and Crichton stood and took their places before the earl and his brother.

"William Douglas, sixth Earl of Douglas, and Sir David Douglas, ye're hereby charged with treason against His Majesty King James II."

The young king worked hard to hide his surprise, sitting up a little taller. "What? Nay!"

The earl glanced at the king with a sneer one gives a child they think deserves punishment. "What charges could ye have against us?" Douglas shouted. "We've done nothing wrong. We are loyal to our king."

"Ye stand before your accusers and deny the charges?" Livingstone said, eyebrow arched, his tone brooking no argument.

"*What* charges?" Douglas's face had turned red with rage, and he stood, hands fisted at his sides.

Livingstone slammed his hands down on the table in front of Douglas. "Guilty. Ye're guilty."

William Douglas jerked to a stand, shoving his brother behind him, and pulled his sword from its scabbard. "Lies!" He lunged forward and would have been able to do damage to his accusers if not for the seasoned warriors who overpowered him from behind.

"Stop," King James shouted, his small voice drowned out by the screams of the Douglas lads and the shouts of the warriors.

Quickly overpowered, the noble lads were dragged kicking and screaming from the great hall, all while King James shouted for the spectacle to cease.

Shaw was about to follow the crowd outside when Livingstone gripped his arm.

"Take care of Lady Douglas."

Lady Douglas. The sixteen-year-old countess.

"Take care?" Shaw needed to hear it explicitly.

"Aye. Execute her. I dinna care how. Just see it done." The man shrugged. "We were going to let her live, but I've changed my mind. Might as well get her out of the way, too."

Livingstone wanted Shaw to kill her? As though it was acceptable for a lord to execute lads on trumped up charges of treason, but the murder of a lass, that was a pirate's duty.

Shaw ground his teeth and nodded. Killing innocent lassies wasn't part of his code. He'd never done so before and didn't want to start now. Blast it all! Six pirates for one wee lass. One beautiful, enchanting lass who'd never done him harm. Hell, he didn't even know her. Slipping unnoticed past the bloodthirsty crowd wasn't hard given they were too intent on the insanity unfolding around them. He made his way toward the arch where he'd seen the lass dragged too not a quarter hour before.

The arch led to a dimly lit rounded staircase and the only

way to go was up. Pulling his *sgian-dubh* from his boot, Shaw hurried up the stairs, his soft boots barely a whisper on every stone step. At the first round, he encountered a closed door. An ear pressed against the wood proved no one inside. He went up three more stairs to another quiet room. He continued to climb, listening at every door until he reached the very top. The door was closed, and it was quiet, but the air was charged making the hair on the back of his neck prickle.

Taking no more time, Shaw shouldered the door open to find the knight who'd escorted the lass from the great hall lying on top of her on the floor. They struggled. Her legs were parted, skirts up around her hips, tears of rage on her reddened face. The bastard had a hand over her mouth and sneered up at Shaw upon his entry.

Fury boiled inside him. Shaw slammed the door shut so hard it rattled the rafters.

"Get up," Shaw demanded, rage pummeling through him at having caught the man as he tried to rape the lass.

Tears streamed from her eyes, which blazed blue as she stared at him. Her face was pale, and her limbs were trembling. Still, there was defiance in the set of her jaw. Something inside his chest clenched. He wanted to rip the whoreson limb from limb. And he knew for a fact he wasn't going to kill Lady Douglas.

"I said get up." Shaw advanced a step or two, averting his eyes for a moment as the knight removed himself from her person, letting her adjust her skirts down her legs.

Shaw waved his hand at her, indicating she should run from the room, but rather than escape, she went to the corner of the chamber and cowered.

Saints, but his heart went out to her.

Shaw was a pirate, had witnessed a number of savage acts, and the one thing he could never abide by was the rape of a woman.

The knight didn't speak, instead he charged toward Shaw with murder in his eyes.

But that didn't matter. Shaw had dealt with a number of men like him who were used to preying on women. He would be easy, and he would bear the entire brutal brunt of Shaw's ire.

Shaw didn't move, simply waiting the breath it took for the knight to be on him. He leapt to the left, out of the path of the knight's blade, and sank his own blade in quick succession into the man's gut, then heart, then neck. Three rapid jabs.

The knight fell to the ground, blood pouring from his wounds, his eyes and mouth wide in surprise. Too easy.

"Please," the lass whimpered from the corner. The defiance that had shown on her face before disappeared, and now she only looked frightened. "Please, dinna hurt me."

"I would never. Ye have my word." Shaw tried to make his words soothing, but they came out so gruff, he was certain they were exactly the opposite.

He wiped the blood from his blade onto the knight's hose and then stuck the *sgian-dubh* back into his boot. He approached the lass, hands outstretched, as he might a wild filly. "We must go, lass."

"Please, go." She wiped at the blood on her lips. "Leave me here."

"Lady Jane, is that right?" he asked, ignoring her plea for him to leave her.

She nodded.

"I need to get ye out of here. I was..." Should he tell her?

"I was sent by Livingstone to...take your life. But I willna. I swear it. Come now, we must escape."

"What?" Her tears ceased in her surprise.

"Ye canna be seen. The lads, your husband..." Shaw ran a hand through his hair. "Livingstone willna let them leave alive. He doesna want *ye* to leave alive."

That defiance returned to her striking blue eyes as she stared him down. "I dinna believe ye."

"Trust me."

She shook her head and slid slowly up the wall to stand, her hands braced on the stone behind her. "Where is my husband?"

Shaw grimaced. "He's gone, lass. Come now, or ye'll be gone soon, too." He'd not been hired for this task, to take a shaking lass out of castle and hide her away. But the alternative was much worse. And he'd not be committing the murder of an innocent today.

Indeed, he risked his entire reputation by being here and doing anything at all, but he was pretty certain the two lads she'd arrived with were dead already, and along with them the rest of their party. Livingstone and Crichton weren't about to let the lass live to tell the tale or rally the rest of the Douglas clan to come after them. That line was healthy, long and powerful.

"I dinna understand," she mumbled. "Who are ye?"

"I am Shaw MacDougall."

She searched his eyes, seeking understanding and not finding it. "I dinna know ye."

"All ye need to know is I am here to get ye to safety. Come now. They'll be looking for ye soon." And him. This was a direct breach of their contract, and Livingstone would not stop until he had Shaw's head on a spike.

But Shaw didn't care. He hated the bastard and had been

looking for retribution. Let that be a lesson to Livingstone for attempting to blackmail a pirate. His men would be proud to know he'd not succumbed to the blackguard's demands. As he stood there, they were already being broken out of the jail at Blackness Bay.

Stopping a few feet in front of the lass, he held out his hand and gestured for her to take it. She shook her head.

"Lady Jane, I canna begin to understand what ye're feeling right now, but I also canna stress enough the urgency of the situation. I've a horse, and my ship is not far from here. Come now, else surrender your fate to that of your husband."

"William."

"He is dead, lass. Or soon to be."

"Nay..." Her chin wobbled, and she looked ready to collapse.

"Aye. There is no time to argue. Come. I will carry ye if ye need me to."

Perhaps it would be better if he simply lifted her up and tossed her over his shoulder. Shaw made a move to reach for her when she shook her head and straightened her shoulders.

"Will ye take me to Iona, Sir MacDougall?"

"Aye. Will Livingstone know to look for ye there?"

She shook her head. "My aunt is a nun there. Livingstone may put it together at some point, but I will be safe there for now."

"Aye."

"Oh..." She started to tremble uncontrollably. "Oh my... I... I'm going to..." And then she fell into his arms, unconscious.

Shaw let out a sigh and tossed her over his shoulder as he'd thought to do just a few moments before. Hopefully, she'd not wake until they were on his ship and had already set sail. He sneaked back down the stairs, and rather than go out the front where he could hear screams of pain and shouts filled with the thirst for blood, he snuck her out the postern gate at the back of the castle. He half ran, half slid down the steep slope, thanking the heavens every second when the lass did not waken.

Though he'd arrived at the castle on a horse, he'd had one of his men ride with another and instructed him to wait at the bottom of the castle hill in case he needed to make an escape. Some might say he had a sixth sense about such things, but he preferred to say that he simply had a pirate's sense of preservation.

Livingstone was a blackguard who'd made a deal with a pirate to commit murder. A powerful lord only made dealings with a pirate when he needed muscle at his back. And when he chose to keep his own hands clean. But that didn't mean Livingstone wouldn't hesitate killing Shaw.

Well, Livingstone was a fool. And Shaw was not. There was his horse waiting for him at the bottom of the hill just as he'd asked.

"Just as ye said, Cap'n," Jack, his quartermaster—called so for being a Jack-of-all-trades—said with a wide, toothy grin. "What's that?"

Shaw raised a brow, glancing at the rounded feminine arse beside his face. "A lass. Let's go."

"Oh, taken to kidnapping now, aye?"

"Not exactly." Shaw tossed the lass up onto the horse and climbed up behind her. "Come on, Jack. Back to the ship."

They took off at a canter, loping through the dirt-packed roads of Edinburgh toward the Water of Leith that led out to the Firth of Forth and the sea beyond. But then on second thought, he veered his horse to the right. When they rowed their skiff up the Leith to get to the castle, they'd had more time. Now, time was of the essence, and riding their horses straight to the docks at the Forth where his ship awaited would be quicker. No doubt, as soon as Livingstone noticed Shaw was gone—as well as the girl—he'd send a horde of men after him. Shaw could probably convince a few of them to join his crew, but he didn't have time for that.

A quarter of an hour later, their horses covered in a sheen of sweat, Shaw shouted for his men to lower the gangplank, and he rode the horse right up onto the main deck of the *Savage of the Sea*, his pride and joy, the ship he'd captained since he was not much older than the lass he carried.

"Avast ye, maties! All hands hoy! Weigh anchor and hoist the mizzen. Ignore the wench and get us the hell out of here. To Iona we sail!" With his instructions given, Shaw carried the still unconscious young woman up the few stairs to his own quarters, pushing open the door and slamming it shut behind him.

There, he paused. If he set her on the bed, what would she think when she woke? What would he think if he saw her there? She was much too young for him, aye. But whenever he brought a wench to his quarters and laid her on the bed, it was not for any bit of *saving*, unless it was release from the tension pleasure built.

And yet, the floor did not seem like a good spot, either.

He settled for the long wooden bench at the base of his bed.

As soon as he laid her there, her eyes popped open, and she leapt to her feet. "What are ye doing? Where have ye taken me?" She looked about her wildly, reaching for nothing and everything at once. Blond locks flying wildly.

"Calm yourself, lass." Shaw raised a sardonic brow. "We sail for Iona as ye requested. And from there, we shall part ways."

She eyed him suspiciously. "And nothing more?"

He crossed his arms over his chest and studied her. As the seconds ticked past, her shoulders seemed to sag a little more, and that crazed look evaporated from her eyes. "Nothing save the satisfaction that I have taken ye from a man who would have done ye harm."

"Livingstone?"

"Aye."

Her lower lip trembled. "Aye. He will want to kill all who bear the Douglas name."

Shaw's eyes lowered to her flat belly. "Might there be another?" he asked.

She shook her head violently. "Ye saved me just before that awful man could..."

"Ye misunderstand me, my lady. I meant your husband's..." Ballocks, why did he find it hard to say the word *seed* to the lass? He was a bloody pirate and far more vulgar words, to any number of wenches, had come from his mouth.

She lifted her chin, jutting it forward obstinately. "There is nothing."

Shaw chose to take her word for it rather than discuss the intimate relationship she might have had with her boy husband and when the last time her courses had come. "Then ye need only worry about your own neck, and no one else's."

He expected her to fall into a puddle of tears, but she didn't.

The lass simply nodded and then said, "I owe ye a debt, Sir MacDougall."

"Call me Savage, lass. And rest assured, I will collect."

CHAPTER TWO

November 1441

Dear Savage of the Sea,

I deplore writing that out, but as it is the name you bid me address you, who am I to give you another? I write on this, the one year anniversary of having arrived at Iona via your impressive ship. And given I am still safely ensconced, I must thank you for seeing me brought here, as well as for keeping the secret of my whereabouts. I am reminded on this one-year mark, that I still owe you a debt, and I did not want you to think I had forgotten.

The nuns at Iona treat me well, though they are irritated I have not yet chosen to take vows. As such, I'm certain they give me the worst of all chores. But I do them with a glad heart because I am alive, and I know more so than any other woman here that life is precious. Except perhaps that of Sister Maria. I've yet to learn her story. She thinks me too young. I am almost seventeen though, and I've been married before, which I'm certain she has not. Does that not make me more of a grown up?

Well, I am rambling, and I'm certain that a man of your trade has no use for ramblings.

I bid you adieu.

Yours in debt,

Lady Marina (I have often caught myself saying my true name, so much so, that I'm certain at least three of the sisters at Iona believe my name to be Jamarina.)

March 1442

Dear Jamarina,

I quite like your new moniker. I was at sea many months, traveling near India. An exotic place to be certain, though too hot for my tastes. I've only just returned and received your missive.

It is good to know you are safe, and trust that your secret is safe with me, for we are both hunted by the same rat. Alas, I am the hawk that feeds on vermin.

Perhaps your Sister Maria has a secret as profound as yours. Perhaps she only toys with you.

I have not forgotten our debt, but I have not had cause to call upon you for it.

As you say, you are only just a lass of seventeen.

Yours in service,

What name would you give me?

June 1442

Dear Gentle Warrior,

Aye, I believe I quite like that.

I confess I was surprised that you returned my letter. I had not thought a man of your trade to possess such beautiful script.

Sister Maria is gone. In the middle of the night. Mother Superior will not tell us what happened, and neither will my aunt. I suppose she did have a dark secret. I pray I do not disappear.

Again, they have asked me if I would take vows to become a novice nun, but there is something holding me back. I shall think on it a little longer.

Yours in debt,

Jamarina

November 1442

Dearest Gentle Warrior,

I hope you are well and that I did not offend you with my last letter. If it pleases, I will not write again. But I must say thank you once more, for it has now been two years since I arrived safely at Iona.

I confess, I long to leave. I do not think a life of servitude is for me. *I am a child of the Lord, to be certain, but I find myself heavy with ~~thoughts that lead me to confession~~ idle thoughts.*

Yours in debt,

Jamarina

April 1443

Dearest Gentle Warrior,

I confess I am much worried over you. It has been over a year since I've heard from you.

What it must be like to sail the sea. Free from walls. Free from judgment. Free. I am still grateful for what you did for me, but I feel a heavy cloud of melancholy. A sadness and loneliness, though I am surrounded by people. Perhaps, what I long for is the open sea.

Sister Maria has come back. I should think she is hiding something, for she avoids me, though not everyone else.

Yours in debt,

Lady J

December 1443

Dearest Lass,

A pirate's life is not for thee.

I bid you good-bye until we meet again. Your last letter was read by someone other than myself.

Your Gentle Warrior

PS. I wish you well on celebrating your eighteenth year. I do not know my own birthday, so I have celebrated mine with you these past few years.

Isle of Iona

October 1445

The nights were normally quiet at the abbey. Lady Jane

Lindsay walked the open-air cloisters between compline and matins when everyone else was sleeping, because sleep rarely came to her.

It was an issue she'd dealt with ever since that horrible night five years before, this inability to rest. And the only thing that seemed to help was walking in the nighttime air, no matter the weather, with no one present so that she could clear her mind, stare at the stars and think of a world outside these confining walls.

Sometimes it worked, and sometimes it did not.

She was Lady Marina now, her birth name of Jane a secret between herself, her aunt and the Mother Superior. Well, and her gentle warrior. She'd not written him since that day he'd warned someone else was reading her letters. And ever since she'd stopped, the scornful gazes she'd been receiving from Mother Superior had subsided. Was it she who read the letters?

Marina had been on Iona since the day the pirate prince had left her at the shore just before dawn so none of the sisters at the abbey would be able to identify her rescuer. And though five years had passed in the company of the devoted women of God, Marina had yet to take formal vows herself. Though not for Mother Superior's lack of trying. She wasn't certain what held her back, only that she felt destined for something, and she'd yet to figure out what. Perhaps the over-arching fear of discovery had been at the heart of that desire to keep herself free and separate from the women who had taken her in.

She'd once thought that she might like a life at sea. Those few days upon the *Savage of the Sea* had been the most peaceful of her life. No one had looked at her as though she were a pawn. No one had expected to use her, as had been her lot since the day she was born. Surprisingly, not even Shaw MacDougall, who she owed a debt.

For now, she knew that their lives could be in danger.

Even that rakishly handsome devil prince of pirates did not know the true danger she was in. The secret that would have made Livingstone want her dead. She'd kept that from Shaw. The less people who knew, the better.

Och, but she had thought of him often over the years. Her gentle warrior. The way he'd gazed at her with barely restrained longing, seeing the shame in his eyes for having done so. The way he'd gone against direct orders from Livingstone in order to save her. And who was she to him other than a lass?

The days she'd spent on his ship, he'd talked with her, played cards and knucklebones with her. She'd even taken two nights to read to him as the sun set. Their connection had been oddly easy and fluid. It had felt right. But then she'd had to leave him, and she wondered if maybe she'd only made up that connection after having an arrogant pig for a husband. Dare she call Shaw a friend?

She thought so. And given the fearsome pirate had been willing to write a naïve lass when she sent him letters, well, that proved it, didn't it?

Jane dropped to her knees where she was in the center of the cloister and stared up at the sky. She had to leave. And yet, she could not leave without the help of the man who'd brought her here. And there was only one way to get him to return to her. To help her.

She owed *him* a debt, and she was certain a pirate would never forget his debts. Especially those owed to him. And now, she would need him to do her another favor. But only if it were worth his while. That morning she'd managed to get a missive sent off with a local fisherman. She could only pray the messenger made it back alive, and that no one intercepted her letter this time. The man had agreed to take her message, but not for free. Especially when he heard where she wanted him to go. But the sight of her ring had been enough for him to agree. She'd given him one of her precious jewels, not only as payment, but also as proof to MacDougall that it was she who'd sent for him.

"Pray, come in time," she whispered to the night air, hoping her words reached Shaw wherever he was.

But it had been five years since she'd seen him, and well over a year since she'd gotten his last letter. She'd not replied to that one, fearful of who it was that had intercepted it, and she'd been waiting every day since then for Livingstone to come crashing through the abbey doors. But her day of reckoning was coming.

The name Livingstone had not crossed her lips since the day MacDougall had saved her from the knight's vicious attack. Not even when they'd been on the ship traveling to Iona. But it had crossed Mother Superior's tongue that morning while the sisters and Jane broke their fast. His name hung in the air, causing Jane's ears to buzz. Her worst enemy was going to be making a visit to the abbey on his pilgrimage across the country. Her hands still trembled at what Mother Superior had relayed to her.

The ladies in attendance had all been pleased to hear it, for it meant more coin would be placed in the abbey's coffers. Perhaps this coming winter, they might all have newly darned hose rather than the threadbare ones they'd used the year before. But to Jane, it had meant something else entirely—certain doom.

It meant death.

For she alone knew that Livingstone was not making a pilgrimage across the country in hopes of redeeming his soul, but instead was ferreting her out. Somehow, he must have gotten word she was seeking sanctuary at an abbey. Perhaps even this abbey.

In truth, she was surprised it had taken him this long to do so. How had he found out? Who'd told him she was here? Was it whoever read had the letter? Mother Superior? Sister Maria who'd disappeared several years before? Or was he just that clever? Perhaps in the last five years, he'd left no stone unturned but those lying atop Iona.

Mayhap for a while, he'd thought her dead, or that the pirate had kidnapped her, ravaged her and done away with her by tossing her out to sea. Part of her had hoped her gentle warrior had taken flight as a hawk and sank his claws into the blackguard.

Alas, none of her dreams that would lead her to freedom had come to fruition.

But something must have made him believe she was alive, and yet, she could not guess at who or what it could be. No one here knew of her identity, save for Mother Superior and her aunt. Even in her letters, she'd not written as Jane or given any other truly identifying information.

There was always the chance that Mother might have accidentally let some piece of information slip, for though she knew that Marina was her aunt's niece and that her name was Jane, she did not know the circumstances regarding why she must be hidden.

She did not know that Livingstone had killed Jane's husband.

That he wanted to kill her.

For Jane held a dark secret. One a man would kill for.

A secret she was willing to sell to a pirate for his protection.

A secret a pirate would be willing to barter with her for.

A secret would be the undoing of an entire kingdom.

If only she could have lived out her days in peace here. But only a naïve lass would have thought such a thing. Even when she'd come here at the age of sixteen, she'd not been naïve. She'd lived the previous three years with the most arrogant of earls—her young husband. He'd treated her like rubbish. He'd disrespected her in front of his men and made sport of seeing her look dejected because it made him feel superior. Jane had been nothing more than a pawn in their marriage bargain. Betrothed at age seven and married at age thirteen, she'd spent three miserable years with William Douglas, and the only friend she'd made was his younger brother, David.

They were both dead now.

Wee David was dead by association, for possibly knowing too much. William was dead for the latter, and for his arrogance. For he'd been the one to proclaim he knew the secret. And from that moment forth, he'd had a target on his chest.

It was only by sheer instinct that Jane had thought to ask William what the big secret was, playing on his need to brag. And then he'd told her.

Now she harbored the most dangerous secret in the country.

And Livingstone knew it.

Castle Dheomhan, Isle of Scarba

There was nothing to spoil a man's debauchery more than a messenger arriving with an urgent missive from a woman. An important woman if she knew where he resided. Besides the wenches lounging on his and his crewmen's laps, there was only one woman who had ever sent a missive to his pirate stronghold.

Gently knocking the two buxom wenches from his lap, who fell in a heap of drunken, naked laughter to the thick fur beneath his throne chair. The same throne chair that had been commissioned from steel and velvet with the Devils of the Deep skull and swords crest at its top and had parts that dated back to the original king of pirates, Arthur MacAlpin, from hundreds of years before.

Rock hard and half-drunk on whisky, Shaw settled his gaze on the messenger and willed his raging cock into submission. But that was almost impossible, given the inebriated state he was in and thinking of precious Jane. She'd be twenty-one now. Old enough that he didn't have to feel ashamed for thinking about her pert breasts and luscious mouth.

Was it she who'd sent this old man to him? Would she dare?

He'd not heard from her since his letter of warning, though he'd hoped to every day since.

But when he unrolled the parchment to behold the looping scrawl of his Lady Jane, he glanced at the messenger who stood cowering before him. This was not her usual girlish letter, but one full of desperation and a bargain.

Taking the steps down from his dais, he leaned down to look the fisherman in the eyes. "Dinna piss yourself."

"I willna, my...my... Your Highness."

Shaw grunted, sneering and not bothering to correct the old man. "How do I know this is not a trick?"

The fisherman stepped forward, reaching for his sporran. A bad idea in a room full of men expecting weapons to be drawn at any moment, and the old bastard was awarded with a dozen sharp blades at his throat.

The bloke raised his arms, glancing around fearfully, knees knocking. His mouth was open in a silent plea before he finally found his voice. "Please, sir, I hold proof."

Shaw waved his hand at his men. When they lowered their weapons, the fisherman continued to reach for his sporran and pulled out a golden ring of emerald and pearls. Shaw knew this ring. He'd given it to Jane as a gesture of friendship. A token of...his affection. He'd told her to send it if she ever needed him. When he'd told her he meant to collect on their debt, he'd never actually meant to take anything from the lass—other than perhaps convincing her when she was of age that she might like to grace his bed. It had taken a feat of pure willpower not to write her back when she'd said a life at sea would suit her to say he was coming to get her.

"Lady Marina," the fisherman said.

Marina... Jamarina... He let out a short laugh.

He'd not heard the name in a long time. It was the one he'd given her before she disembarked his ship. The lass had plagued his dreams for five long years. More beautiful than a woman had the right to be. He'd always felt guilty about his desire for her. For she'd been so young at the time, and pirate or nay, he had a code when it came to women. But not anymore. Now she'd be a woman grown, and the curves he'd felt when he carried her aboard his ship would have blossomed.

Shaw grunted and went back to the letter, the women on the floor pawing at his boots all but forgotten.

Dear Gentle Warrior,

I am prepared to pay my debt straightaway. 'Tis most urgent that you come now. Else, the balance will never be repaid, for there are others who wish to lay claim to the treasure I alone possess. I trust that your desire for adventure and thirst for the greatest of prizes will allow you to make haste to me. And know that I do not flatter myself that any sense of honor would bring you forth.

Most urgently yours in debt,

Lady M

"When did she give ye this?" Shaw demanded. The man stank of fish, his face the color and texture of dried leather.

"Early this morning, my laird. When I dropped off the fish at the abbey."

Shaw grunted. "And what was your payment for daring to step foot on my island?" He kept his voice calm, low, but it still had the power to cause the man to quake.

"The ring, sir."

"The ring," Shaw mused. He held the emerald jewel up to the candlelight. "So ye'll be wanting it back?"

"I'd be happy to leave with my life." The man's knees knocked together.

Shaw grinned, baring all of his teeth as he did so. "I suppose ye would." He closed his fingers around the ring. "Go then. Afore I unleash my beasts to feed on your bones. Ye were never here. Ye never saw this place. If anyone so much as lands on my beach by accident, I will hunt ye down and kill ye."

The old man nodded violently, then turned and ran toward the wide double doors that made up the entrance to Shaw's keep.

"Wait," Shaw called and two of his crew stepped in front of the old man to bar him from leaving. "Ye forgot something."

Trembling visibly, the fisherman turned, and Shaw tossed him the ring. But his reflexes, or his nerves more like, weren't expecting it, and the ring fell to the stone before his feet. There was a measure of held breath in the air, and Shaw wondered if the man would pick it up or if the moments would tick by to the appropriate count that his men knew meant free game for whatever treasure had been dropped.

Seeming to understand the urgency, or perhaps just wishing to get the hell of Shaw's island, the fisherman scooped up the ring.

But instead of rushing out, he asked, "What should I tell my lady?"

"Ye needn't tell her anything," Shaw said. "I'll be there before ye get the chance."

With that, he blew a whistle to assemble a small crew and marched past the old fisherman, thinking at the last second to grab him by the scruff and drag him down to the docks before he was robbed for having overstayed his welcome.

Soon Shaw would lay his gaze on the beautiful lass again. Only this time, she would be a woman. Had the years at the abbey done her well? Was she now a child of God as she'd often struggled with deciding upon in her letters? And if she was, would he have the ballocks to corrupt her?

At that thought, Shaw laughed aloud as he gripped the helm.

Of course, he would.

He was Shaw Savage MacDougall. He took what he wanted, when he wanted. And never had he shied from debauching a willing woman.

Better yet was the question regarding what was this prize she claimed to possess? This treasure that he would not be able to resist?

He imagined a mountain of jewels and gold. A key to the king's own treasure stores. But truth be told, those were not the treasures he'd been pining over for years since last seeing her. Nay, the treasure he wanted was *her*.

In just a few hours time, he'd know what it was she was offering.

"Where to, Cap'n?" Jack asked, eagerness in his eyes.

"Iona."

Jack frowned. "Ain't nothing there we want, Cap'n."

Shaw turned a fierce glower on his crewman. "There is indeed something I want there. And ye best not be telling me again what it is I want, else I'll have ye hanging from the jack and make good on your name."

"Aye, Cap'n. Willna overstep again."

Shaw growled. "Make certain no one else does, either."

*Want to read more? Check out **Savage of the Sea** and the rest of the **Pirates of Britannia** series wherever ebooks are sold...*

ABOUT THE AUTHOR

Eliza Knight is an award-winning and *USA Today* bestselling author of over fifty sizzling historical romance and erotic romance. Under the name E. Knight, she pens rip-your-heart-out historical fiction. While not reading, writing or researching for her latest book, she chases after her three children. In her spare time (if there is such a thing...) she likes daydreaming, wine-tasting, traveling, hiking, staring at the stars, watching movies, shopping and visiting with family and friends. She lives atop a small mountain with her own knight in shining armor, three princesses and two very naughty puppies. Visit Eliza at http://www.elizaknight.com or her historical blog History Undressed: www.historyun-dressed.com. Sign up for her newsletter to get news about books, events, contests and sneak peaks! http://eepurl.com/CSFFD

facebook.com/elizaknightfiction

twitter.com/elizaknight

instagram.com/elizaknightfiction

bookbub.com/authors/eliza-knight

goodreads.com/elizaknight

MORE BOOKS BY ELIZA KNIGHT

THE SUTHERLAND LEGACY

The Highlander's Gift
The Highlander's Quest — in the Ladies of the Stone anthology
The Highlander's Stolen Bride
The Highlander's Hellion — Fall 2018

PIRATES OF BRITANNIA: DEVILS OF THE DEEP

Savage of the Sea
The Sea Devil
A Pirate's Bounty

THE STOLEN BRIDE SERIES

The Highlander's Temptation

Eternally Bound
Breath from the Sea

THE HIGHLAND BOUND SERIES (EROTIC TIME-TRAVEL)

Behind the Plaid
Bared to the Laird
Dark Side of the Laird
Highlander's Touch
Highlander Undone
Highlander Unraveled

WICKED WOMEN

Her Desperate Gamble
Seducing the Sheriff
Kiss Me, Cowboy

UNDER THE NAME E. KNIGHT

TALES FROM THE TUDOR COURT

My Lady Viper
Prisoner of the Queen

ANCIENT HISTORICAL FICTION

A Day of Fire: a novel of Pompeii
A Year of Ravens: a novel of Boudica's Rebellion

$\underline{4}$ = 3 times a day NO.12
before meals

$\underline{8}$ = 3 times a day NO21

can be taken
together .

$\underline{Mon}$ Oct 19 9:30am

Dr. Liu

Made in the USA
Middletown, DE
06 October 2020